T0114544

FONDRICA JONES

authorHOUSE®

AuthorHouse™
1663 Liberty Drive
Bloomington, IN 47403
www.authorhouse.com
Phone: 1 (800) 839-8640

Published by AuthorHouse 07/29/2016

ISBN: 978-1-5246-2151-3 (sc)
ISBN: 978-1-5246-2150-6 (e)

Print information available on the last page.

This book is printed on acid-free paper.

Chapter 1

Travis was this big time dope boy from my hood. He was one of the realist niggas I knew. He was every woman dream and had much money and a lot of hoes. I was one of Travis main bitches. I was a young brown skin female with a shape that would make any man turn his head the other way if I was walking by. Travis was my main man for the most part of it. I mean he had bitches and I used to do my little thing too. But, it was the dreads and gold's with the money and presents that had me fuck up about Travis. In the beginning Travis was sweet to me. But, at the end he cheated a lot and the disrespect had me in the state of mine where l could not stand for me. His sister Kreme was a good friend though-out the whole time we was in a relationship and decided to teach me the game. Kreme and I would ride around and get money. Every nigga in L.A. knew us. In the club we were always hot topic. That's were all the money came in when Kreme introduced me to this pimp name Jay Jack. Jay Jack had hoes all over L.A. working making money from local gang members and dope boys. Some on the hoes from Jay Jack corner had side lines jobs

working at local strip clubs. You know something to make extra money. Kreme and I was one of them. Kreme and I spent our time doing big girl shit with niggas like taking trips out of town and buildings a dream in the game. The name of the club Kreme and I danced at was called The Roxy's. I made a lot of motherfucking money in The Roxy's. It was owned by this older nigga name Pimp. Pimp used to sell drugs back in the days and came across enough money to open up a business and it was a strip club which was The Roxy's. All kinds of rappers used to be in The Roxy's. My first dance getting introduced to the game I was eighteen years old. I had just had my first daughter Money and I needed the money support her. Travis had moved on with his life and Kreme was teaching me to survive on my own. The owner to The Roxy's didn't give a fuck if I was young dancer. All I had to have was the body. Kreme took me to the owner and put me down with him. He was a cool ass dude. Shit sometime he used to let Kreme and I dance in the club for free. My first night dancing in the club I worked the poll. Hoes was surprise to see a young bitch like me come and the club and have that much power over niggas. Niggas paid their money. In a couple months I got the hook up in the project and got Money and I an apartment. Shit was sweet, I was able to bring my little niggas friends over and I used to make extra money on the sides. In the daytime while Money was in daycare I used to work the streets corner in L.A. with Kreme. That's when we would work Jay Jack corner. Jay Jack was the type of pimp that would wait on the corner for his hoes to make his money. I can remember my first trick like it was yesterday. It was a nigga name Major. Major was a nigga from cross the water, who moved to L.A.

to work in the dope game. He was a dark skinned nigga with waves in his head. Major had money and cars out the ass. He used to park his Bentley on the side corner and when all his rounds were over he used to come up the ally and trick with me. We would go to old apartments where people didn't live and make out. I made love with him. He was a nigga that made me want to make it to the top. Major game was like that. Every time I used to sleep with Major I had to give Jay Jack half of my money. So, out of the five hundred dollars I used to keep two fifty. That was good money for me. Shit, after about five pops I had myself one thousand dollars. I worked the corner for a whole year and got my apartment fully furniture and bought me a two door Lexus. Most, hoes my age couldn't understand how I was doing it. They were still sleeping around for free and getting took care of by their parents. As, for me I was a corner bitch with much swag. Major and I fucked around so much he used to come to the apartment I had in the project and chill. After, a couple of months he found out it were a safe place to keep his dope and start keeping his work at my house. I used to love the thuggish shit Major and I would do and how he showed me attention on the corner block. Being with Major for six months I was over Travis. I had a nigga in the game just like Travis. Major was a nigga to understand. He knew I needed money so he didn't look down on me for having a pimp or stripping. Major also used to give me thousands of dollars and I used to hit the mall whenever I wanted too. I was one of the best dress females in L.A. When, Kreme and I first started The Roxy's we had older bitches that looked up to us. It all started when a nigga name Man came in with a gang of niggas and they all had money. Some of them even came in with millions of dollars in a duffle bag. When, Man and his crew walked in The Roxy's the D.J. asked for all bitches that could work the poll to come to V.I.P. Kreme and I was one of them with this bad as bitch out of Miami name Candy. When, I got in V.I.P. Man thought I had on bad lingerie and wanted me to dance for him. My ass was hanging out and I was looking gooder than a motherfucker. Niggas thought I was bad and start tipping me hundreds at a time. I was making the cheeks to my ass clap and bounce up and down. It was other bitches in a Jacuzzi eating fruits off each other and putting on a freak show. While, Man was tipping me he asked for my number. Man wanted to become a fuck friend. I had wanted Man since I was younger. I had dreams of fucking with him and it was finally about to happen. After, I gave Man my number I told him to keep in contact with me and to get at me when the club was over. Major, was uptown L.A. so that gave me time to pop things off with Man. In the club that night I end up making a lot of money. Ten grand was good for a young bitch like me. Shit, I was trying to come up. My first night in the club I saw a lot of shit. Hoes was tricking in a small motel that was next to The Roxy's. When, Man got the word that it was a side motel to pay money to trick he went in rented room 120. The owner to The Roxy's gave me permission to walk out and make that extra money. When, I got in the room Man had three grand and some cocaine. Man grabbed me by the waist and pulled me close to him. He turned me around to check how sexy I looked in my stilettos. He wanted to see my body with my clothes off so I took my lingerie off. Man, liked everything that he saw. I took the three grand in but it in my hands and laid on the bed. Man laid between the inside of my legs. Up and down Man pounded my pussy. That, was the second nigga I had tricked besides Major. While, I was on the bed Man asked to continue fucking me. So, from time to time while I would dance Man would rent a room at The Hideaway Inn. Most dope boys from L.A. used to trick at The Hideaway Inn. After, Man and I fucked and I made him happy I went back in the club. It was my turn to dance on stage. I went on stage and worked the poll fast and slow. Niggas was paying to see me dance. I was looking greater than most bitches in the club. After, my first day dancing at the club and tricking Man at The Hideaway Inn Man wanted me to go to one of his dope spots where he made money. I didn't have a problem with it shit he had already paid me three grand. Man was a fine ass nigga with gold's in his mouth. He had dreads to top it off. I used to love grabbing a whole of Man dreads, while we used to fuck. However, when we left the club I gave Kreme the word that I was going to one of Man ally apartments to chill with him. He was a cool as dude for the most part of it. An, the nigga got me on so much cocaine. His hood friend Eddie was working dope out the apartment late night. Man and Eddie went half on the bills once a month. Man usually worked the corner and used the apartment to store is work. The first night with Man I ate steaks from this dude name CeeLow that sell food to people that stay up late after the club. Man treated me like a queen. He kissed all up on me and he had the ally apartment fixed up like a woman lived there. It had a Jacuzzi in it and I loved how the bubble bath from Bath& Body Works felt while I was in the Jacuzzi. Man made love to me. All night we fucked and he put his dick inside of me. It was so hard and good. He made me moan all night long and I wanted to stay with Man forever. While, I was chilling with Man I was thinking I was going to love working the streets. You know why? Because street niggas show you love and they have frame. After, the trick for three grand at the club and the fuck at the ally apartment Man gave me some money to get a cell phone. My pussy was that good he kept spending money. That next morning I went and got Money my daughter to spend a little time with her and went to the phone company. Shit, that was good for me to have a side line phone to keep my tricks numbers in. As, soon as I got the phone I called Man and gave him my number. Man gave me the word that he was going to keep in contact with me. After, I got off the phone with Man I called Major on my other phone. Major had been uptown L.A. selling drugs all night. When Major answered the phone he was like baby what's up. I started the phone conversation by asking Major what time he was going to stop by my apartment. Shit, I wanted to see my man and hug and kiss all up on him. Major told me he would be over to the crib around noon. That's was cool with me that gave me time to leave the cell phone place and get myself ready for the day. The next phone call I made was to Kreme phone. I called her to see what she had going on for the day and Kreme was already on Jay Jack corner tricking making that fast money. I gave Kreme the word I would be on the corner as soon as Major stop by the crib and I see him. Money my daughter was still with me for the day. She was getting older and Money was almost two years old. For the most part of it I was doing good taking care of her. Time went by and Major had made it to my apartment. Major came in with a money bag and gave me a kiss on the cheeks. Major made his self feel like he was home. He did that every time he came to my house in the projects. Major looked at how sexy I looked and start telling me all kinds of sweet things like how much he loved me. Then, he counted all his money up. Major had made a total of fifty grand Friday night. He went in the back room where he was keeping his money in a safe at my house and put the fifty grand up. My nigga was getting much money in the game. After, talking to Major for about one hour I asked him to buy me a new Gucci bag out the mall. Major went back in the safe and got the money with no problems for me. I called Reese my sister after Major left and asked her could she watch Money for me while I go on the corner and to the mall. Shit, that's all I have my mother die when I was five years old to a drug related crime. My father has life in prison for a murder at a bank when he tried to rob it. Grandma was in my life but I really didn't want her to babysit that much because she was old. Shit, that's all I had and I didn't want to come between that. I took Money over to Reese apartment in this nice gated community in L.A. My sister was older than me and she worked as a nurse at one of the best hospitals in L.A. For the most part of it, Reese was doing well for herself. After, I drop Money off I went to the mall and then I went on Jay Jack corner. The first trick of the day was this dude name Dell. I went in the ally looking like a nigga wanted a trick to look and got on my knees and suck Dell dick. As, I sucked Dell dick Dell stood there with a gun in his pocket just in case someone tried to rob him. Dell always carried a gun because he was a major dope boy on Jay Jack corner. I finished up the head job and got my money last. The tricks on Jay Jack corner got their money last because some time hoes would try to run off without doing the job. I fucked Dell and put his number in my new cell phone just in case he wanted to trick when I was off the clock. You know so I could make some extra money. I gave Jay Jack his half and put the other half in my car. Shit, the streets of L.A. were so rough I never kept money on me. Kreme taught me a nigga would rob you on the streets. I never been robbed and don't plan too. After, I came from my car Jay Jack told me he had a thousand dollar lick for me in the upstairs ally apartment. It was some of Dell homeboys. When I got back in the ally apartment dope was everywhere and money too. That's how high rollers did it in L.A. They made money all day long. When, I got there I had to fuck two niggas for a grand. As, I was fucking the two niggas Major walked in the ally apartment. Shit, he was friends with the dudes and Dell. Major was hurt from the expression on his face. His feelings were involved with me. But, hell I was a trick when I met him. That's how the game went. Mark the nigga I fucked in the ally apartment was breaded up. Mark had money out the ass and he was a Florida boy. He was out of the hood in West Palm Beach. I heard for time to time Mark would traffic dope from West Palm Beach to L.A. But, as Mark pounded my pussy he told me how good it was too. As, time went by I was in the ally to long and Jay Jack came to the walk way to get me. Shit, Jay Jack didn't allow his hoes to trick a nigga over thirty minutes. Shit, the clock was the clock. An, he would say that from time to time. I loved my job making money on the streets and working at the strip club. My second day on the corner I went uptown L.A. and made twenty thousand dollars with some niggas. I was doing show after show and money was coming fast. That was my first time getting introduced to eating pussy so I got on cocaine. I was scared to go uptown L.A. by myself so I had Kreme come with me. Kreme was about that life and start feeling on my ass in front of all those niggas. Dell was the nigga to take us uptown to his cousin Bird house. Bird, was a rich nigga that made it out the game. He had a mansion with a pool, a Jacuzzi and flat screen televisions hanging off the wall everywhere. Bird house was a hang out a female would want make money at. I walked in Bird house and the first thing he did was gave me the twenty thousand dollars upfront. Shit, I tricked those niggas and got money all day long. When, night came around I left Bird mansion and went downtown L.A. so I could dance at The Roxy's. Kreme and I separated for a minute to get ready for the club. I gave her like an hour and then I hit her up on her cell phone. For some reason when Kreme was in the building she made my night go by better at the club. At the club that night Man was in the building. Man was looking gooder than a motherfucker his dreads was standing in the air and he had on an urban outfit out of one of the hoods stores. A fashion that all dope boys where wearing at the time. Man, had money and his hand and he gave me my first couple of tips for the night. Another person that was in the club was this rapper name Rich Homie Quan. I danced for him and he showed me a good time. After, dancing for Rich Homie Quan I was able to open a bank account the next day. I didn't even need the job working on Jay Jack corner, but I still kept it. I wanted all the money I could get I wanted nice shit for me and my daughter Money. With some of the money I made with Rich Homie Quan I went and

re- furniture my apartment in the projects. I was living large to be from the hood. I left the furniture store the next day then I went and got my hair done. It was a must I look fly on the corner. My next stop of the day was to the nail shop to get my toes and nails done. You know to look fresh for the dope boys on the corner block. Leaving the nail salon I went directly on the block. Dell was the first nigga I saw for the day. He asked me did I want to make some money. I was like hell yeah. Shit, Dell was the nigga to take Kreme and me uptown to his cousin Bird house and make those twenty thousand dollars. The same night I danced with Rich Homie Quan at The Roxy's. Some of my money was still in a safe. That's how bitches out the hood did it. They always had money in the bank and money in a safe at the crib to blow. While, I was at the ally apartment Dell gave Jay Jack his money and I was suppose to get my half when I was done with the job. Dell put the pound game down on me. He was calling my name out and he kept telling me how good my pussy was. I was smiling from ear to ear to see a nineteen year old nigga make love to an eighteen year old bitch like me. Major was there but my nigga didn't give a fuck. Shit, that's how I had start buying Major dope. That was his main focus. After, the quick trick with Dell I went outside to get my half from Jay Jack. Shit, Jay Jack gave me the full amount. I had only been working for Jay Jack a couple of days and he had already started letting me keep all my money. When, I got a break Kreme had just made it on the corner for the afternoon. My girl had been up all night making money and needed some rest so she was late getting on the block. As, for me after the club I went home and counted up my money and did some running around this morning to get ready for the block today. I wanted niggas to see me looking good. Dell, and I finished fucking and a couple minutes he wanted some more pussy on the spot. So, Dell went outside to pay Jay Jack for another section. Shit, this time he gave Jay Jack three grand. Jay Jack asked Dell why he was spending so much money on me. An, Dell told him because Kreme got good pussy and she looked good as fuck with that lingerie on. Dell, and the corner boys had a strip poll in the ally apartment and Dell wanted me to work the poll. I got on the poll and danced fast and slow for Dell. Dell couldn't believe I was young in age and he didn't give a fuck. All he wanted to do was sticking his dick inside of me and give me money. After, I fucked Dell for a couple times he gave me some cocaine on the side. That's how it was on the corner niggas got you fucked up. After, the second pop with Dell and getting on cocaine I was in my zone. By, that time Major had made it on the block. Major was getting a little upset about me stripping and tricking niggas. He started having thoughts I would leave him alone and find a new nigga on the dope corner. I talked to Major and kissed all on him and put my game down. I told Major he was my main man and he told me to keep it like that, after, kissing me Major put word on the streets that he was going on the next block and selling drugs from now on. His feelings was involved with me and decided to let me do my thing and sell dope somewhere else. Shit, time had pasted and he didn't want to work the same street corner that I tricked on. Shit, that was cool with me now I could really do my thing. I didn't want my nigga seeing me work my ass for other niggas anyways. I just wanted to bring the money home. Major, was just a cool ass nigga and wanted to be with a bitch that was street like me and I wanted a thug ass nigga like him. Major had a bitch and the game and he wanted to keep that. That's why I respected Major because he didn't look at me different for being a stripper and having a pimp in the game. Most, niggas would have lost all respect for a female like me. After, fucking Dell twice on the corner that day and talking to Major and he coming to the decision on changing up corners to sell dope Man call the phone. Man was calling to check in on a bitch and to make sure I haven't forgot about him. That's what type of gangster Man was. Man, gave me the word that he wanted to eat lunch with me and talk about future plans as being friends. We end up eating at a soul food restaurant eating some chicken and rice with cabbage and corn bread. Man gave me a small gift which was a tennis bracelet with a ring and some diamond cut earrings to go with it. The bracelet was all gold with diamonds on the inside of it. Man talked a little bit and he wanted to know what kind of person I was. I told him he was dealing with an easy going person that didn't like drama at all. Man told me that the kind of friendship he wanted. I also told Man I was a ride of die chick and he liked that part the most. I told him I was new in the game. Shit, Kreme taught me if a nigga was spending money like Man was it was alright to tell him I was new in the game. Man was doing big shit so that rule applied to him. An only a week Man had bought me a cell phone, a bracelet with earrings and a ring. Not only that he had given me three grand at The Roxy's the first night he met me. So, I trusted Man as a person to tell him about my life as a new beginner in the game. Man, gave me the word that I apply to the rules he set when talking to a female and told me he wanted to keep talking to me. After, eating at the soul food restaurant man showed he asset to his other apartment that he don't hustle out of. He had a pool table and it was a nice place to chill and get high and make money. Man took up most of my day so I was done working the corner for the day. Man was a lot of man and I wanted to chill out with him as much as I can. Kreme always told me if a nigga showed a good time you should do the same for him. So, from that point Man and I start doing our thing on the side while Major was on the corner selling drugs. I was getting the same treatment from Man that I was getting from Major. The only different was I was in a relationship with Major. Night came around and it was time to hit the club. I went home and Major was standing next to my front door I had five missed calls from my sister Reese. Money was still at Reese house and I thought something was wrong or she wanted me to pick Money up because she had to work at the hospital overnight. That wasn't the case Reese was just calling to check on me because she haven't heard from me all day. I walked in the house worried about how Major would feel about me being pregnant. I had gone to one of those walk in clinics because I missed my cycle. I mention to him that I would be having a baby and he was happy about things. Right then Major talked about moving into the apartment. Major wanted to know how I felt about having my second baby and I told him things was going to be great if the baby was going to be raised in a house with both parents. He had questions about me still dancing and tricking. I told Major that I was going to work the block and the club until I start showing. He looked at me crazy then Major asked me how my day went. Shit, I lied and told Major I was on the corner all day.

I didn't want my nigga to know I was hanging out with Man. Anyhow, Major went for the lie I told him. My nigga wasn't worried about me being in the streets leaving him for another nigga. While, talking to Major in my projects apartment I got my lingerie and heels ready to dance at The Roxy's for the night. My phone rang in the process and it was Kreme. Kreme wanted to know was I dancing for the night. While, I was on the phone with Kreme I told her I was pregnant from Major. Kreme was a little bit disappointed because Travis was her brother and she wanted Money to be an only child. Kreme say she wanted the best for Money and me and I was still young. But, I told her shit happen and Major and I wasn't using protection. I got ready and walked out the door to head to The Roxy's. When, I got there Kreme was already in the building dancing and making money. An, niggas was ready to spend their money on me The DJ was just calling all females to the VIP room. It was some local rapper in the club that just had made it big. Kreme went in VIP and start dancing with him. As for me the first little money I made for the night came from a trick. I went to The Hideaway Inn and made that little extra money. I needed every penny I could get being that I was pregnant. Man was in the club when I got back in the club and he had a lot of money his hands. He was spending it on some stripper name Candy out of Miami until he saw me. I danced for Man for about one hour and made five grand until Kreme called me in VIP to dance with the local rapper that had just made his first album. I went in VIP and start shaking my ass clapping both cheeks together fast. Niggas was giving me money out the ass. For one part of the strip section Kreme ate my pussy in the VIP room of the club.

Niggas had out video cameras and they was videoing us. I was getting money I wanted my face on as many videos as possible. At age eighteen I had my own apartment a car with money in my pockets. I was straight. Shit, that's all I needed. The next day on the street word had got around that I was two weeks pregnant from Major. Travis had found out and came over to my apartment in the projects to see what the deal was. Shit, Money was two years old and I had no dealings with Travis. When, Travis knocked on the door shit I was surprise. Shit, I had been in the projects for a while and that was my first time seeing him come by my house. Good thing I had just got Money from Reece house so he could spend some time with her. I knew Kreme had to be the one to tell Travis I was two weeks pregnant and gave him my apartment to one of the most drug related projects in L.A. Travis came in the apartment and the first thing he wanted to know was I pregnant and notice Money and picked her up into his hands and start kissing on her. I was like yeah am two weeks and it's from my new boyfriend Major. Travis was a little bit upset. Kreme had put that Money need better shit in his head. Shit, I was straight and didn't give a fuck who thought different about my life. I had saving in the bank and money in a safe on the side. I wasn't trying to hear what anybody had to say about me. Major, Money, and I was about to be a family. Travis, start getting fly out the mouth. He started telling me I had turned out to be a trick in L.A. About thirty minutes of Travis bullshit I put him out my apartment. Travis had no need to be telling me I needed better in my life. He wasn't a good father to Money. He left the house and I called Reese to tell her about Travis visit to the projects and to see was it okay to bring Money back to her apartment. Reese didn't have a problem with Money returning for a couple more days and I got into my Lexus and took Money back to Reese place. While, on the way to Reese place I phone Kreme to tell her about her brother fuck up surpise visit. I also told Kreme to keep that nigga out my businesss. Shit, I was doing grown woman shit. When, I got to Reese apartment she was still surprise that I was pregnant. Shit, Reese thought it was a good thing. Then, we got on the conversation about who was the daddy of my child. I told Reese some fine ass nigga from cross the water that I been in a relationship with. Reese wasn't in the dope game or tricking business so she didn't know Major. Shit, when Reese visited me in the projects she wouldn't even stay that long because of the dope, violence, and guns. I left Money at Reese house and before I left I gave Reese some money to get Money some Jordan shoes. Money stayed fresh. After, leaving Reese apartment I went back home and took a shower for the day. I had a couple of missed calls when I got out the shower. Dell, Man, and Major had called me on the phone. I returned all their phone calls and they all wanted to spend some money. Major, wanted to know was I back home so he could come count some money up. Major was selling more dope than any nigga in L.A. That's where all the local dope boys got their drugs from. Once, Major came to my house and I let him count his money up I went on Jay Jack corner. Major counted up one point five million dollars in total. When I got on the corner Jay Jack was making sure all his tricks get paid. Dell, had made all his rounds and wanted to spend a grand on me. Jay Jack got his half and I did the quick fuck. Kreme was on the corner smoking loud and making niggas want to spend their money on her left and right. She had on this new Louis Vuition lingerie. Then, Kreme got a call on her phone to come to the ally apartment. When, Kreme got upstairs Dell had made a deal with Jay Jack that Kreme and I would do a show for him. Shit, that was straight with me. More money plus I was getting pleasure with Kreme eating my pussy. Kreme knew she knew how to eat pussy good ass fuck. I came three times in twenty minutes while Kreme was eating my pussy. Dell, made a couple of sells out the ally apartment while Kreme and I was putting on our freak show. Then, he gave me some cocaine. As, for Kreme she had some loud and didn't need a supply from Dell. After, about forty-five minutes Kreme and I went on the corner. When, we got on the corner the L.A. police department was everywhere. A nigga name Biggs had been shot and killed. Biggs was a dope boy in the game. Niggas say that a nigga robbed him and took one point two million dollars. Shit, was crazy in L.A. on days like this and I would go home and chill. I told Jay Jack I was off the clock. A nigga had been killed and lord knows I didn't want to go to jail for tricking on the corner. I went home and put the little money I made on the corner up for today. I sat down and called Man. I wanted to get a little time in with him while Major was still on the block making money. On the phone with Man I told him about the murder with Biggs that happen on the corner. Man, wanted to know who I was talking about so I phoned Kreme on three way to get Biggs full name and age. Come to find out Biggs was Man cousin. He wanted to know full details about what happen. All I could tell Man was some niggas robbed Biggs and took one point two million dollars. He asked a lot of questions like did the police have a suspect.

I told Man there was no weapon and the police only had Biggs body. Man, was pretty upset to hear his cousin had got murdered. Before, the club that night Man gave me a visit to my apartment to get a little more news. We even went back to the murder spot. Man gave Biggs mother a call on the phone to let her know his heart went out to her. Come to find out Biggs was older than I thought and had kids the same age as me. After, Man made a couple calls about Biggs death I put on a show for him to make some cash at my apartment. Shit, Man did something to me that Major had never did and that's fuck me all over my apartment. I really gave him the business in the room where I had a strip poll. I danced all over the poll for him. I smoked a couple of stank joints. Then, Man got a call from Ceelow. Ceelow wanted to buy some drugs. I didn't even know he was a drug dealer too. I thought he just sold food late night. When, I got from the back room in my apartment Ceelow was already in my living room. Ceelow scene like a pretty nice dude. When, he left Man and I finish getting our freak on. He relaxed and let me fuck the shit out of him. I put down so good he told me I had the best head game in the world and gave me some extra money. It made me feel like falling in love with him how good the sex was. Every nigga I came in contact with in the game always made good loving to me. That's one thing I didn't have a problem with was my sex life. Night rolled around fast and it was time for Kreme and me to get ready for The Roxy's. Kreme call just as I was getting ready. She wanted to come to my house and get ready. But, as she was on the phone she was already at the door so she knew it was okay. Kreme started to put on her make-up and she had a sew-in in her hair with her toes and nails done. She really looked great and it was her birthday. Kreme was having a party at The Roxy's where all kinds of dope boys was going to be in the building showing mad love. Kreme was twenty-one years old today and was legal to buy liquor. Kreme had a bottle of Grey Goose and she was getting fucked up for the most part of it. The way Kreme was partying for her birthday made me turn up with her. By, the time we made it to The Roxy's we were fucked up. When we made our entry to The Roxy's all kinds of balling ass niggas was in there. Hoes was already tricking out The Hideaway Inn. Bitches were in VIP making money and I was ready for my night to start. Niggas from the corner block was on the second level of The Roxy's balling out of control and when Kreme and I walked in they gave her a birthday shout-out and some money. So much money got handed out I even got some. Junkies were in and out of the club getting crack I mean the night was turned up. They all were on this new drug call molly. The first hour in The Roxy's I made three grand. As, the club was getting more pack I went to the locker room and put my money up. Man wasn't in the club so while I was in the locker room I called him. Man, was taking care of some drugs deals and was running a little late. Time went by after I talked to Man and he made it to the club around four thirty in the morning. That shit kind of made me upset because that was money I was missing out on. I had only made three grand. When I finally saw Man I asked him did he want to go to his apartment after the club. I needed the money being that I had the baby in my stomach in due time it would be time for me to stop dancing and tricking. But, for now am going to get money. Man didn't have a problem with me going

back to his apartment and making some money so I got in my Lexus and left. When, we got to Man apartment I had a personal sack of cocaine and I got lace up. Man was in a rush to fuck so I put the cocaine up and fucked him. He was fucking some pregnant pussy for the first time. All night Man fucked me and enjoyed it. After, a couple of hours of fucking I finally gave Man some head he was curling up his feet it was so good. We fucked again and I got on my knees and start giving Man some more head service. He liked the entertainment. I was so into Man I called Kreme so she could help put on a freak show for him. When, Kreme got there she smoked a couple loud joints and then we put on show for Man. Man was so into us and made it rain all over us. Each time Kreme would make me cum Man would give us a couple more hundreds. I were loving what Kreme was doing to me. Then Kreme got from between my legs and start fucking me like a nigga with two fingers. The two fingers felt good inside of me. Kreme was making me feel good so I stopped her from fingering me and start licking her from the back. Man, liked the entertainment of seeing two women in bed. That made Man pay us all his money. After, Kreme and I got our freak on we teamed up on Man. Man eyes was close from the head service I was giving him I was loving every minute of what I was doing to Man. After, I gave Man head he start hitting my pussy from the back the way he was going in and out felt so good I came two times. On the other hand, Kreme was licking Man balls from the back. Man was loving that freaky shit and stopped us to give us some more money. This time Man went in his safe. He gave Kreme and I both twenty five thousands a piece. I was on top of my game with Man. I continue to please him. As, the night went on Man, Kreme and I party came to a end. I got up and headed to downtown L.A. When, I reached the project it was quite because it was early in the morning. All the dope boys and junkies were asleep. The only nigga that was on the corner was this nigga name Red. Red was looking for a trick. I was the only female left on the streets so he asked me could he pay me a couple hundreds to fuck. I got out my Lexus and got the twenty five grand Man had just given me in tonight section. Red was standing next to me waiting on me still to give him an answer so I told Red yes I would trick with him. When, we got in the apartment Red had an ounce of cocaine. That was my first night being introduced to putting cocaine up my nose. Before, that I use to just smoke cocaine in my joints. The rush to my head made me feel good so I put it up my nose all night. Red started to kiss on me and before you knew it I was having sex with Red and daylight was coming. Red had a ten inch dick and I couldn't believe it. He was packing and I was surpise to see that. At first I didn't want Red to stick his dick inside of me. But, I found the power in me to relax. I laid back on the bed and let Red stick his ten inch dick inside of me. Red, kissed and licked around my neck to make my pussy get wetter. In about fourty minutes Red and I were done fucking. Red pulled out his wallet and gave me the money. Being, that it was morning time I didn't lay down I got in the shower and put on some clothes for the day. I got out the shower hit the cocaine before I hit the streets. When, I finally put on my clothes and hit the corner Major Bentley was the first car I saw parked in the hood for the day. First, thing I did for the day was stop by the hair dresser to get my appearance back on.

By the time, she was done doing my hair it was three thirty in the afternoon. Man gave me a hit up on the phone after having a long night with Kreme and I. He wanted me to know that he had a good time. I walked to my car and drove to the L.A. Square Mall to go to Forever 21. A lot of bitches were in there buying some dresses that was on sale and I got five of them. Then, I left the mall and went back on the corner to trick up on some money. My pimp Jay Jack was out on the corner making sure everything was in order when I go there. An, my first trick of the day was Red. The nigga I had fucked for a couple of hundreds early this morning. I guess the pussy was good to him because Red wanted some more pussy. He went up to Jay Jack and asked how much it cost to pay for some ass from Kelly. Then Jay Jack wanted to know how Red knew of me. Red told Jay Jack that niggas had word on the streets I had a good fuck game and I worked the corner for a pimp service. Jay Jack was suripise to here that and liked what Red had told him. That meant I was doing my job. For the compliment Red gave Jay Jack about me Jay Jack gave me a little of half over the amount he usually gives. Instead of going to the ally apartment Red and I walked to his Bentley and handle business. Red put the pound gave down and when he was finish I continue my day by walking up and down the corner for another dope boy to trick with me. While waiting on my next pop I got on a little cocaine and watched junkies run up to dope boys for crack. Then, as I was watching the block CeeLow came thought to serve food and sell crack out of his food truck because I saw some junkies run up to his truck and by some crack when he first pulled up. Then, as I was standing on the corner Reese called me to put Money on the phone.

Money, was at the age where she was talking and asked about her mother so Reese gave me a call on the phone. Shit, money wasn't coming like that so I went uptown to get Money. When, I got there Reese ex-boyfriend Qunicy was over there. I was surpise to see him Reese had been in a relationship with Qunicy for five years and the dating game between them was suppose to be over. When, I walked in Reese house Money had on the shoes I had sent Reese to the mall to get. Money ponytails was on point and Reese had my baby girl looking like a million dollars. While, I was at Reese house she talked to me about my future goals. Reese was a nurse and ever chance she got she would talk to a young bitch like me. Reese wanted me to get an education bad. I figured I had heard enough of Reese talk and left her house. Leaving Reese house I went back on the corner to see was money coming yet. When, I got there niggas say Major had been looking for me. Word on the streets was Major and Travis had been in a fight about Major having me pregnant. I didn't know Travis was going to do some fuck up shit like that. I called Major and he was fussing his as off. Major was mad and wanted to talk to me he was telling me he didn't have time for the bullshit with me or Travis. Then he got on the subject of me stop working the block. Shit, but money had to be made. I was upset from what Major was saying on the phone because he was going to have to deal with me working the corner for a few more weeks I need the money. Shit, nine months was going to come fast and I wanted to have a couple hundred grand saved up in my account so I could buy both of my kids nice things until money pick up again. The most important thing was me not doing cocaine while carrying the baby and I needed to stop. But, Major

didn't know that part about me. Major got off the phone and the next minute he was on the block I trick on. I thought Major was going to still be fussing but he started hugging up on me in my Forever 21 dress. Niggas was surpise to see us in love. While, we was standing on the block Travis did a drive by shooting trying hard to kill Major because my nigga had got off in his ass. I was thinking damn he that mad because I done moved on with my life and found a better nigga then him. He was acting a fool and soon or later one of those old ladies that sit on their porch was going to call the police while he was with all that gun play. I hated the fact that Major and Travis was going though it because Major was my nigga. He was someone I could ride with. After, niggas found out I was pregnant from Major they start to chill out on the tricking level. So, I start spending most of the days I was pregnant in the house. Kreme would come by the house everyday and see me. As, for every nigga on Jay Jack corner I didn't see them until I had my baby. Months had went by and I didn't go on the block. I had gained to much weight and couldn't trick. By, that time Major had begin to spend a lot of time at the house. After, I found out I was having a baby boy Major would give me money daily to go to the mall. When, my son came into the world he was a nine pound baby and I name him Major Jr. after his father. Major Jr. looked just like Major when he was born. He had that good hair like him and everything. Kreme was the godmother of my son and she gave me a baby shower before I had him. When, Major Jr. born I had just turned nineteen years old and had two children. A few days after having my baby I was back on the corner a bitch didn't give a fuck about a six weeks check up money had to be made. Dell was the first nigga to see me back on the street and he showed love. He gave me nine grand on the spot. He said he wanted to make me feel like I was home again. I took the money looking fly ass fuck and put it in my Dooney& Burke bag. Then, I walked into the ally apartment and there were some new faces. I walked to the back room in the ally apartment and Dell followed behind me. As, soon as we got in the room Dell pulled out his dick, I got on top of Dell and rode his dick. As, I was riding him he watched because I was giving him the business. While, Dell and I was fucking Jay Jack was waiting for his half of the money because for the first time Dell put the money in my hands. My plans were to keep the money but Jay Jack saw Dell when he came up to me and gave me the money. Dell, told me that while I was gone off the block pregnant tricks had start to keep the whole thing. He said niggas wasn't in the business of paying Jay Jack money to be a pimp in the game but some way Jay Jack got his half. After, I fucked Dell my G-spot was hot for the rest of the day and I fucked back to back making money. Niggas was getting at me left and right in the game I thought I was going to be making less money because some new hoes may have came on the block in my spot. Plus, I was thick ass fuck after I had my baby. Niggas was giving me cocaine and money all over again and I was happy. Money and Major Jr. was in daycare so I made the best of my time. Time went by and my day for working the corner was over, but before I left Kreme pulled up in a junky car. She said the junky had rented Travis the car because his car was hot. But, Travis had the car because he was hot on the corner and those old ladies called the police on him and he had a warrant for what he did a couple months ago. Word on the streets that the police had a picture of Travis and would come though and look for him daily, by the time I got done talking to Kreme I had one more trick for the day which was with this nigga from Orlando. His name was Tony and he was in L.A. visiting one of his cousins. Tony and I walked like five blocks away to handle business. It didn't take that long and once I was done I went to my kids daycare and picked them up. Then, I went home and word for the rest of the day was the police was back looking for Travis.

Chapter 2

The police finally picked Travis off the streets and my son from Major was a month old. Travis had a gun charge and Kreme say they were trying to jam him up. Shit, at first I wanted Travis locked up and jail but once the police pick my babydaddy up I felt bad for him. It was Friday and I had woke up early. I put Money on her new Roca Wear outfit that was made by the rapper Jay-Z. Then, I took out a Polo made by Ralph Lauren and put it on Major Jr. By the time I got the kids ready it was almost time for their daycare to start so I put on something simple for the day. I left the house and took the kids to daycare. My next stop was to the hair salon to get fresh for the corner. It was a must that I kept myself up. This time I had Nikki my hair desser do me a sew-in. When, Nikki got done with the 20 inch had I was on point. Then, I went on the corner on my way to the corner the club owner to The Roxy's called me. He wanted to know was I coming back to the club. I was like hell yeah that's money. Mainly, he was calling because it was going to be a big rapper in the club and he wanted all his top of the line dancers to be in the building. After,

getting the call from Pimp that a big time rapper was going to be in the club I changed the direction I was going and went to Tricks a stripper store and got me some new lingerie. Inside Tricks the lady that own it had a deal on tatts and a tongue ring so I got a few tatts and a tongue ring. They say it made a nigga dick feel good when you gave him head. My tatts was a picture of some butterflies. When, I got done at Tricks I went on Jay Jack corner. Jay Jack was on the corner and hoes were making money. I went up Jay Jack to let him know I was on corner just in case some money came. I worked the corner all day long and while I was on the corner I got a surpise visit from Man. I was happy and excited about seeing him I haven't seen Man in months since I first had got pregnant. Man was like you finer that a motherfucker that baby got you thick ass fuck. My shape was on point and Man was ready to trick with me. I took Man upstairs in the ally apartment in downtown L.A. and sucked his dick. As, I was giving Man head he got freaky and wanted to hit me from the back. At age nineteen I was fucking like I was a grown ass woman. Shit, it made my pussy get wetter by getting fucked. It was so good Man wanted to still be a number one fan in my phone. After, we fucked Man told me to check off the block so he could take me to the L.A. Square Mall. I was dressed to the tee at the mall and when I left I put on one of my new outfits which was a Lacoste fit. When, I left the mall I went to Man apartment I gave him some pussy for twenty- five thousand dollars to save up for a new apartment. He wanted me and the kids to get out the projects Man said he would even put the apartment in his name. Shit, I didn't have a problem with a nigga giving me money to save up for me and my children to live in a better community. Man, and I got our freak on for a hour and the sex was so good. When, Man and I got done fucking I went back to the corner. Man went to the bathroom to get a rag to wipe my cum off the inside of my legs. Before, I left he grabbed on my ass. I couldn't even believe he could tell I had gain weight. Man, had made my day by giving me that much money to save up to get out the projects. When, I finally made it to the corner Red walked up to Jay Jack and paid for a head job from me. I walked up the ally to the apartment and went to the spot and gave Red a head job out this world. As, always Red had a gun on him then he told me to get on my knees and do my thing. Then, he pulled out a condom for protection. Red pulled out his ten inch dick and he was already on hard. Red started to kiss me to get me in the mood. He stopped for a moment and took some money out his pockets. Red walked to the front door and gave Jay Jack his half of the money. When, he walked back in the room where I was I sat on Red dick and start riding him. Back and forward I moved on Red dick. My stomach was in pain because how big it was. From the way Red was looking he was feeling what I was doing. Red had just got gold's in this mouth and he was grilling me like a real thug nigga would do while getting some good pussy. Red had me fucked up about his swag game. I was really feeling him with the gold's in his mouth. After, fucking Red I got on my cell phone to call Reese so she could pick the kids up from daycare. Reese was down for that so I was able to stay in the streets. I chilled for another hour put money wasn't coming though so I went home for the day. When, I got home I went to safe and counted up all my money. I had a total of sixty- five grand in cash. I put the money back in the safe and sat back and felt good about how much money I had and smoked a blunt. That was enough money to move out the projects but I had to save up more money. Shit, I wanted to have my shit decked out in the inside. There was nothing wrong with my apartment in the project but Man wanted me to be uptown L.A. with him. He was tired of coming downtown just to get some pussy. Plus, a bad bitch like me should be in a gated community. Man said since my credit wasn't staight he would sign for the apartment. After, getting high I decided to get up and head to my grandma house and see her for the day. I thought it was time to see grandma. I wanted grandma to always think the best of her grand-daughter Kelly. I headed a couple blocks down the road to grandma house. When, I got to grandma house she was happy to see her grand-daughter. I went in the house and before I could sit down grandma gave me a big hug and a kiss on the cheeks. That's how it was with grandma she loved to hug and kiss on her grandkids. After, giving grandma a hug I sat and watched television at her house for a couple of hours. When, I was at grandma house she always made me feel like I was at home even though I had moved in my own place in the projects. And, just I was sitting down it reminded me it was grandma birthday. I went in my purse and gave grandma a couple hundreds of dollars. That made her feel good for the day. Then, I sat at her house until night came around. When, it start getting dark outside I got up and left grandma house so I could hit the streets and work The Roxy's for the night. I walked back to my crib and got some of my best lingerie. I grabbed me some condoms just in case I had a couple of tricks for the night. Then, I got on some cocaine for about two hours before I left to go to The

Roxy's when I got there Major, Mark, and Dell alone with some more niggas was in there. They all was smoking hanging out tipping strippers and having a good time. I walked in and my first stop was to the DJ boost to get a time to dance on stage. Then, I walked to the back locker room to change into my lingerie to get my night started. When, I finally walked back on the floor I had on some three inch stilettos and right then niggas was trying to spend their money on me as I walked the floor with my perfectly shape frame. I started off with a couple of table tops then, I made it to the second level of The Roxy's. On the second level of the club I worked the poll and made a couple hundred dollars. Major was on the second level of the club making his rounds and watching me dance. After, Major made his lick he walked past me and tipped me a thousand dollars. By, the time he got to the bottom level of the club Major was on his way back up on the second level I was working my ass that good. Before, he walked back upstairs he gave me a shout out at the DJ boost. To one of the baddest bitches in here tonight this shout out go to Kelly is what he said. Niggas was turning their heads to see who Major was talking about and I start waving my hands in the air. One nigga was like look at that fine ass bitch Major is in a relationship with. My face was the best looking face on the scene and niggas start giving tips because I was Major lady. Major was a top of the line nigga. Rich Hoime Qaun was doing his damn thing in the club that night. Kreme had a VIP past to dance with him for the night. I was praying the owner gave me a VIP past to dance for Rich Hoime Quan that night too. Pimp the owner to The Roxy's finally gave me a past to get in VIP to dance for Rich Hoime Quan. So many big time niggas was in VIP out of Alanta G.A. They where tipping a bitch good and giving out their money. They took lots of pictures and post them on their phone as us being some of the baddest dancer they knew in time. At one point in the club Rich Hoime Quan paid all the dancers ten grand to dance for him in the club. We entertained him so much he made a request for all the strippers to meet with him in The Hideaway Inn so we could trick with him for one hundred thousands dollars. When, I got in the room I did a threesome with Rich Hoime Quan and some more strippers like Strawberry that dance at The Roxy's. Before the night was over we had balled so bad pictures was posted of me all over online. By the end of the night I had so much fun I still wanted to entertain Major so I beat him home to my apartment in the project took a shower and put something sexy on. I treated Major like a king and he treated me like a queen for the rest of the night. We made love and Major broke much bread with me. After, giving my man some pussy I decided to count up my money that I made with Rich Hoime Quan in VIP that night. I counted up all my money in front of Major and he could tell that his bitch wasn't fucking off she was bringing much money to the table. Seeing how good I had been doing Major broke me off some more money. After, I finish counting up my cash I saw I had enough money to get out the projects. Then, I put the money back in the safe and had a little talk to Major about moving out the projects. He was down with that but he talked me into keeping the apartment so he could hustle out of it. Shit, that was gravy with me but I damn sho was about to get out the hood. All night I laid down and made love to Major with the thought of me moving into a better community. His sex was the best and for the first time in our relationship Major ate my pussy. I was so surpise. Not only that Major had a Fendi purse on the side for me. Before, Major put the purse in my hand he hung it on the door nob and ate fruits off my pussy. I loved what Major was doing to me. Morning came and Major and I was still at it until I told him I had to go uptown. I didn't tell him for what but I was going to meet Man and see about getting a new apartment. When, Man answered the phone he was surpise I had came up with the money so fast to get an apartment fully funituned in a gated community. He had been wanting me to move uptown and we had even talked about it but it was finally about to happen. I asked Man was he down for still getting the apartment in his name and he was damn sho down. I talked to him and told him that Major would be living with me in the apartment. He was upset but he still put it in his name. That was a favor for me and the kids. Man and I went to some apartments call Up Living and got a four bedroom apartment. Man, was down for me moving closer to him in L.A. I told Man that I was still keeping the apartment in the projects so Major could hustle out of it. The rent man in the Up Living apartments told me I could move in the same day I paid the money. I told him that I had to buy new funitune and he let me borrow a bed he had in the storage area in the apartment buildings. After, I left Up Living I went to the Gucci funitune store. Shit, I had one hundred thousands dollars to spend on funitune. I thought to myself I could spend the hundred thousand grand on all Gucci and save the money I had in my safe. I had already paid the rent up for the whole year which was eighteen thousand dollars. At, the funitune store I spent thirty thousand dollars on the set that I wanted. I even got a pool table out the Gucci store. The salesperson said that he couldn't make a special delivery because they were backed up so I would have to wait two weeks. I called Reese as soon as I left the funitune store and told her that I had move in a gated community in Up Living close to her. Reese was excite and all happy for me. Kreme got the word from Man that I was no longer living in the projects. Kreme liked the fact of me moving uptown. She thought that was a way to meet some high rollers. Kreme always was thinking of a way to meet some new ballers to ball out with. I went back to my apartment in the hood and packed all my clothes up to move in Up Living. When, I got there Major was hustling out the apartment. I put on some clothes to move all the things I was going to take out the apartment. Reese came over and put a lot of the stuff in her SUV truck. Night came so fast and I found myself still at the apartment under packing me and the kids clothes. Then, out of the blue Major called to see was I working the club. Being that I had move bills was on my plate I thought it was a good idea to go make the money so I stop what I was doing and went back to the hood to get ready for the night because that's where all my strip gear was. It would be easier to leave those things in the projects instead of taking them uptown with me to my new place. I could just change in the hood every night. By, the time I got to The Roxy's every nigga from the hood was in there. Man was the only nigga from uptown there that night. He was looking at me while he was selling dope out the corner of his eye. Major was in there selling dope to the local dope boys so they could sell to the junkies. Major was getting much money that way in the game. He made more money than the local dope boys because he sold them dope at a high price just so they could double it and bring him the other half again. Shit, he had to we had bills at two different apartments now. My rent was fifteen hundred dollars in Up Living so both of us had to be making money. Even though I paid it for a year. Anyways as the night went by I did table tops I was bouncing my ass all over the tables getting tips. Niggas was walking by telling me to bounce that ass up and down. I turned over and made my ass clap for three minutes at a time before stopping. When, I did that Kreme would always stop and tip me in the club. Kreme was on the basement level of the club and looked up to the first floor and saw me up on the table bouncing and stop what she was doing and came to tip me. The owner had a surpise party going on for all the strippers that danced for Rich Hoime Quan in VIP and after I got done with table tops I went in VIP to party I got so many shout outs that night. As, I was dancing Dell walked in VIP and I start grinding my ass on him slow off Avant. By, the time I got done dancing with Dell I had made five hundred dollars. That was some good money to buy me and my kids something from the L.A. Square Mall. I know the night was young and it would be money to add to the five hundred that I had made. After, the dance I gave Dell he went upstairs to the second level in the club so I followed him so I could make more money off him. Dell always was a nigga that tipped me good. Upstairs hoes was getting busy and making money Kreme was on her way to The Hideaway Inn to do a trick. She was in good spirit Kreme was always that way when she was about to make extra money. She was a bitch that was always on top of her game. Especially, being the only one at her grandma house to pay bills being that Travis was in jail. Anyways, upstairs I start shaking my ass for Dell again and after a while Dell whispher in my ear that he wanted to trick with me at The Hideaway Inn. When, we got in the room Dell wanted some head so I gave him some head service. He came in about five minutes and then I wanted some dick because my pussy was wet and he stick it in and gave me the business for about thirty minutes. Before, I left the room at The Hideaway Inn Dell gave me three grand and that was a plus for me then I went back in The Roxy's to shake my ass. When, I got in the Roxy's Kreme was looking for me. I went to find Kreme as soon as I got word she was looking for me. I knew it must be important. Kreme was looking for me because she had a lick for us uptown with this dude. I didn't mind going uptown to make some extra money plus I had just moved that way. Kreme was all excite because the nigga was paying thirty thousand a piece for some females to do a freak show on Dee block in uptown L.A. Shit, I heard the price and told Kreme I was about to grab my bag so we could be out the place. Shit, it wasn't that much money left in the club. Kreme said the night was still young and the nigga with the money wasn't ready to go yet so I went back to dance. While, I was dancing I saw still girl name Robin that I once got in a fight with over Travis buying crack from Major. I was surpise because I thought she was suppose to be some bad bitch. An, now she was on rocks. It amazes you how people let their life go down. The night was still young so I went backstage to the locker room to change my lingerie. I wanted my appearance to stay on fleek. I didn't want to go down and be looking like a crack head like Robin. As, I enter back on the dance floor Major gave me a hundred dollars to do a table top dance for him. I got on the table put on a sexy look and begin to dance for my nigga. Major had much money in his hands giving it to a bitch so I took all my clothes off and shook my ass backward and forward on top of the table making both ass cheeks clap. Major and I was putting on a show in The Roxy's other niggas came over to the table and start to tip me. By, the time I had got done dancing on the table The Roxy's was about to close down. When, the DJ made the last call on the microphone Kreme found me so we could go with that nigga uptown to do the freak show for thirty grand a piece. These was some new niggas I didn't know. Kreme had just met dude in the club but we wanted to make the extra money so we packed all our lingerie for the night and headed uptown in my Lexus. On the way there I had Kreme do some more calling around about Tae. From the converstion Kreme was having about Tae he was one of the richest dope boys in L.A. Kreme friend girl said being invovled in strip parties with strippers was the type of shit he liked to do. I just wanted the money out his ass. When, we got to Tae house it was a nine bedroom house with a game room, a swimming pool, and a Jacuzzi in the inside of it with a bar. Tae wanted to chill in the game room and watch us dance on the pool tables. We had a bunch of liquor and got fucked up. I was down for that shit plus I had a little of cocaine left to get high with. In, for the first time Kreme got on cocaine with me. My girl was high after a couple hits to the head but she kept going. When, Tae got back to the game room with the liquor he wanted Kreme and I to take off our clothes and get started with the show. The, first thing he wanted to see were Kreme and I eat each other pussy so I got on the pool table and opened my legs. Kreme got on the pool table and climbed on top of me and open my legs wide and began to eat my pussy. Kreme wet lips made my pussy get even wetter. As, we was doing the freak show Tae started to tip us more money on the side. I end up staying to Tae house to five thirty in the morning. When, the party ended at Tae house I took Kreme back to the hood because I wanted peace at my apartment in Up Living. I dropped Kreme off in the projects and then I went back uptown to my apartment in Up Living. The air was on when I got there and I went into the guest room and laid in the bed that the landlord had let me borrow. I laid down until that Sunday afternoon and watched how the church people talked and gather around after church from the window in my apartment. Then late that afternoon I got my first call from Major. He was upset because he was in the hood looking for me Major had forgot all about the apartment in Up Living already. I told Major I was uptown to my new apartment and told him I would call him later when I get up. When, I got off the phone with Major I had three missed calls from Reese. When, I called Reese she wanted me to come and get the kids because her and Quincy was going on a date. Shit, that wasn't a problem so I call grandma to keep the kids for the day. I got up brush my teeth and but on a rumper for the day. I went two blocks to Reese gated community and got the kids. When, I picked them up I rode downtown L.A. to grandma house so she could watch the kids for the day for me. When, I got to grandma house she was cooking some neckbones and rice. I sat at the kitchen table so I could get me a plate of food. The taste to grandma food always made me feel good.

While, grandma was watching the kids I went in my old room at her house and got me some rest. But, before I could lay down Kreme called me on the phone because she saw my Lexus parked outside my grandma house. Kreme must be was already on her way to grandma house because as I was on the phone I heard her in the front living room giving grandma a hug. My grandma sounded as if she was happy to see Kreme. Shit, my grandma had stuggle to raise me and after Kreme showed me the game she was always one of grandma favorite people. For, that reason grandma had the up most respect for her. After, talking to grandma and Kreme for a while I was awake. While talking to Kreme she mentioned she was going to take the thirty grand she made at Tae house and buy a car. She was tired of getting rides from people or renting junkies cars. I asked grandma one more time before I left to keep the kids. She was in a good mood and decided to watch Money and Major Jr. I took Kreme to the dealer ship and after being there for about an hour she got a 2014 Acura truck. It was a four door with some black leather seats. The next stop in Kreme new truck was the rim shop were she got some twenty- eight inch rims. Niggas all over the hood wanted to know who was driving the Aura truck when we pulled back in the hood. Kreme was doing the right thing by getting a car. It was something for her and her son to get around in. Kreme parked her Acura truck in front of Jay Jack corner were bitches was tricking and making money and I pulled my Lexus in behind her. Niggas was looking around to see who was pulling up in the new truck. When, they saw it was Kreme they made comments like damn Kreme you doing it big like that. Kreme first stop was up to Jay Jack to let him know since she had the new truck she will not only be working the corner as a trick but she will be selling a little dope on the side too. Shit, Jay Jack gave her the okay on her request and I was excited about it because Kreme was trying to come up in the game. By any means I respected a bitch like that. Once Kreme got out on the corner selling drugs most niggas respected her and they divided the sells with Kreme daily so she was making double the money she was before. As, for me, I worked Jay Jack in the daytime still and at night I worked at The Roxy's. That day on the corner everything was humping from tricks to crack sells. After, being on the corner for hours selling pussy and watching Kreme sell dope I watched her sell her last piece of rock to Robin. While, Kreme was doing that my cell phone rung and it was grandma. Grandma was calling because Travis had called her house from the jail house. Grandma say Travis told her he wasn't facing that much time. I told my grandma that was bullshit and don't listen to anything he had to say. Grandma said he talked to Money for along time and he asked about me. That was bullshit to because Travis just thought it was chances of me and him still fucking around that's why he asked about me. But, that was good the no good ass nigga called to speak to his child. I got off the phone with grandma and called Reese to see if she was still on her date with Quincy. Reese was done dealing with her ex Qunicy for the day. So, I asked Reese to go to grandma house to get the kids to give grandma a break. When, Reese made it to grandma house she called me on my cell phone so I could meet her in the projects at my house to see the kids before they go uptown L.A. When, I got to the apartment Reese and the kids was still on the way and the first thing I saw was a new Gucci bag that Major had got for a gift for me. Major was in the kitchen cooking up dope and when I walked in he grabbed his gun really fast. Major thought I was some nigga trying to rob him and was about to shoot me in the face and killed me if I wouldn't have holler his name out loud to tell him stop and put the gun down. Major had scared the fuck out of me. While, I was waiting on Reese to come I went in the back room and got some lingerie to dance in for the night and got my stripper bag ready. Reese came like twenty minutes later and knocked at the door when she got there Reese didn't come in the house she stayed at the front door while I gave Money and Major Jr. a hug. After, seeing the kids and Reese I walked over to Major where he was cooking dope in the kitchen and gave him a kiss and asked him what my little gift was about. Major told me he was just thinking about me and decided to get me a new bag. He was so excite to give me the Gucci bag. The Gucci bag Major gave me was a large size bag that I could start taking to the club with me at night to store my lingerie and stitettos. I went to the backroom and took the lingerie and three inch stilettos off the bed and put them in my new bag. By, the time I went to the backroom and finish getting my clothes ready for the night Major was done cooking dope. Then, as Major kissed on me he lead me to the next room where he had a dozen of roses and ten grand for me. That kind of shit made me proud that Major was my man. Bad as I wanted to spend time with Major I had to hit the club and it was almost time for me to go. I called Kreme to see what was up with her for the night and she was still on the corner working. Jay Jack was on the corner asking where did I go because I had promised him I would

work the corner some more today. I told Kreme that I would be on the corner and about fifteen minutes. I finish loving on Major and gave him a hug and kiss on the cheeks and headed to the corner. When, I got on the corner Dell was walking up to Jay Jack to pay for a trick with me but Red had already paid his money. "Come on baby let's make moves, "Red said." "Okay daddy", I said." Then I walked up the ally to the apartment and started to suck Red up. Red dick was still big but I had got use to fucking him. Shit, I had fucked Red a couple of times. As, I was sucking Red dick he tipped me more money and dropped it on the floor in the apartment so I could see it. After, I sucked Red dick for an hour I gave him some pussy. When, I got done I could hear Dell foot steps come up the stairs. He had already paid Jay Jack and the first thing he did when he walked in was give me an ounce of cocaine and five hundred dollars on the side besides the money he had gave Jay Jack. I put the money in my new Gucci bag and went in the room where Dell was. I got on my knees and start giving Dell head. It was my second head job since I had been back on the corner. When, I got Dell in the position I wanted him in he relaxed and let out his cum into my mouth. When, I got back on the corner Jay Jack was fussing with some new girl for getting money from one of the local dope boys without fucking him. Jay Jack told the female to get off his corner and don't come back. By, that time Mark was on the corner hustling and wanted to see what a chick was working with for the day. Everything was cool with me as usually and I was trying to make money. Mark walked up to get a closer look at me in my lingerie and decided to pay Jay Jack for a section. He paid five grand on the spot I was looking so damn good. I walked back to the ally apartment and gave Mark a fuck out this world. Mark was a nigga I never mind fucking. He was a fine ass Florida boy with a swag game like a L.A. nigga. When, I got upstairs Jay Jack was behind me he had made it his business to finish watching his hoes for the day after that chick tried to run off with some money. It wasn't a problem with me I still was going to get the job done. As, Jay Jack was watching I sucked Mark up. When Mark and I got done he asked for my number so we could trick on the side then he asked was I in a relationship. I told Mark yeah I was in a relationship. Shit, Major was my heart so I couldn't lie to Mark about him. Even though Mark was a paid ass nigga in the game. Mark whispher in my ear two can play this game, then he told me he was in a relationship also with this girl name Tasha. I knew Tasha well from around the way. An, when Mark told me that he was in a relationship with her it explained well to me how Tasha kept the money to keep herself up. Plus, she was a bitch that sold a little drugs on the side herself. I mean Tasha was a fly ass chick she had a mouth full of gold's and whenever you saw her she was clean from head to toe. After, peeking Mark game and seeing he didn't give a fuck about me being in a relationship with Major I decided to fuck with him on the regular. I walked outside of the ally apartment and had double of what I had before I went in there. I walked to my Lexus and put my money up. As, I was putting my money up Major was making his way around the corner to check on me for the day. He walked up to me and the first thing Major did was give me a big hug and kiss. All the niggas on the corner was peeking us out and loved the fact that Major was my ride or die nigga. That was everyday life in L.A. Night came rolling

around and it was time to clock off Jay Jack corner. So, I went to my apartment and took a shower to head to The Roxy's. By, the time I made it to The Roxy's it was thick as fuck. Every nigga from the hood was there and the DJ was doing his thing on the ones and twos. I went back stage to the stripper locker room and put on my lingerie to dance in. As, I walked on the dance floor the first person I saw was the owner to the club. Pimp was headed my way and when he finally reached me he wanted me to work VIP. When, I got in VIP Kreme was already in the room shaking her ass and making money with niggas. As, I walked though VIP several niggas wanted to dance with me but I gave this dude out of uptown L.A. a dance, I grinded my ass all over his dick. Wayne was his name. He was a brown skinned dude with dreads in his head and he had a mouth full of gold's. That was the type of shit I liked about a niggas. Wayne was giving me compliments on how good I looked in my all black lingerie. Then, out of the blue Major wanted though the VIP room and grabbed my hand. He guided me to the dance floor and we start dancing in the middle of the floor while he made money rain on me. After, dancing with Major for an hour or so he was ready to get his freak on. So, Major asked me did I want to go to The Hideaway Inn to fuck. I was down for some action from my man so I told Pimp the club owner I was leaving VIP for a minute and to find some else to work my spot. Candy came rushing in VIP shaking her ass before I could even leave. As, for me Major and I walked to The Hideaway Inn holding hands. He wanted niggas to know I was his main bitch. I was wearing and all gold lingerie with some gold stilettos. I got from a popular strip store in L.A. When we went into The Hideaway Inn

Major rented the room with the Jacuzzi in it. I took off my lingerie and start dancing on the poll that was in the room. Before you knew it Major dick was sticking up in his boxers kissing on me with a hard dick. I put my hands on Major dick and start to jack it to make sure it was hard all the way. After, jacking Major dick I got on my knees and start giving him some head. As, I was giving my nigga head he put hundreds of dollars on the side of me for a tip. Like always Major paid more money than any nigga in the hood even paid. Major and I finished fucking and I went back in the club. When, I got back in the club Candy had VIP turned up and Pimp continue to let her dance in my spot so I went on the second level of the club. When, I got on the second level Mark wanted a bitch to dance for him so I did my thing for him. Tasha was in The Roxy's for the first time dress to the tee, she had on an all black Gucci dress. I got on the table and did a table top for Mark and the local dope boys start to tip their money to me. T-Pain I' am in love with a stripper came on and the club went crazy. I begin to shake both ass cheeks and bounce up and down on the table and Mark was slapping me on the ass while I was dancing. After, thinking about all the niggas looking at me in The Roxy's I got turned up. Then, out of the blue Dell walked in the club at the peaks of the night hours and wanted a quick fuck. I told Dell he had to pay me double to go to The Hideaway Inn because the club was jumping. Inside The Hideaway Inn Dell pounded my pussy good and I was enjoying it too. It was the first time a nigga licked cocaine off my pussy. Dell gave me ten grand and that made thirty grand in total for me for the night. I walked back in the club and went back in VIP and start dancing. The night ended and Reese was on my voice mail to come and get the kids. My baby daddy Major rode out to Reese house with me. When, we got to Reese house the kids was asleep so I packed up their things and carried them to the car without waking them up. Then, I gave Reese a hug and told her I would bring the kids back once the sun came out for the day. Reese told me that would be okay and don't worry about bringing them clothes because she went shopping for them. As, we rode back to my apartment in Up Living we listened to music in my Lexus having a little family time. That's how I liked things to be. I drove to Up Living and for the first time Major, and the kids and I stayed at my new place. The funitune was still on the way so we slept on the bed the rent man let me borrow. Major walked in the apartment and took a look around it and when he got done he gave me a hug and kiss and told me that's the kind of shit a bad bitch like me should be living in. I unpacked the kids bags that they had from Reese house and Reese had some new clothes in there that she let them bring home from Child Place. When, I was done I went in the master bedroom and laid next to Major and had a long talk about being together forever. We told each other how we were meant to be. Then, in the middle of the conversation the phone rung and it was Robin. She was looking for a hit and Bae told her he wasn't on the corner working. When, Major got off the phone it was five thirty in the morning and Major started to kiss on me. I loved when my man loved on me it made me felt like a real woman on the in and outside of my body. As, we laid in bed Major Jr. begin to cry. It was time for my son to get his morning bottle and that meant I couldn't lay down for the rest of the day because he was up. While, feeding Major

Jr. Major had us in his arms hugging up on us being a family man, minutes later Money got up and wanted some cereals. While, I was up with the kids Major finally got some rest in the master bedroom. My day wasn't going to stop now for me to get some rest both of the kids was up so I put them on some clothes and thought to myself that was part of being a mother you work hard while the man lay down in the bed in get rest. While, me and the kids was chilling Kreme called the phone and wanted to now what I was doing. Kreme was still out from last night and wanted to come and smoke a morning joint with me. I gave Kreme the address to my apartment in Up Living and waited for her to come and with the way she was driving she was to my front door in no time. When, Kreme arrived at my apartment she was fully dress for the day and had much weed to smoke. She talked very loudly and end up waking my man up. After, seeing my new place Kreme gave me a big ass hug. Everyone was hugging me about my apartment. It was so nice and big. My girl was proud to see me doing my thing living large and doing good not being in the hood. From the hug she gave me it was one of those big sister little sister hugs that meant she cared about me doing better for myself. I had came a long ways since I was eightteen when I first start fucking with Travis and my new man was a big help to me in our relationship. For a chick that didn't have a mother or father I was doing good for me and my kids. Kreme, and I talked about plans for the future and she told me how we needed to go back to school. I was down for what Kreme was saying but I still wanted to wait before I get my GED. Shit, as for now I was still dancing and making the strip club my second home. As, Kreme and I was smoking the blunt I saw the six pack to Major chest walk up the hallway in my apartment. He went into the restroom and brushed his teeth. Major was big on making sure he was always clean. That's why I fucked with him. On the way from the restroom Major came in the living room where Kreme and I was and hit the blunt, Major told me he was surpise to see me still at the house. I told Major it was only nine in the morning and it was to early for me to hit the block. After, Major found out what time it was he went back and the room and laid down. Kreme and I stayed up talking and smoking. While, talking to Kreme I got on my cell phone and called Reese. I wanted to know was it okay for me to bring the kids back over to her house but Reese was on her way to Sak Fifth to do some shopping. Reese made me laught at the thought of her going shopping. That's something she loved to do. So, I got off the phone with Reese and called Man. Man was up for the day and was laying low chilling. Shit, he said he wasn't going to get on the clock to later on that day. So, I tap Kreme so she could take me to Man apartment in uptown L.A. It was only two blocks away from my apartment in Up Living. Kreme and I got Money and Major Jr. and headed over to Man place. When, Man saw me he was surpise and decided he wanted to start the day off with tricking me for a couple grand. He had an eight ball of cocaine in a white bag for me. Man was trying to get me in the room fast so I had Kreme sit in the living room area and watch the kids. He gave me ten grand to see where my head game was. I hit the cocaine a couple of times and got on my knees and gave Man some quick head. That was mainly because the apartment was in his name. But, I know Man was just fucking me to give me money because that's what type of nigga he was. Man was the type of nigga that loved for his bitch to stay straight on money. So, when we got done fucking Man gave me another five grand so that was fifteen grand in total. Kreme and the kids were in the living room watching television when we got done. By, the time I had got done with Man and made it to my apartment Major wanted to know where we was and Kreme and I already had our lie together. We told Major Kreme needed a tire change on her Acura. Then, Major called me in the back room and when I got back there he was ready to hit the streets for the day. So, I gave Kreme the word that I would get up with her later Kreme left my apartment and I put on some clothes to get ready and take Major to the hood for the day so he could hustler.

Chapter 3

Yesterday, I didn't make any money on Jay Jack corner. All, I did was chill out and watch out for Kreme while home girl sold drugs and some pussy to Mark friends out of Florida. That was some shit I missed out on. Last, night Major and I had the best candle light dinner at the new apartment in Up Living. I had on an expensive lingerie with some stilettos to make it look good and I put on a show to make my man smile all night. Major, had plenty money in a Gucci bag that was indentical to the one he bought me and for the most part of it he gave me money all night to shake my ass. We were doing shit that those hoes in a flick would do and Major loved every bit of the action. Before, I could leave the house Major asked me to go with him for the day to get a passport to go to the Islands to see his family. When, I got to grandma house I didn't stay that long because Major was with me. But, that was grandma first time meeting Major and she treated him like a child of hers. Major and I left to go get the passport for the post offices. I had never been outside of L.A. and I was so excite about taking my first trip outside of L.A. to the Islands to see Major family. When, Major and I got to the post office the building was pack with so many people. It took a whole hour before I got to the clerk to fill out the information to get a passport. But, after I got to the cerk it only took her five minutes to give me a blue booklet with a passport in the inside. After, getting my passport I smiled my whole way back to the corner. I called Reese before I got on the other side of town and drop the kids off with her. When, I got back on the corner those Florida niggas was still out there with Mark and one of them wanted to know who was driving that nice ass Bentley and I told him it was my man car. "Damn baby yo man got a car like that." By the time I got out the car Mark had paid Jay Jack one thousand dollars to fuck me. After, hearing the price that Mark paid I got a condom out my Gucci bag and walked to the ally apartment. When, I got upstairs I went in the back room and got on my knees and start licking Mark nut sack. Mark was making all kinds of faces as I looked up to see did he like what I was doing. All Mark home boys out of Florida were checking out my head game. After, seeing me do my thing they paid Jay Jack upfront some money to get some action from me. Mark and I were finished in five minutes and he gave me a fifty sack of cocaine to get a little hit before the next trick. I walked outside to Jay Jack and got my half of the cut. Then, Kenny was the next nigga I gave some head service and he had a regular size dick so it wasn't that much for him to cum. Next, was Dread which was also a nigga out of Florida. Unlike, my nigga Dread had locks in his head with six gold's to the bottom of his mouth, he was one cute ass nigga I even played around with him after I did the head job for him. Word, on the streets it was time for Mark to go to West Palm Beach to traffic drugs whenever Kenny and Dread was in town. That day on the corner Mark had lots of Grey Goose and niggas and hoes were getting fucked up on the corner. Fucking with those Florida boys was dope and I thought I had missed them and they were gone back home but that wasn't the case. L.A. was still jumping and hoes were out on the streets tricking left and right. While, chilling on the corner that day I got a call from Travis using someone one time free phone call at the jail. Shit, the name the operator said was unknown but I knew it had to be Travis. I press zerc on the phone and some male that was in the county let Travis have his one time free call. Travis was calling my phone to see was Kreme around. Shit it was a small world I didn't even know he knew my cell phone number. Grandma or Kreme had to give it to him. I walked down the ally quickly to give Kreme the phone plus I wanted to be noisy and see what Travis was about to say. Travis told Kreme the state was only giving him six months and to tell haters to mind their own business and he would be out soon. Kreme got off the phone all excited about the state not sending Travis ass to prison. I was even happy for my babydaddy. That was a good thing he wasn't going down the road. Maybe he could get out and be a better father to Money. The corner wasn't moving that fast since those three tricks I did so I left and went to my apartment in the project. When, I got there I told Major they gave Travis six months and Major was even happy for him. Major was in the kitchen cooking up crack like always. As for me I went in the back room to my safe and counted up all my money. I had so much money I was balling. A young bitch like me had one hundred and sixty six thousands dollars just sitting at the crib. I got fifty thousand out my safe to go and get a new Bentley. I called my grandma to see could I pay her to put a car in her name. Shit, my grandma was down for me paying her to put a car in her name for me. I took out another ten grand and put it in my Gucci bag. I got in my Lexus and drove a couple blocks to grandma house. When, I got there grandma was up and ready to go to the car dealer I opened the Gucci bag and put ten grand in cash in grandma hand. Grandma took the money and put it in her secert hiding place where she keep all her money. We got in the Lexus and drove to the Bentley dealership when I got there I saw several cars that I wanted. I picked out an all black on black Bentley and the car dealership did a credit check on grandma I paid my cash and we were on the way. Grandma drove the Lexus to my new apartment building and got in the car with me and we drove back to the hood. Niggas was looking to see who was in the new Bentley riding thought the hood and Kreme spotted me from a mile away and start yelling that's my dawg in the new Bentley. I still had factory rims on the Bentley. I told Kreme to hop in so we could take a spin to my apartment in the project so Major could check out my Bentley I just got straight off the car lot. When, we pulled up on Major he was on the corner selling dope. He stopped what he was doing in walk over to my new ride. "So I see you in a Bentley with factory rims on it." "Don't tell me it's yours." "Yeah baby its mines and I paid cash for it. "Major hopped in my new whip and drove it around the block to show it off. Shit, I was happy Major was driving my car I wanted him to be seen in my car. I wanted niggas to know my nigga was driving. I told Major I had to get something fresh with all the money I was making I wanted to upgrade. I went on telling him I still had the Lexus and I put the Bentley in grandma name. After, Major got thought showing my Bentley off I hit him up on his cell phone so Kreme and I could slide. When, he pulled back up on us for the second time he had the music blasting to the max in that bitch. The factory speakers sound so loud and clear. He jumped out my new whip kissed me in the mouth to let me know I was doing my damn thing and went back to selling dope. Niggas start hitting me up on my cell phone telling me Major was in a new black Bentley. I told them it was my new ride and to put the word out to everyone on the block. I drove to the spot I had picked Kreme up from and let her sell her dope for the rest of the day. An, my next stop was uptown to Man place. When, I let Man see my new Bentley he was happy for me. I told him I paid fifty grand in cash for it. Man and I enjoyed the rest of the day with each other. I showed off my new ride with all the ballers uptown the kids was with me uptown and the kids was fresh in their Polo Ralph Lauren. Every nigga uptown wanted to know who I was. While, I was uptown I phoned Reese to keep the kids for me and Reese had just made in back in from the mall and told me I could bring them over. When, I got to Reese house with Man I showed her my new ride and she had all kinds of designer gear on her bed from the mall. I was thinking to myself that Reese had been doing a lot of shopping lately. Reese even bought me something I like out the Jimmy Choo Collection which was a dress. After, driving all over L.A. in my whip I went back to the hood. When, I got back to the hood I went to the drug man and got me some cocaine and chilled out until it was time for me to dance at The Roxy's for the night. Before the club

I went to get a sew-in. Hoes in the shop was talking about who they fuck with and talking about everybody business as usually. As, for me I just sat there and got my sew-in done. They even were talking about Mark and how he got a new Mustang stunning with those niggas out of Florida. I just sat there quite shit I didn't need some messy ass bitches in my business. Shit, it was bad enough they knew I was a stripper at The Roxy's. My girl put me before any of her customer because I gave her and extra hundreds dollars and I was done in no time so I could head to The Roxy's to dance. I pulled back and the project ran into my apartment and got my lingerie ready for the night. After, I got done I rode to the club when I pulled up to the club it was pack and niggas was everywhere. The, owner to the club was outside making sure all the strippers made it in the club safe because someone had just got robbed outside the club. My man was in the building alone with Mark and Kenny and Dread those niggas out of Florida. Kreme was already at the club and when I walked thought the club it seemed like every nigga in the club was trying to get at her. When, I got in the club I walked thought the club and went to the DJ station like I always do and got a turn to dance. Then, I went to the locker room and put on my lingerie. I went back on the dance floor and by that time Pimp the club owner was back in the club and wanted me to work VIP with Kreme. I was down for that because that meant more money for me. When, I got in VIP Mark and his friend was inside with ten grand in a money bag. Five was for me and the other five was for Kreme. These niggas wanted to see Kreme and I put on a freak show with each other. I stood on the table and start shaking my ass in front of Kreme to get the party started. I clapped my ass for Dread and Kreme at the same time. I don't know why but for some reason I liked his swag. When, Kreme finally start eating my pussy camera phones was flashing everywhere. In VIP the niggas out of Florida was making it rain. They bought the liquor bar and they spent so much money. By the end of Kreme freak show with me Dread wanted to take me to The Hideaway Inn and fuck. I gave the word to the club owner Pimp as I always do and asked him could I step out to make some extra money. Pimp gave me the okay and Dread and I left to get the moment started. When, I got to The Hideaway Inn Major was in there fucking around with Candy. The first thing came to my mind was this nigga got me fucked up. Major and I start fighting and Dread didn't know what the fuck was going on. I hit Major so many times in the face until he finally got away from me. He had me fucked up with talking to another bitch. I told Major everything was over between me and him and to come to my house and get his shit. The same way I saw him with Candy I walked in The Hideaway Inn with Dread. Dread asked me what that was all about. I told Dread Major was my people and I caught him fucking another hoe. I was upset with Major ass. It's no telling how long Candy and Major had been fucking around with each other. All while I was fucking Dread I was thinking about how I just saw Major fucking another female. Candy wasn't an ugly girl in fact she was cute with a nice shape. I finished up the trick with Dread and went back in the club. When, I finally got back in the club I changed my mind quickly about Major coming to get his shit from my house. I walked up to Major and asked him did he still love me. He was like yeah Kelly. "You mean the world to me Kelly and don't never think different." "Candy was just a trick you are my lady." Then, he went on talking about all the niggas I had tricked with. That kind of disappointed me but I had to stand there and take it like a grown woman. I wanted to keep things straight with Major because he was leaving the country in a couple of weeks and I still want to go. After, Major and I talked and got an understanding I went in the VIP room and start dancing on the dance floor. I felt better Major wasn't leaving me for another bitch or hoe. For the rest of the night I danced in VIP. Then, Major walked in VIP and it reminded me to tell him to get the money back from Candy that he had paid her to trick with him. Major, did just as I told him to do. An, after that he knew not to trick on me again that why I was his main bitch for him to get pussy from. Now, that was an understanding I knew I wasn't going to have problems out him again. That night I finish VIP in the club and instead of tricking after the club I went home for the night. Major was there with me. The night went by fast and it was daylight outside before you knew it and I was getting a call from the funtiune man. He was calling because he found time to bring the funtiune early. I got up and called Reese and told her I would be running a little late because I wanted to rearrange my funtiune safetly without the kids being in the way. After, the funtiune man left Major fucked the shit out of me and promise he would never cheat again. I suck Major dick and he kissed all up on me with the new gold's he had just got in his mouth. Major tongue tasted so good and I wanted to keep fucking him all day. I laid down on the bed for the last time that the rent man let me borrow and Major whole my body. He wanted me to know what he had done in the club with Candy was wrong and he was still my man no matter what. And nann bitch couldn't come between that. Directly, after Major and I had sex the furniture man came to the house. I got up and put on some clothes and finally answered the door for him. When, I got to the door the furniture man had a receipt for me to sign for dropping the Gucci furniture off. Then he and one other man moved the Gucci designer in the house. I called Kreme to tell her the furniture man was there with the Gucci designer set and she rushed to my apartment to see my new set up. When, my friend saw my apartment with all Gucci in it she was so shocked she told me how nice my shit was. All, Kreme could do was hug me on what I had done. That was a big step moving out the projects. The furniture was white and gold. An, I had white and gold all though my apartment. I had a couple pictures of 2Pac in the game room. Other than that I had photos of the kids in my apartment. By, the time I arranged everything in the apartment Major was up and called me to his presents. I told Major to get up so I could put the new bed in the master bedroom. I moved the used bed that the rent man had let me borrow out and moved the king size Gucci designer in my room. I called Reese so she could bring the kids home and so she could see the new furniture I had got. Reese didn't take long at all to get to my apartment and when she got there she was surprise to see it with some thirty thousand dollars furniture. Reese had nice shit in her apartment but nothing like what I had in my place. Reese didn't stay that long and in fact when she left she took the kids with her because she was off for the day. Kreme, left directly after Reese and that left Major and me at the apartment along again. I put that pussy on Major in our new king size Gucci bed. My nigga hit my pussy real good from the front and back and then he hopped in the shower. I got in the shower with Major and my body felt damn good feeling the warm hot water go done my back. Major rubbed Victoria Secret all over my body and bath me up and down. When, we was done taking a shower Major dried my body off and lotion me up. Then, my nigga help me put on my clothes. Next, Major put on his clothes and we headed to the hood for the day so I could work the corner and Major could hustle. When, I got on the corner those Florida boys were still out there. Mark came down the ally to see what was up with me for the moment. Shit, like ant trick nigga he wanted to pay for some pussy. I went upstairs to fuck Mark and he gave Jay Jack five grand to fuck me. Mark was surprise at how good the head was and gave me some money on the side. When, I finish Mark gave me some cocaine to add with the money on the side. Mark wanted some chicks to travel to West Palm Beach and traffic dope back to L.A. the trip was going to be only for three days. He was going to take us to a strip club that makes much money and dance at a club called The Kings of Diamonds. It was some big time club owned by the rapper Trick Daddy Dollar father. I asked Mark could I take Kreme with us. Mark was down for that type of shit. On the way there he was going to stop in Jacksonvillie at the Skyline. It was a joint were local niggas from Jacksonvillie get together and pay hoes to dance. Kreme was down for going when I called her on her cell phone and asked her. That afternoon I called Reese to see could she keep the kids for three days while I hit the road on my road trip to Florida. Reese told me yeah and don't worry about bringing the kids clothes she had clothes for them at her house. That afternoon I finished working the corner because I needed to get up enough money to go to Tricks to get some lingerie to dance in while I was in Florida. I wanted to be on point. My two biggest tricks of the day were Dell and Mark. Then, I clocked off the block. I went back to my apartment in the projects and counted up my money in my safe for the first time after I bought the Bentley. I paid fifty thousands for the car. An, gave grandma ten grand for putting it in her name so I still had a little over a hundred grand left. I had one more night to dance in The Roxy's before I went to Florida and I wanted to make like ten grand to take with me. After, I counted up all my money and put it back in my safe I called Major up to let him know about the deal going down in Florida. I told Major I was going to traffic some dope back to L.A. and I would bring him a key of cocaine back. Major was down for that and had much respect for me telling him about my trip and me bringing him some work back. This was going to be my first time trafficking dope and I wanted the trip to go well. Kreme was going with me so that was a plus. When, I got off the phone with Major and put the money back in the safe I went to Tricks to get me some lingerie to dance in while I was going to be in Florida. I wanted those niggas in the Skyline and King of Diamonds to remember a bad bitch like me. Mark had gave me five grand and Dell had gave three grand and that's the money I was going to lingerie shop with. Uptown L.A. I bought six lingerie outfits with the matching stilettos. One of them had a picture of dope and guns on it. It was some hot girl type shit to dance in. Next, I got a pair black stilettos to match all six outfits. As, I was going in Tricks Kreme was walking out she gave me the word that she had been to Florida with some niggas before and was nice there. Kreme was looking fly ass fuck and had went and got six gold's in her mouth with some diamonds and home girl was unstoppable. After, shopping in Tricks I headed to the mall to get some summer short sets out of Aeropostle. I also went in Forever 21 and bought some more of those dresses. Being in the mall took awhile but when I was done I was ready for my trip to Florida. My next stop was back to the crib to get ready to dance at The Roxy's. When, I got back to the crib in the hood and pack my things for the night I still had a little time before the club start so I grabbed my safe to take it to my apartment in Up Living. I didn't want anyone to notice I was gone and come in and steal all my money. By the time I was done taking the safe to my apartment uptown the night was still young so I went back to on the block and niggas was still hanging out. Robin was out there looking for a hit and the crack was taking her down each day. She was looking badder than a motherfucker. Kreme and I made it back to the block at the same time and some new niggas that was on the block was trying to see who were pulling up and the all black Bentley and pink Acura. When, Kreme and I jumped out the driver seat niggas was like damn they doing big things. Then, Kreme and I walked up on Jay Jack and gave him word that we were both going to Florida for a couple days so we wouldn't be on the corner. The ally apartment was clear and all the dope boys we knew were gone to The Roxy's. So, I left the block and didn't trick with any of those new cats hanging out. I went to my apartment and parked my whip and got my Gucci strip bag and walked blocks over to The Roxy's. On my way there I saw junkies buying crack and srtippers going to their second jobs. When, I got to The Roxy's I walked in and every niggas in the club turned their heads around to see who I was. Mark was the first nigga I saw that night and I gave him word I was ready to go to Florida. Major came in the club with some Roca Wear on with the matching boots hoes and niggas was trying to see who he was he was so clean. Major walked in after his grand entry and gave me a hug and a kiss on the lips. That shit made me feel good ass fuck with Major kissing up on me looking that damn good. I finish hugging Major and went and got a VIP pass to dance VIP for the night. Those Florida boys was making it rain in the club for their last night in L.A. The DJ was playing Timthony Harris song twenty fours and all the stripper was on the dance floor making their ass round off. Then, in the club that night they had this gay couple name Roonie and Rhonda dance on stage. They did a nice freak show eating each other out. Niggas paid them a lot of money for the show they did. I even tipped them a couple of hundreds. They had candles on stage with them to make the club light up and I ready think they did wonderful. It was a marvelous thing to see. Then, right after the show with the gay couple it was my turn to dance on the stage. Major gave me ten grand in all hundred just for being his bitch and Mark stood in front of the stage and watched me dance the whole time and tipped a couple grands. I stood in front of Mark at one point and made my ass round off hard ass fuck and he threw money all over me. I dropped on the floor so he could get a close up then I came down the poll and came into a splint. I got all my money off stage and went to the back locker room to put my money in my locker. When, I went back on the dance floor Major had an attitude because I was dancing in front of Mark. The first thing he said to me was don't let me fuck you and your fuck boy up. I act like I didn't hear him and went back in VIP. In, VIP for the rest of the night I dance and put on a wonderful show. Every nigga in the club was giving me money. The night came to a end and I went back to the project where I stayed for the night. When, I got there Major was still in the streets but walked in twenty mintues later after me. He still had and attitude with me. So I went in the back room. I got a phone call from Mark and I tried to act like it was Kreme on the phone. Mark was calling to tell me we were leaving first thing and the morning. So, I decided to get some rest and morning came before you knew it. The first person I called was Kreme because I know she had a long night but she was already up and packing her things. I asked Kreme to ride behind me so I could take my Bentley to Up Living. Shit, I didn't want any junkies selling parts off my car so that would be the best place to take it. No junkies the better it would be. I got in my car and Kreme followed me uptown. When, I got uptown I park my car in Up Living and went back to the hood. On the way to the hood Mark phoned me and told me to meet him at the airport he was ready to leave town. Mark said our first stop would be in Jacksonvillie, Florida to get a rental car and the other way we would drive to West Palm Beach. Kenny and Dread was with us and I enjoyed their stay in L.A. they really should me they was some real niggas and they spent some money with me. When, Kreme and I got to the airport Kenny, Mark, and Dread had their bags pack and on the flight ready to go to Florida so his homeboys could go home and we could get the dope and come back to L.A. We rode Delta First Class to Florida. On the plane Kreme and I sat in the front of the plane. It was a long flight to Jacksonvillie but when we got there Mark paid for the rental car with a credit card. After, we got the rental car we stop by a soulfood place and got us something to eat. Then, we went to one of the finest motels in Jacksonvillie to get a room. When, we got to the room we unpacked our things and we rode clean to Florida so we had to go in the hood which was on the Northside of Jacksonvillie to get some weed and cocaine. In the project we went to females and niggas knew we wasn't from there by our swag. Mark went in the projects and went to this dude he knew in got the supply. On the way back to the room we stop to get some blunts and our night was on from them. Mark, drove into the motel parking lot and we had already smoked our first blunt. When, we got in the room we got out the camera phone and took all kinds of pictures and made a private facebook page so we could talk direct to each other without anyone knowing. That was for Major and his girlfriend Tasha wouldn't be in our business. All on the beach I got on cocaine and Mark took photos of me and made me feel like I was his woman. It was like he was my dream man and I was hid dream woman. On the beach in Jacksonvillie it was a curise call Main Street Cruise and Mark paid one thousand dollars so I could go on the cruise with him and have a couple of drinks. Kenny and Dread was booed up with Kreme and my friend was about to show them some of her stripper moves and put on a show for them. On the cruise Mark paid for a private room for two hours and we had sex and I danced on the strip poll that was in the room. In Jacksonville after the cruise we went to something called the Florida Fair and I rode on a lot of rides. Night came round and it was time for us to go to the Skyline. In the course of being in Jacksonville for those couple hours I got to know Mark and he had nice conversation and he really was a cool dude to be around. When, we got to the Skyline Mark parked the rental car and Kreme and I got out with our bags. I had a fake I.D. because you had to be twenty one to dance at the Skyline. My I.D. said I was twenty one years old and I was able to buy liquor that night. At the Skyline when we got there the music was different from L.A. the DJ was playing a lot of booty shcking music but I could vibe to that. Kreme and I were high as hell from the weed and cocaine we got from the projects in Jacksonville. We, went to the back locker room and it was nice in the inside with a lot of mirrors so you could get a view of your whole body. When, we got back on the dance floor we start working the club like we had been there before. Mark went to the club owner and told him there were some new females in the building and we wanted to work VIP. We had to pay and extra fifty dollars but it was worth it because we made the money back. The disco light was on and the colors from the light made our outfits look even better. After, we paid to go in VIP Kenny and Dread went to the bar and got ten thousand dollars in ones to tip us. Kreme and I were in VIP making our ass jump up and down for some Florida boys with a mouth full of gold's. In the Skyline I worked the strip poll like crazy that night. It was all kinds of niggas in there and they was buying you drink after drink all night. Unlike at The Roxy's there was no side line motel to trick in. Hoes in Florida had to travel miles outside of a club to trick. Kenny found a little hot baby to take back to the motel and trick with. Dread and Kreme hooked up for the first time and

Mark and I had a room alone. Back at the motel Mark and I hugged up on another all night long and he wanted me to know I was going to be his ride or die chick. That was fine with me I could be his ride or die chick. Long as he knew that Major came first. I took off the Jimmy Choo dress that Reese had bought me and as I took the dress off Mark watched the frame of my body. Mark looked at my body and told me I looked like a grown ass woman I didn't look like I was nineteen years old. Mark went telling me that Major had a fine ass bitch for a old lady and he didn't mind sharing her. All that night I was balling out I was chilling with a major dope boy in the game and I end up making twenty thousand dollars at the Skyline. Anyways, by the time I took the dress off and Mark watched to see my body his dick was already on hard and he struck it inside of me. It reminded me of the candle light dinner that Major and I had a couple days before I came on the trip. Mark made love to me and made me feel like a grown woman and I liked that. Alnight Mark and I had sex and when we got done it was morning time and we didn't get any sleep. We got up and put on clothes and I put on one of those Forever 21 dress I got for the mall in L.A. Mark thought I looked sexy than a motherfucker. We rode miles away from Hotel Duval to fine a Waffle House to eat breastfast at. Kreme and I smoked our first blunt of the day before we ate and we were higher than a motherfucker. Mark told us that we would be heading to West Palm Beach after we eat. At, the Waffle House I ate waffle and eggs with bacon. Kreme, Mark, Kenny and Dread had the All Star meal. After, we finish eating we got on interstate seventy five and headed towards West Palm Beach. It took us a couple hours to get from Jacksonville to

West Palm Beach. While we were on the way to West Palm Beach and Mark was driving I decided I will give Major a call. I told Major that I was in Florida and I was on the way to West Palm Beach to get the dope. Major was excited to hear from me and told me to make sure it some good dope before I buy it. My man had never had a whole key of cocaine bought by me. I only bought him a couple of ounces before but this time I was doing it big for my man. After, a couple of hours on the road we finally made it to West Palm Beach. When we got there palm trees was everywhere and the city was so big and nice. I was happy to be in Florida with some dope boys spending money and having fun. The first thing we did was drop Kenny off at his babymama house. Kenny babymama had a manison builded in the hood of West Palm Beach I mean home girl was doing it big. Then, Dread and Kreme went to The Hoilday Inn and got them a room. That gave Mark and I some time alone. When, Mark and I dropped off everyone we went on the beach in Miami and hugged up. Then we went to the Wellington Mall it was suppose to be one of the biggest malls in West Palm Beach. I did a lot of shopping and balled out. Next, Mark took me to Fort Lauderdale. In Fort Lauderdale I went to the Galleria, Coral Springs, and The Sawgrass Mall. Mark was just showing me around in Florida and I was having a lot of fun. The weather was nice in the Sunshine State. I did a lot of kissing and hugging up on Mark and he made me feel like a queen. Next, after shopping at the malls down south Mark and I went and got a room. We took a lot of pictures and posted them online. At the Courtyard by Marriott I made love to Mark and I rode his dick and gave him head and made him feel like I was suppose to make him feel. I treated him that special because Mark had beat Major to the punch and took me out of L.A. first. Mark and I end up fucking for the rest of the day. It was our second day in Florida and on our third day we were going to get the dope before we leave. By the time night came Mark and I had did so much we wanted to contunie to spend time with each other but we had plans to go to the Kings of Diamonds. Mark did a little talking to me about the Kings of Diamonds and told me that only big time strippers worked in there but I had the shape looks and body so I would do good. We called Kreme on her cell phone to see what the deal was with her going to the Kings of Diamonds and working with me. As, usually Kreme was down for making another dollar. We drove from our motel we had got in Fort Lauderdale and went back to West Palm Beach. When we got to the Hoilday Inn where Kreme and Dread was staying my girl was dress and already had on her lingerie. Kreme was showing most of her body and her nipples was still on hard from where Dread had been kissing on her at. We jumped in the rental and headed to Miami, Florida. Mark said it should only take us fourty five minutes to get to Miami for West Palm Beach. When we got to the Kings of Diamonds niggas was everywhere and they all knew Kreme and I was some new faces. I had on another Jimmy Choo dress that I had recently got back home in L.A. Kreme had on her lingerie gear and niggas was trying to get at us left and right. When we got in the club the owner saw how sexy Kreme looked in her lingerie and asked us to work VIP for Plies. I went to the back stripper locker room and put on my lingerie and went back in VIP. The Kings of Diamonds was so big and it was nothing like the Skyline in Jacksonville. I had my duffle bag to keep my money in the inside of it. I danced on the poll in VIP and played with my pussy with some sex toys to make extra money. Mark watched to make sure my dance moves was straight and he tipped at the same time. Mark gave me a thumbs up to let me know I was doing a wonderful job. The thirty inch weave I had in my hair made me look like a model on television. Before you knew it I had made twenty grand from some local dope boys from Miami in the Kings of Diamonds. They had never saw a bitch and decided they would tip big. Mark walked around with my duffle bag to keep up with how much money I was making and to make sure I didn't get rob and Dread did the same for Kreme. After, working the stage by myself for about two hours I went back to VIP with Kreme. When, I got in VIP Kreme was in a freak show with one of the females that worked in the club. I mean they were getting their freak on. Niggas had out their camera phones taking pictures of them. I was surpise to see Kreme eat another female pussy beside mine. But, I liked what I saw so I tipped her and the bitch a little money on the side and took some photos of them myself. After, the club we took Dread and Kreme back to The Hoilday Inn in West Palm Beach. At the motel Kreme got her duffle bag and counted up all her money that she had made in the club. She counted a total off one hundred thousand dollars to the little twenty thousands that I had made. We posted all our money online to let niggas and hoes know we was making big bank. As, we was posting our money and having fun online a video of Kreme flash cross the phone, a nigga name Cash had a video of Kreme eating that female stripper out in the Kings of Diamonds. There were so many people making comments on Kreme. Niggas

was like damn she eating the fuck out of her. Mark, and I stayed at Kreme and Dread motel for about an hour then we left. On the way to our room Mark asked me how did I feel about trafficking. I told him it was new to me put I was down for it and I would do it anytime. By, the time Mark and I got done talking and having sex once it was a brand new day. I got up put on some clothes because I didn't want to lay around the room all day. While, I was getting ready Mark put on some clothes and called the dude about the ten kilo's of cocaine. The dude told Mark and I to meet him in Miami in about a half hour. It didn't take long at all to get the dope and I checked it to make sure it was some good cocaine just like Major told me too. By, the time we got the cocaine Kreme and Dread was calling us to see what time we was leaving down south to head back up north. When, we got to Kreme and Dread room they already had on clothes. We took Dread home and got on the road. Mark, Kreme, and I drove all the way to Jacksonville and took the same route back to L.A. When, I got to L.A. the weather was different and it was cool. I got off the plane and the first thing I did was called for a cab. Next, I called Major to see where he was and Major was in the projects waiting on me to come over. Thank god I had made it back safe with the dope and I was about to give my man a key to sell. I got in the cab and rode to my apartment in Up Living to get my car and my next stop was to deliver Major the dope. In Up Living I put the fourty thousand dollars that I had made in Florida up. In Jacksonville I had made twenty thousand and Miami I made twenty thousand so that was fourty thousand in total. Before, I left Up Living to go to the projects I called Mark to let him know I had a good time out of town. When,

I called Mark he was at the ally apartment cooking his dope up already. Being on the phone with Mark made me feel good all over again about the experience I had just had in Florida. I put the money I made up and did a couple things around the house like make up the bed and wash the few little dishes Major left in the kitchen. I went to the project gave Major the dope and went back to Up Living. When, I got to Up Living I did the most important thing and that was call Reese. When, I called Reese it was late and her and the kids was in the bed for the night. I told her I would call her the next day or she could call me when she get up tommrrow. Night had come and L.A club life was about to start. I know all the ballers was about to be out. It, was my first night back in L.A. but I knew I was going to work the club for the night. I know Pimp missed a lot of money while Kreme, and I was out those three days. When, I got to the club it was a lot of people as always and niggas was paying cash. Different night same niggas paying money to see a freak show, Pimp was happy to see me back in the club. He knew niggas was about to pay their money. I saw Candy and she had a frown on her face when I saw her. I guess because I made Major take the money he tricked with her at The Hideaway Inn. I made the bitch even madder I danced next to her made the most money them went in VIP and worked the poll and made the most money and there too. I got a call on my cell phone and it was from Dell. An, from the background he sounded like he was in The Roxy's. Dell had missed my face for a couple of days and was trying to trick something. He wanted to go to The Hideaway Inn. I told him I needed five grand off top. Dell walked over to where I was standing and gave me the money and we went to fuck.

Dell asked a couple questions like where was I for the last couple days. I really didn't want to tell him but I told him Florida anyways. I got on my knees and Dell pulled my hair back and I gave him some head. When, I was done I went back in the Roxy's and danced for the rest of the night.

Chapter 4

At The Roxy's last night everything went well and I end up making some money. Dell was surpise to see me back in town and for the first time I stayed at The Hideaway Inn with him. Major have been calling my phone all night long. Now, it's morning I'am about to get up with my man and see what's going on with him. As, I called Major the phone rung and he answered it with an attitude. "Where the hell you been at Kelly." "I have been calling your motherfucking phone all night long." "Major I stayed at Kreme hous." "Last night we spent the whole night talking and counting up money." I had to throw Major a lie. If not he would have been fussing the whole day. I asked Major where he was in he was in Up Living at the new apartment. I got up and headed towards Up Living. When, I made it to the door Reese had dropped the kids off because she had and emergency at work. Sometimes things like that happened at Reese job. Money was getting so big and Major Jr. was about to be two months in two weeks. I couldn't believe time was pasting like that. When, I made it to the back room Major was sitting on the bed smoking his first joint of the day. Then, he jumped up hit me so quick and blacked my eye Major had surpise me with that one. I thought he had went for the lie I told him. I start yelling and crying at the same time. I told that no good motherfucker to get the hell out my apartment. Major wouldn't listen to me. Then, I called Kreme so she could help me. Kreme answered the phone by saying "Bitch where you at because Major been riding throw here in his Bentley looking for you." "I told him you were at the club.""Kreme don't worry about that hurry because Major just hit me in the eye and it's black." "I promise if he don't leave my house am going to cut his ass." "Whole up am on the way Kelly, you two don't need to be carrying on like this." Kreme rushed to Up Living and made it just in time before Major and I start fighting again. Everytime Major hit me he called me a lying bitch. I really didn't give a fuck about what he had to say. So, what I had lied. I was out trying to get money. Shit, he was a dope boy and Major gave me cash put I needed my own money for me and my kids too. Kreme told me to pack some clothes so the kids and I could get out the apartment for a couple of days. I rushed and packed some clothes. Then, I asked Major for my key. The nigga didn't even give it to me. I guess Major was going to stay at the apartment. So the kids and I left and went to the projects. Things was so much better there I didn't hear all that fussing. Kreme kept me company. My home girl would never forsake me. Kreme rubbed my eye and knew I was hurt about Major hitting on me. Major hit me but I wasn't leaving him because I knew I was wrong for staying out with another man. Kreme called Major on the phone and told him I was with her last night and home boy told Kreme to get her lie straight and hung up the phone. Major called me and asked me was I still playing games and did I want him to beat my ass again. She could have called me when Major came looking for me. The sun was shinning and my day had started off the wrong way. I was full of worries. I called grandma to see could she keep Money and Major Jr. I still needed to work the corner. That's how it was being a trick you wanted all the money you could get. By, the time I got off the phone with grandma Major was calling me with the same bullshit. I continued to tell him I was with Kreme to the end. Major talked on the phone with me for a long time then he came to the apartment in the projects. Major saw my eye and thought that I needed to stay out the streets until it go down. Shit, that would take two weeks. Then, he slap me punched me in the room and fucked the shit out of me. Things were getting serious between Major and I. Major gave me some money after we had sex. I was beginning to be in Major pockets a lot. I got and took Money and Major Jr. to grandma house. I put of a pair of Dooney&Burke sunglasses that Reese had purchase for me months ago. The fact of having to wear sunglasses to grandma house because I had a black eye felt bad. I drop Money and Major Jr. off at grandma and jumped in my Bentley and rode uptown to my apartment and counted the squares of money that Major had just gave me. I counted one hundred thousand dollars in total. The fact of Major giving me that much money made me cry. Major was really in love with me. All this time I wanted him to love and care for me he was finally doing it. At age nineteen I had two hundred and twenty six thousand dollars. For a minute I just sat there and thought how I was broke before I got introduced to the game. In a minute if I kept up with what I was doing I would be a million dollar bitch. I needed to go to the L.A. Square Mall to get some sunglasses to match up with the different outfits while my eye was black. It was around three o' clock so I called Kreme so she could tell Jay Jack I would be running late. Kreme put the word on the streets and told me to hurry up because money was coming fast. My head start hurting thinking of all the money I was missing out on. I finally made it to the mall. I went in Sunglass Hut and bought six pair of different designer shades. That should be enough while my eye is black. I rushed out the mall and drove all the way to Jay Jack corner. Niggas and hoes were on the corner selling drugs and selling pussy. When, I got out the Bentley niggas was running up to me like I was about to buy crack from them or I was some famous bitch. Mark was on the corner and he was showing Red our private facebook page. After, Red saw all the photos he was like damn Kelly that's how you do it. I told that nigga he know I do it big. Then, that made Red want to pay for some of my pussy. Red went up to Jay Jack and gave him a couple of hundreds. Shit all he wanted was a fifteen minute section. I went to the ally apartment and I laid on the bed in the backroom. Red struck his ten inch dick inside me. It felt good to the have all that hard core dick inside me. Then, I finish Red up and went on the corner. Robin was back on the corner asking and begging for crack. Kreme was the only one on the block that gave her some crack. She felt bad to see one of Travis ex-girlfriends begging for a hit. Then out of blue I asked Robin how did she end up on crack. She gave me this sad story on how she lost her family in a ally fire. Then, she turned around and asked me for some crack. After, I told

Robin I don't sell crack or give junkies crack I continued to walk up and down the corner for the afternoon to trick. Dell was on the corner looking finer than motherfucker with a Ralph Lauren Polo outfit on. Instead of tricking me he pasted me off some cocaine. I went down the ally apartment and took a couple hits. Damn that was some good shit. I went back on the corner and Mark paid Jay Jack some money so I could dance for him for a whole hour. I put on another lingerie and went upstairs. I got on the pool table and start doing table tops for Mark. Mark was making money rain on me I was looking that good. I had on the sunglasses I had just got from Sunglass Hut and it matched with my lingerie. Mark felt on my ass and hit me on the ass hard. As, Mark hit me on the ass he gave me money, Jay Jack was standing at the door to watch out for nine. Nine came on the corner on the block while Mark and I was doing our thing. Everyone in the ally apartment ran and dope and everything was left in the apartment. The only person that got caught was Robin and she was smoking crack when nine got her. Robin was cussing the L.A. police department out. In the ally apartment niggas had left so much crack Robin got charged with all those charges. Possession of cocaine and attend to sell crack was two of her charges. The next day of the streets word was that feds picked up Robin case. I was like that's a damn shame feds picked up a crack head. That was kind of mess up a junkie getting charged with all that dope, Major had stayed at my apartment in Up Living and I stayed in the projects. So, I didn't get a chance to tell him what happen to Robin. But, I thought it was good Major and I was getting a little space. I laid down most of the day after I went and got Money and Major Jr. from grandma house. Money reminded me so much of the pictures of me at grandma house when I looked at her. She was so pretty. By the time afternoon came I had got several phone call one was from Kreme telling me about Robin and the other one was from Reese telling me she was home from work if I wanted her to keep the kids. Reese had worked a sixteen hour shift. I got up and went to this local store that sold urban clothes and got the kids something to put on for the day. The sun was shinning bright late November in L.A. and I was surpise. Junkies were all over the corner and I was ready to spend my day chilling. After Robin got charged yesterday I made a decision to stay at home for the day. I figured I could used some rest for the day. After, I drop the kids to Reese house I went to Up Living to see what Major was doing for the day. Major was so excited to see me. He took a look at my black eye and gave me a kiss in the face. Major look at me with a serious look and told me he would never hit me again. Next, we start talking about what was happening in the hood and I told him that the police had got Robin out the ally apartment. I also told Major that Kreme had called me this morning and told me that feds had picked up Robin case. Major couldn't belive that the ally apartment had a drug bus. Major said in cases like that junkies usually start to work. I got out some cocaine and took my first hit to the head for the day. The cocaine had me feeling gooder than a motherfucker. The sun was going down and it was time for me to head back to the hood to get ready to work The Roxy's tonight. Before, I went back to the hood I went to Tricks and got me some lingerie to dance in. After, I left Tricks I went to the hood and hoes was working the corner still or going to their second job. I parked my car on the corner of Jay Jack block to see Kreme. I was killing time before the club start. Kreme was dressed in her lingerie and niggas was paying her to hit the ally apartment and have sex with them. After, seeing Kreme make like two or three licks on the block I decided to leave and go to my apartment in the projects. I chilled there for two or three hours by myself before Major came in the hood. By the time Major got there it was time for me to get ready for The Roxy's. He tried to talk me out of dancing with a black eye. Major went in the kitchen and got his dope to make his rounds for the night then he hit the streets fast. When, Major left I called Man to see what he had going in. On the phone with Man I told him about all the excitement that had been going on downtown and how the police busted the ally apartment. While talking to Man on the phone he wanted to see me so I set a date with him for tonight after The Roxy's. I called Kreme to let her know I was going to be with Man after the club so if Major called her to make up a lie. I got up because it was close to twelve o' clock and I needed to be hitting The Roxy's. When I got to the club niggas was parked on the outside of the parking lot with Bentley's and all kind of shit. I parked my Bentley in VIP parking balling harder than a motherfucker and jumped out with my stripper gear for the night. When, I got in the club Candy was already working VIP for some thug ass niggas with a mouth full of gold's. I thought to myself same shit different night. I changed quickly and walked back on the dance floor and start bouncing my ass to some old Pastor Troy. A song call pop that pussy made for stripper only. All hoes were dancing to the down south dirty music. After, my first song I went to the second level in the club and start doing a freak show with this stripper name Strawberry. Mark was watching me hard and had no choose but to tell me my game was top of the line. I was shaking my ass and nipples. Then, out of know where Major came on the second level of the club and asked me could he tip me and Strawberry at the same time. I was like yeah and he started to spend money. I mean he made it rain with money. Major was balling out with Strawberry and me. After, I made money with Major I went on the third level in The Roxy's. This was my first time on the top last level of the club. U.S.D.A. was on in the club and every stripper that worked in the club was on the dance floor. On the third level of the club there was nothing but doctors and lawyers. They all looked like professional men and they tipped more money. I really enjoyed myself. They treated me like a lady and I made more money because it was my first time on the top level. The night came to a end and it was time for me to go. I called Man because I told him I would spend sometime with him. Man was more than happy to see me. When, I got to Man house I took off the sunglasses and right then Man got upset when he saw my black eye. "What the fuck happen to your eye." "Major hit me the other day because I lied to him." I told Man Major said it wouldn't happen again. Man really wasn't feeling that part about Major made a mistake. All he wanted to know was why my eye was black. I explained to him that I didn't come home after The Roxy's. After, talking to Man for an hour about how a man isn't suppose to hit on a woman we finally had sex. Man missed me for the most part of it. It was seven o' clock in the morning and I still was having sex with Man. Man and I made love for the last time around seven in the morning and

I jumped in the Bentley and headed to Reese house to get the kids. I got to Reese house and got Money and Major Jr. Directly, after I got the kids I called Major to see did he want to watch the kids for the day. Major told me he didn't have a problem with keeping the kids he said it was a first time for everything. Major was in a good mood. I guess he was feeling his self in the streets and had some more pussy outside the house. I knew that was a lie because Major had been downtown making money all night. When, I got downtown with the kids Major had sold the whole key of cocaine that I had got him from Miami. I walked thought the door and Major was selling his last ounce out the package. He gave me ten grand out of the money he had made. I then asked Major again could he keep the kids so I could hit Jay Jack corner. Major told me yeah he would watch the kids for the second time. I got on the phone and called Kreme to see where she was and Kreme was at her grandma house. I walked down the block to Kreme grandma house and when I got there I found my bestie in the back room counting up money. Kreme had counted a million dollar and cash that she had made the night before. With the money Kreme told me she was about to get her grandma out the hood and build her a house. I was happy for Kreme and was waiting on my big break to make a million dollars to. After, talking to Kreme for a hour I went back to the trap apartment. My landlord had got the word that I been doing crack deals out the house and took the rent up two hundred dollars a month instead of putting me out. When, I got in the trap house Major was still watching the kids and he looked like a family man. I kissed him for being the man that he was. I loved Major and nothing could come between that. Being round Major and the kids made me feel good. But, I had to get ready to hit Jay Jack corner. Before, I left I gave Major the note that the rent would be going up. Major gave me the word that he would handle the two hundred dollars every month. I left the trap house and went on the corner when I got on the corner niggas was back selling crack and the drug bus deal with Robin was over. Mark was on the corner making deals with the nine keys of cocaine that he bought back from Florida. Niggas was coming all that day to buy cocaine from Mark and it was grade A because I had a couple hits. Kreme called my phone while I was on the block to let me know she was going to be running late getting on the block. Kreme had some business to handle and was going to work afternoon shift. Jay Jack usually was cool with that for some reason he had an attitude. Niggas on the corner had a block party planned and Kreme was suppose to work it. I called Kreme to let her know that niggas wanted her to do a block party. Kreme said it would only take an hour for what she had to do. I hung up the phone and directly after I hung up with Kreme Mark called my phone so I could come up to the ally apartment and give him some head service. I walked up to the ally apartment and Mark was sitting on the chair waiting on me. I slow danced to Mark and I had on one of the baddest lingerie outfits ever. Mark had a sexy look on his face and he was licking his lips. I blowed a kiss at Mark and got on my knees. When, I got on my knees I pulled Mark pants down. I licked on the top of his dick and sucked it up and down. As, I gave Mark head he had my hair pulled back with his hands. Mark came in about five minutes and the feeling of the cum going in my mouth felt good. I got up off the floor took off my lingerie buttoms and pulled a condom out to fuck Mark. I sucked Mark penis again to get him back on hard. As, I got Mark on hard I put the condom on him and start riding his dick up and down. I finish fucking Mark and Dell walked in the room. He came in gave me a gram of cocaine and told me he had paid Jay Jack for a section. I hit the cocaine a couple of times and then I got on the pool table and start dancing for Dell. I danced off the block is hot. While dancing I worked my ass fast and slow and then I would go to the floor and make both cheeks clap. Dell tipped me fives and ten at a time. By the time I had got done fucking and dancing I had made a couple grand. I danced until it was time for them to go to Kreme block party. As, I got in my Bentley all the niggas were checking me out about to head to Kreme strip party that her and the hood boys had going on. As for me, I was on my way to check on Major and the kids. I reached my apartment in the projects and the police was everywhere. Someone had been shot and killed. Blood was everywhere on the sidewalk. Major was standing outside to see what was going on. I walked around the yellow tape and walked up to Major. I asked him what was going on and he said some older cats killed this nigga name Bud. Bud was a heavy weight drug dealer. It was crazy in L.A. as soon as the streets kill one big time dope boy another come alone to make twice the money the last one made. I gave Major a hug and kiss and told him thank god it wasn't him laying on the sidewalk dead. The kids was in the apartment sleep. I talked to Major for a while then I told him I was going to hit up Kreme strip party. I put on a mint jacket with some leather pants and some knee high boats. I curled my sew in and put on some MAC make up with the matching eye shadow to match my pink mint jacket. I grabbed a lot of ones. I wanted to tip Kreme for the night. I walked outside to my black Bentley and got in the car. I rode blocks over to the strip party. When I got to the strip party niggas was all over Kreme and she had some deep wave hair in hair that stopped to her ass. Niggas were enjoying her take off her clothes and damn did she have a pretty body. Kreme would swing from poll to poll and bounce up and down and make her ass clap. As, she danced I would tip her some on the ones. Money was all over the floor and Jay Jack was all over the building collecting money for the freak show. While, Kreme and the other girls danced I stood in the corner with Mark as he hugged up on me with my new ten thousand dollar mint jacket on. Mark gave me a grand in all ones to tip Kreme. Kreme danced in front of me like I was a nigga. At the party it was two sideline DJ's in the building for a whole four hours niggas and females watch Kreme and some more bitches dance and shake their ass. For a minute it was so much money in there I started to dance. Kreme party ended around twelve and I rushed home so I could get ready to dance at The Roxy's. I went in the projects that I was now paying rent to trap out and put on a lingerie. I got ready quickly and drove to The Roxy's. I parked in the VIP parking lot where nothing but ballers park. I walked in the club and Kreme had ended her freak show and was already in The Roxy's with a million dollar Gucci lingerie on made by Gucci. I ran up to Kreme and asked her where the fuck she got the money to buy a Gucci lingerie and she told me Rod bought it for her a couple months ago. Then, I gave her a hug and kiss and complimented her on the strip party and told her she did a wonderful job dancing. She was fly ass fuck. I walked back stage to put my bag up and walked back to the dance floor. All my regular tricks were in the club. It was a different night but the same old shit. Thinking about Kreme success as a millionaire made me want to tighten up on my game. She had so much going on for herself, she was about to build her grandma a house outside of the hood, she had a fly ass shape and she was a down ass bitch. As for me I had two cars, an up scale apartment and two kids but I wasn't a millionaire. After, doing so much thinking about Kreme I went up to a nigga that I knew would tip and that was Mark. I asked him to buy a couple drinks before I began to work my ass. As, I danced Mark posted a couple photos online and I made a couple grand and then I walked to the second level of the club. On the second level of the club I worked my way though the crowd and as I walked by nigga looked and slapped me on the ass. Some of them even gave out tips. The night was still young in the club and I only had made a couple of grands. I made it to the spot I was going to dance on the second level and Red started to tip me. After a couple moves Red wanted to go to The Hideaway Inn. When, we got there he ate my pussy and I sucked on his dick doing the sixty nine. I finished Red up by riding him. Red was yelling out my name and telling me how good the pussy was. Time past and I was done tricking Red I walked back in The Roxy's with the money Red gave me in my hands. When, I got back in the club all kind of niggas was up on Kreme tipping and giving her money to work the poll in that Gucci she had on. I went to the first level were Kreme was by the stage to make some of the money niggas was tipping. All night for the rest of the night I danced in the same spot with

Kreme to make money. After, the club I drove back to the projects and the police had cleared the scene where the murder had happen earlier. Niggas was still out selling dope and junkies were all over the project parking lot. When I open the apartment door Major and the kids was asleep. I woke Major up and told him to let's get the kids out the projects for the night. With all the killing that went on I want them to stay somewhere safe. Major got out of bed got Money and Major Jr. car seats and followed me to our apartment in Up Living. We went in the house put the kids to bed and in the next five minutes Major and I was in the shower making love. Major was making me feel good. Major was all over my body kissing on me and making love to me. Major and I got out the shower and went in the master bedroom. When we got in there Major dick was still on hard. Major, pulled me close to him and asked me to suck him up, he knew I was the queen of a good head job. Then, Major told me if I got him to get on my knees and suck it to it cum. I told him as long as he make me a promise and Major wanted to know what the promise was. I told him the only way I would give him some head if he gave me ten grand. Major got off the bed and went into his personal safe and got the money. After, Major gave me the money I got on my knees and gave him head. He came so quick and then I sucked it some more and got him back on hard. When, I got Major back on hard we made out until the sun light came out. As, the sunlight hit our eyes Major and I went to sleep until Money came into the room to wake us up to give her something to eat. I feed Money and called Reese to babysit for the day. Reese was off work for the day from the hospital. She said her and Qunicy was going to sit around the house all day and watch movies and it was fine if I bought the kids over. I finish cleaning up the mess Money had made in the kitchen and took them over to Reese place. At Reese house the whole time I had on sunglasses because I didn't want her to see my black eye. Reese wanted to know why I had the sunglasses on. It was hard to tell her the truth, she was a little upset but not like Man was. Before we left Reese house she told Major don't let it happen again. Reese said she had already knew because Kreme had called her and told her about my black eye. Shit pissed me off when other motherfucker's tell bitches business. Anyhow, Major and Reese end up talking to each other about the whole black eye deal and he gave Reese his word he would never do it again. Major and I went back to Up Living and both of us put on some clothes so we could hit the corner for the day. Major had gave me ten grand last night and I wanted to hit the mall before the sun go down today. I knew for a fact I had to work Jay Jack corner. I called Kreme up even though I was still a little disappointed with her for telling Resse Major had black my eye. I asked her did she want to hit the mall with me or did she want me to just bring her something back. Kreme was down for me taking her on a shopping spree. Shit sometime a bestfriend had to show love. Kreme told me to meet her at the L.A. Square Mall and she wanted to go inside of Pink and get her a couple things. Pink was a new designer that most hood females were wearing. I put on a Fendi dress that I had in the closet for a couple months. The Fendi dress was a knock out for the day. Major didn't want to drive to the hood so I had to take him to the projects to trap for the day. When, I got to the hood I saw Kreme pulling out the hood to head to the mall. Major got out the car and before he get out he gave me a kiss on the cheeks. As, Major was giving me a kiss Kreme called me on the phone to let me know she was going to ride with me since I was already in the hood. She got in the car and before we could drive off Kreme told me she had a lick. It was a head service job and it would only take thirty minutes. The dude she had to meet lived an uptown L.A. when we got to his place Kreme had a small conversation with him and did the head job and we was out in know time. At the mall we start our shopping spree by going in Foot Locker, Macy's and Victoria Sercert. Last, we went to Pink and racked up on some outfits. Leaving the mall we stopped by the weed man Kreme knew outside of a gated community uptown L.A. and got some to smoke on. Next, we rode downtown L.A. in the hood we stopped by the corner store and got some blunts to smoke out of. As, for me I had some cocaine in my pocketbook to put up my nose. Kreme and I went back to my apartment in the projects and got fucked up. While chilling getting high Travis called on the phone. Major was there so I didn't get a chance to talk to him even though he showed his ass before he got arrested for shooting up the block. After, Kreme and I got fucked up we hit Jay Jack corner. On the corner niggas was happy to see us hanging around each other. Kreme was my ride or die chick. Mark was on the corner looking for a quick fuck. He wanted Kreme and me to do a freak show. Mark say he had three grand. I called Jay Jack from out the car he was sitting in and had him collect the money. Kreme and I followed Mark up to the ally apartment. Dressed in all black lingerie I took off my pants and kept on my bra. I kissed Mark neck until he got a passion mark on him. Mark felt on my ass until

Kreme put her pussy on Mark face. He put his tounge up the whole of Kreme pussy. That shit looked so good I tap Kreme on her shoulder so I could eat that pussy. I completely took over. After the quick section with Mark, Kreme and I had done something we haven't done in a while and that was fuck each other. I went back on the corner and walked up and down the block during the course of me walking I tricked Red a couple of times. Then Dell was my last trick of the day. As usually Dell gave extra money to fuck. The section with Dell went by fast and right before I was about to leave Mark paid Jay Jack another three grand for me. I walked back up to the ally apartment and fucked Mark. Out of the blue Mark got between my legs and start eating me out. Jay Jack watched the whole time just in case the police came to the ally. I finished Mark up and left the corner for the day. I drove a couple blocks to my apartment in the projects. When, I got there Major had the apartment jumping with junkies. That's how my man was making money. Most of Major junkies were home owners. I called Reese to see if she wanted me to get the kids while I was waiting on Major. Reese and Quincy were enjoying the kids and they were on their way to the new water park that L.A. had recently got. As, for me I had tricked my regular three clients of the day and it was time for me to head to my apartment in Up Living. Major sold the rest of his crack to a nigga that sell dope and hopped in the Bentley with me and we rode home for the afternoon. All the way there he kissed on me while I was driving. By the time we made it home Major wanted to know was I working the club. My answer was yeah as always. Shit I had to make money if I wanted to be a millionaire like Kreme. She was banking in the game. I only had two hundred twenty six thousand dollars. He talked to me and he was proud I was making money with a black eye. Because usually on the block a female couldn't work with a black eye, anyways I sat around the house until twelve o' clock and then I got ready to hit the club. I drove to The Roxy's by myself but nine times out of ten Major was going to come to the club. As usually Kreme and Candy were the first two females at the club working VIP. I walked to the DJ station first for the first time in a long time and got a time to dance. My set time was for one o' clock so I had a hour to do lap dances and table tops. I decided I would work VIP until them. Niggas was already touching and feeling on me before you knew it. I danced slow to some Avant while niggas tipped me. As, I was dancing Major made his way to the front door of the club. He made my night because when he came in he had plenty of money in his hand. Major broke me off twenty grand. That kind of money made me get loose. My man was the only nigga that showed that kind of love to me. I rubbed all on Major and dance while dancing I moved my ass up on him. Major set the motherfucking night off. Niggas saw how he was slapping me on the ass and throwing money next to me and decided they would join. I mean my niggas spent twenty grand on me in the club. I already knew what I was going to spend that on. After dancing for Major I danced with Kreme and made money with her for the rest of the night. The night came to an end and Major walked up to me smiling and hugging up on me. Major wanted me to follow him home so we could make love. As, I was leaving the club Kreme walked up to me gave me a big hug and told me thanks for the support that I give her and it a wonderful feeling to have me as a friend. My life was always full of excitement with Kreme she made things so easy I loved having her on my team. Kreme got in her Aura and drove a couple blocks to her grandma house. Kreme and her gramdma were still in the hood until the home builder finish with the home. As for me I followed Major to the apartment where he had candles around the fireplace and roses for me. I put on some sexy to entertain my man and laid next to the fireplace. Major start licking on my pussy and eating me out, then I reversed the sex position and we start doing the sixty nine. While eating on me Major was talking dirty than a motherfucker, we fucked all over the house until morning then I cooked him breastfast in bed. While I was cooking his morning meal a female called his phone. I wanted to say something but I just told the chick he was asleep and to call back. The sex we had was so good I kept my mouth close about a female calling Major phone. I didn't want to fuck things up. I went in my pocketbook and got a few hits of my cocaine before I took Major his food. We, ate and then we fucked twice back to back. He kissed all up on me and told me how he was going to get me a manison in L.A. I was believing everything my nigga was telling me. I knew Major was a man of his word. Time past and Major got up to leave the house for the day to trap in the projects. As, for me I called Man because it had been awhile since I saw him. I know he was way over due for some pussy. When, I got to Man apartment he didn't waste know time laying between my legs feeling the wettest of my pussy around his dick. Man and I got it down for a couple of hours then I took him back to Up Living to show him the apartment and how it looked for the first time since I got funtiune. Man, liked the fact that I had Gucci all the way though my place. My apartment was like a small manison. Man started to kiss all over me in my place and I got hot. I bent over and let him hit me from the back. The feeling of Man hitting that pussy was a damn good thing. As, he hit the pussy I prayed that Major didn't come back and find us doing the nasty in the apartment even though it was in Man name. After, Man got done waxing on my ass I hopped in the shower while I was in the shower I could hear Man telling me that he was about to walk back to his place blocks down. Thank god that was over I thought to myself if Major only knew the things I did behind his back. I put on some clothes and decided I would go to the hood and hang out for the rest of the day. When, I got to the hood small children was on the sidewalk playing chicken heads was sitting on the porch talking about everyone that past by and the local street niggas was hanging around selling drugs. Then from a distance I saw a bitch with real Gucci on. It was Kreme she was doing big girl shit since she was sitting on that million dollars. I got out the car went in the ally apartment to see what was popping for the day and nigga was ready to spend money on me. There was ten niggas out of Washington D.C. trying to pay a hundred grand a piece to trick with the baddest bitch on the corner. Niggas gave then word it was me and I did what I had to do to get that money. The niggas was gone over my head job. They wanted to know who taught me the game. I told Rich Boy my girl Kreme was the one who put me down with my head and fucking skills in the game. I went back on the corner and gave Jay Jack ten grand out of the hundred racks I had made. I left the block for a minute and went to my apartment in Up Living. I added the money to my safe and took some out so I could go to the mall. A bitch did have a blast with the cash I took to the mall. I got all kinds of shit for my out of town trip with Major Cross the Water. In the mall I went in the Gucci store and did some shopping. In the Gucci store I bought all kinds of shit. I wanted to be fresh going out of town with Major. When, niggas and hoes saw me I wanted them to be like damn who is that. While in the mall I got a call from Kreme and she said Rich Boy had money on the side walk of Main Street with bitches dancing. I finished up what I was doing went back on Main Street and made another hundred thousand. Now, my saving was at four hundred thousand I was on the road to being a million dollar bitch.

Chapter 5

Weeks past and my black eye that Major gave me went away. Now, finally Major and I was about to prepare to go Cross the Water to visit his family. The trip was a delay so many times in the process of going but now we are making steps. All day I have been in the nail and hair salon getting all done up to go Cross the Water. Last night I drop the kids off at Reese house so she could watch them for my stay out of the country. In the nail salon the Chinese woman that did my perfectly box nails and toes got me out of there in no time. Now, am at the hair salon in the hood listening to these same nobody ass females that trick and get their hair done for the club and don't take care of their kids talk about every damn body business. While waiting I looked at a couple of Jet magazines and watch BET on the salon flat screen television for entertainment. Noting was going on in the rap business and rappers were still making money off gangsta music. After, I got my ear full with the music business it was time for me to get in chair. My hair stylist wasn't in the shop she was out sick with the flu so another girl that was next best to her did

my hair in a short cut. I sat while she glued the double zero seven onto the tracks and put them in my head. As, she did my hair she put Pump It Up on the tracks so they could stay. Once she glued then down she cut the layers and flat iron the weave and she was done less than an hour and a half. I paid her sixty five dollars and a ten dollar tip. I looked at my hair in the small mirror in the shop before I left. An, boy did she do a good damn job. As, I was leaving the shop I called Major to see what he was up to and of course Major had already been to the barber shop and got a hair cut. Now, he was in the hood getting off the last little bit of crack he had before we catch our flight. I hung up the phone with my nigga and called Man on the phone. Man was in uptown L.A. at the liquor bar having a few drinks by himself and I decided to join him. When, I got there he had two Sex on the Beach drinks already at the table for me and him. I kiss Man on the lips and took a seat at the table. He had on my favorite Ralph Lauren by Polo Colonge. I sat closer to him so I could smell the frangance on his clothes. After I got confortable I got in a conversation with Man and told him that I would be leaving the country with Major to go see his family Cross the Water. Man thought it was a good idea for me to go to a different region and experience something new in my life. He talked about a experience that he had with a school teacher he used to date and told me how they went Cross the Water and the ocean waves are so deep and beautiful. Then Man asked if it was okay with Major could I bring him some insents back for one of the people that sell them on the Island. He went on saying how he knew they would last longer than the cheap insent he get out of Dollar General. I start laughting and told Man I would see what I could do. But I really didn't think that would be a problem. I sat there with Man for a couple of hours talking about building a closer relationship and being there for another. Man told me how he was working on a project of building his own strip club in L.A. Man said it would be a million dollar business. He said he already had the spot and the company had already been paid to remodel the building and it costed him one point five million dollars. It was going to be bigger than The Roxy's. His dream was to make all the money he invested in the club over once he opened it up. The name of the club was going to be called Riders. An, he gave me an ups that I could come and work at his spot. After, drinking six Sex on the Beach with Man I ended our small date and returned to my busy day of getting ready to leave the country. I walked outside the bar and got in my Bentley when I got in the car the music blast my ear because I forgot to turn it down before I got out. I turned the volume down just a few and rode to my apartment in Up Living. I went in the house and start looking though the closet to find something to wear I was having a hard time doing so. I got on the phone and called Major as I called him I put the phone on speaker phone so I could do two things at once. "Bae, what should I take on our trip Cross the Water.""Oh, get a club dress for every night your there and outfit for the day time and a couple of bathing suites for the Island." After getting a idea of what to pack I decided to pack half of what Major said because it sounded like a little to much. I figured I could do a little shopping while I was there if I needed too. On the part about going out every night I knew that was something I wasn't going to do. Major could club at all those tent houses on the Island and maybe I could get closer to his mother. Even, I may talk her into coming to L.A. to visit Major and I. Then she would get a chance to see her first born grandson from her lovely son. I packed my bags and drove to Wal Mart to developed some pictures of Major Jr. for his grandmother and Major other family could have some memories of him. The development department at Wal Mart took about one hour. It was three o' clock in the afternoon and I still had to eleven o' clock tonight before I leave for my trip. After, spending an hour in Wal Mart getting the pictures developed I decided to take a trip downtown L.A. and see what was going on around the corner. When I got on the corner Mark, Red and a couple other dudes was hanging out selling dope. Kreme was doing her thing on the corner as well selling dope and tricking niggas to make a way. I gave Kreme the word that I would be leaving the country with Major. I told her I wasn't going to be working the streets for a week or two. I sat around the block and for a minute I didn't make any money until some of the boys got off their dope and wanted a freak show. I told every nigga I tricked that day it had to be quick because I had a flight to Florida. Tim was the first nigga I fucked for the day he was this young nigga that had just dropped out of school to support his family after his mother pasted. I was Tim first trick this was his first time learning or even being on Jay Jack corner. Time gave Jay Jack five hundred dollars which was regular price and we went up to the ally apartment. Jay Jack gave me the money first and I went upstairs to handle my business. Tim other homies say that was a little to much money so they would hold out on the fucking tip and make them some more money. When, I got upstairs with Tim I told him to take off his pants so I could

give him some head. Tim was excited about getting head for the first time. He wasn't used to a bitch like me and it kind of made me want to give him his money back. But, my mind change when I saw his largely size dick. Tim was packing for his age. From the looks of things he wouldn't have any problems in a relationship he had something under his pants to make a female love him. I got on my knees and grabbed a whole of Tim dick and put the soft meat in my mouth until it was hard. My head moved backward and forward until it was hard then I started to jack it. My jaws were tight around the head of his dick when Tim came and I swallowed his cum. He was like dam bae I like what you did to me. A nigga wouldn't mine getting some more of that. I told Tim that I was leaving to go Cross the Water with my man and I would be back in a couple of weeks but as soon as I get on the block anytime he want to spend some money my name is Kelly just ask for me. "Okay Kelly nice to meet you and damn once again you put me in the game bae." I went back on the side walk and told Kreme that Tim had a perfectly shape long and round dick. She smiled at me and told me good luck on some new meat on the corner. Mark had finished up his last pack of cocaine and was ready to spend a couple thousands for the day. Mark wasn't new to the streets so he showed love like that. Mark went up to Jay Jack and gave him the money and Jay Jack told me to report to the ally apartment. I walked directly upstairs and got my half of the cut. I knew Mark had tip big. I got in the ally apartment for my second time of the day. Mark gave me a straw and some cocaine to get high on while he hop in the shower that we used in the ally apartment. Mark had been making money in the hot sun all day and wanted to get refreshing up. He was in the shower about thirty minutes and by the time he got out I had done a gram of cocaine. By that time I was ready to give him a fast head job. Mark wanted pussy to but I told him I couldn't mess up my new hair dew. He laughted at me but took my word. I told Mark all about my trip and he was shocked ass fuck that Major was taking me out the country. I gave Mark a head job and decided that I had did enough on the corner for the day. It was getting late and I wanted to catch my grandma before the streets lights come on because that's usually when she goes to bed. I got to grandma house just before she was about to lock her door. As soon as she saw my face she start smiling and gave me a big hug. As grandma was giving me a hug I told her I was leaving the country to go Cross the Water to meet Major family. Grandma was more excited than me and told me to take good care of myself and my family and to make sure am saving the money that am making on the streets. I hugged grandma as tight as I can and didn't let her go. I went in my pockets and got the money I had made on the corner that day and gave it to her. It was a couple thousands plus the two fifty I had made from Tim a new coming in the game. She was more than thankful for the cash. I told grandma I loved her and to call her granddaughter my sister Reese and check on the kids while I was gone. Grandma said okay she would make sure she call Reese and put it on her to do list. I walked out the house jumped in my Bentley and blasted my five thousand dollar music system thought the hood. That should give the streets something to talk about for a couple weeks while am gone. I called Major on his cell phone and he answered it very quickly. Major had just got off his last couple rocks and was on his way to Up Living to pack his bags so we could make our flight to Florida. I got off the phone with Major and told him to be at Up Living around the same time as me or a little afterwards. An, as soon as I was about to hit the expressway and blast the music in relaxation Reese number came flashing across the caller I.D. of the phone. "What's up Sis?" "Nothing Kelly just making sure I talk to you before you leave the country." "Oh Reese thanks and how are my babies doing?" "They okay just got done eating." "Now they are looking at television." "Okay that's what's up?" "Well Kelly I was just calling to here you voice before you leave." "Okay see you when I get back." "Okay Boo." Then Reese told me to be safe and to remember she love me and all other kind of good stuff and she also reminded me not to get over on the Island cheating on Major because there is a lot of good looking men over there. Reese made me laught at the last part of our conversation because she said she would hate for Major to kill me on vacation in another country. I couldn't say nothing but you crazy girl and I promise to be on my best behavior. It felt good talking to Reese on the phone before I left. I had told Reese I love her and the kids. By the time I got off the phone with Reese Major was behind me on the expressway. Major got behind me and followed me to Up Living. As, I rode in my Bentley I listened to Promise by Jagged Edge. I was in the mood of making love to my man. An, decided to pick the phone up and call Major and run some of my game lines. On the phone I promised to stay true to Major and never leave him. We pulled up to Up Living and Major walked up to my Bentley and opened the door and start kissing me off the end of the song. We walked upstairs and Major packed his

clothes for our trip. I sat down and the living room table and got on some cocaine. Major walked past me a couple times and in no time he was ready to go. We sat round and waited on a taxi cab to come by and get us. We decided to sit at the airport for a few hours before our flight took off. At the airport Major and I decided to catch up on some talking. Major told me how no one could ever do me the way he does me and I told him he was right. He treated me like a queen and that's what I liked most about our relationship. I told Major I never meet someone that make me feel as ready as he does and nann man could take his place. Next, I explained to him that he was the love of my life. We kissed and got in a conversation about how the trip was going to me amazing. Major said his plans were to hang out with one of his close cousins and his hopes was up high that I loved his family. I told him not to worry that his relationship was about having fun and experiencing what the other person like and experience. The conservation Major and I was having were so long we talked to the end of the flight. The fight came fast and we were in Jacksonvillie in no time. Getting off the plane all I could remember was how pretty the sky was flying in the air. The first thing we did was went and got our bags that we had bought on our trip. Next, Major and I went to Dollar Rental and rented a yellow Mustang to get us to Miami to get in our boat. After, we got our bags we road to get something to eat, then we got on the expressway and headed towards Miami. Major looked fly ass fuck driving the Mustang. It took us six hours to make it to Miami. When Major and I made it to Miami we went to the beach where all the ships go cross the water and headed for our ship. A lot, of people was going on there honey moon. Couples were kissing and I saw a lot of Hawaii hats with flowers on them. Major and I went aboard and found our cabinet where we would be sleeping for a day and a half until we get Cross the Water. There was a swimming pool on deck and a bar to drink liquor. Major and I went to the cabinet number that was on our ticket put our bags away and had fun for the rest of the day. Instead of getting a little sleep we grabbed a couple hundreds and went to the bar and drunk. I had so many double spots of Henessy and Grey Goose. I was fucked up and went back to the cabinet and put on my bathing gear to swim on the level deck where you could watch the ocean front with the deep waves. It was so beautiful and Major sat on the side of the deck and watch me playing in the pool water without getting my hair wet. From time to time Major would turn around and look at the sea waves. After, awhile I got out the water and hugged on Major in the night air. It was a card table with a couple of whites mens playing for money with one older black guy who keep losing all his money until Major came to join him at the table and they start playing a couple hands of spades. I left the swimming area and went back to the cabinet to put on some clothes because the night air to the ocean winds was making me cold. At, the cabinet I changed to lay down and get some rest. I didn't rest on the plane or on the ride to Miami. So, I figure it was time to get my sleep on. I laid down on my back and rocked myself to sleep in about thirty minutes I was knocked out. I slept two hours and when I got up I found myself still in the cabinet by myself. I got refreshing and went back on the level deck. When, I got there Major and a couple other passagners on the boat was turned up listening to some ray gay music and they had

started a casino dance on the deck with Hawaii fruits and drinks in there mouth. I walked up to Major on the deck and start doing the ray gay dance on him. As, I moved around in circles I made sure Major watched my perfectly shape body. Time went by and the sun was coming up. Major and I decided to go to the cabinet and get some sleep. Shit after dancing and drinking for hours that night I needed some rest. In the cabinet Major and I laid next to each other and it felt good to lay next to a man that cared and love you. As, the boat took us the rest of the way to the Islands Major and I laid in out cabinet and look at television and made love, the next thing I knew was the driver to the ship was calling for all passagners that was visiting the small Islands our stop was coming up. When, I got there I didn't know what to expect I thought Major mother would be waiting to pick us up. But, it was Major cousin Sam and his sister Leshay that came and picked us up. They wasn't in a big body car like I thought they were going to be, it was a small Totoya. Major sister LeShay and him looked just alike and she was a very pretty girl with the shape that most girls on a lslands have with a nice tan. Major and I loaded our bags in the small vechicle and rode to a small neighborhood that was builded out of small wood. When, we got there Major told me that was his cousin house and since we where going to be doing a lot of clubbing it would be a good idea to stay there. When, I got inside of the cabinet it was a three bedroom and Major cousin had small candles lit to make the cabinet have a sweet scent. I looked at Major and gave him a big hug. Already, I knew this was going to be a wonderful trip. I was finally on the Islands and Sam Major cousin wanted to know did we want any rest before we hit the beach club. I told him I didn't need any rest because I was ready to have the time of my life. I asked Major what would the club be like and he told me it was a small wooden tent area that play music outside. LeShay Major little sister said she had to go to Major mother house to get a small sun dress for the night. She said everyone on the Islands knew her and she wanted to get Jazzed up to go to the music tent and dance. I asked Sam for a towel and rag and got dressed to go out to the dance. Sam already was dressed for the event and it didn't take Major that long to get dress. The beach was just a couple minutes away from Sam place and Major mother lived in a nice house on the way. We stopped the car and Leshay hopped in the car and we headed to the joint to have a good time. I was excited about going to a tent house dance. We walked to a tent wearing clothes that you walked around in America in. Nobody was worried about the dress code and the DJ was playing Ray Gay music. Everybody was dancing and having a good time. That really wasn't my type of dancing but I fitted right in. It was a little table set up with someone servicing drinks and I had a couple spots of Rome. Major was already tipsy from the boat trip on the way Cross the Water but he still got some more drinks. There were so many people at the tent and the people from cross the water was drinking. Major and I danced and kissed on the dance floor. So many Island boys were trying to get at Leshay Major younger sister. After, dancing to the Hawaii music we walked the beach front and talked while we talked his cousin and sister was at the tent dancing. Major asked me were I enjoying myself and I told him I had just got there but so far everything was cool. Then we kissed and made out. The sand to the beach felt good and Major went to a

stand where they were selling goods to rub on my body. He told me that what made most island girls and boys skin was so smooth and soft and I should buy a couple of them and take back with me. I liked the way they made me feel and by the time we was done Leshay had timed us and guided us back to the tent house. I danced to music I couldn't understand for the first time in my life. As, I was dancing with Sam I saw some girls laughting and pointing at Major like they wanted him. I laught at how people on the islands like to flirt with each other. The next thing I knew she was all over Major dancing and putting her hands on his chest. I for once thought that was cute and kept doing what I was doing. It looked like a picture in a movie. Le Shay talked very loudly next to me and asked me was I having fun. I told her I was getting the hang of things but needed a few more drinks. LeShay heard what I said and rushed over to a guy she knew and had him buy me a shot of liquor. The dance with Sam was over LeShay and I even danced and bumped each other booty on the dance floor. Major sister LeShay was a peoples person for the most part of it and I really liked my baby auntie. I wish I had brung him over to his father country so he could see his family. But, Major said not to rush thing because it's not like he would remember the trip because he was to young. Night life cross the water had went by fast and it was five in the morning and the spot was still jumping. LeShay and Sam told Major it close at seven in the morning for a new shift to come on the beach to play music for the morning time. Major, mind was focus on getting me back to the room we was standing in at Sam house so he could make love to me. I gave him a serious look so he could know that sex could wait and that it was best to stay out with Sam and LeShay. From the look I gave Major he decided to party longer. As, the couple hours went by we had drink after drinks and we was feeling a little to good to drive back to Sam cabinet so we got in a cab. When, we got back to Sam cabinet Major gave Sam word that I did cocaine and I got turned up until the time it was time to go to Major mother house for a fish fry. Sam put on music and we watch television. He also cooked a big beastfast and by the time everything was done Major hold family was at the cabinet introducing theirselves. He had one cousin name Kesha that was so hood. I really lilked Kesha a lot. Kesha and I smoked a couple of loud joints and I thought Major mother would have something bad to say about us smoking but I got alone with my mother-in- law because she was a smoker too. The party started at Sam house and we end up at Major mother house were we did a fish fry. We talked and I meet Major whole family which I got a chance to give them the baby pictures that I had made copies of. When, I showed Major mother the picture she start laughting and got a picture of Major out when he was a baby and him and my son looked just a like. After being at the fish fry for hours Major gave his family word we had been up for twenty four hours and we needed some rest. For the next couple days we spent time alone and walked the islands and made out. I bought Reese a purse from the islands that this man was selling which was made out of leather. Then, I got the insents Man wanted me to get for him. Sam and LeShay both had jobs so Major and I spent most of our days shopping and going places he used to go when he lived on the Islands. The wheather was so nice that I told Major if he every married me I wanted my wedding to be there. We even talked about having a daughter so she could be a flower girl but we both said that would be in the future. On the end of our first week I saw Major mother for the second time which was at her job because she wanted her co- workers to see her son. Major mother co-worker hugged all up on him she told him about how is mother always talked so good about him and told her he had a wife name Kelly. I guess she called me Major wife because we were in a serious relationship. Shit, I was so in to this man it was no way around it but to call me his wife. We talked and she made plans for us to come back to her house for dinner. It was going to be this Saturday and I couldn't wait to spend more time with her. She mentioned that she wanted me to help her set up an all ivory and white silverware for the dinner. She went on telling me how she wanted me to learn just in case I had to set up a dinner table for Major which I didn't mind doing. Major mother Shonda was a nice person and I enjoyed her conversation a lot. We end our small talk with hugs and kisses and Major and I went on the beach to ride on some jets. When we got to the beach we went and rented a jet for a couple dollars and got on them and rode far out into the water. We was so far I thought a shark was going to get us but we made it back safe. Major taught me how to ride a jet and I rode him for like an hour. I was having so much fun. It was Thursday and we only had two days before the dinner. Major and I didn't have and ivory outfit so we went to an outlet close by the beach and bought something nice to wear for Shonda dinner. By the time we got something to wear it was night and we went back to Sam place were we got ready and went to the tent for a night out. Before, we went to the tent we got high and drunk some Gin at Sam place. Then, we went to the tent house. At the tent house I was used to things so I dance and enjoyed myself. I drunk ten Sex on the Beaches and I even smoke with this Island boy. Major saw some guys he knew and they went to some place in the Islands and they talked for a long time by the beach. As, for me I kept getting my party on to sun rise. Now it's Friday and I been sleeping all day and making love to Major at Sam place. Sam been at work but LeShay took the day off and she was over Sam house with us and had a little friend with her to keep her company. By the time Sam had got off work Major and I had put on some clothes and was ready to hit the casino to play cards. At, the casino Major and I won so much damn money until I went to Sam cabinet and fuck the shit out of him all night long. Saturday came rounding in and I had to go to Shonda Major mother house and help with the table. Shonda called early that morning for me to set up the table. I got up and put on my clothes for the day. When, I got to Shonda place she had some weed rolled up and we smoked. Shonda got a little personal and talked to me about being a parent. Shonda and I talked about my family and I told her about my grandma and she was happy to hear that I had a grandma to support me because Major had lost his grandma years back in a hurricane. That was sad for me to hear something like that. By, the time Shonda and I had done the table and talked it was time for dinner. I put on my ivory outfit and called Sam and Major to see was they coming. Shonda had cooked pasta and garlic bread. Everything was tasty and I got very full. The table was set up nice and it wasn't so different from the way my grandma do things but she had real damn diamonds on the table that was a gift from Shonda to me. After, dinner Major and I hooked back up and smoked a couple joints on his mother back pourch. Everyone that didn't have a long day on the beach made plans to go back to the cabinet and party. I put back on the same dress because the tent wasn't really like a night club in L.A. where you needed a new outfit every night. If you know what I mean. I drunk and enjoyed myself at the tent house. An, for the next couple days Cross the Water I went on the beach alone. I meet some guys and hung out and they were very friendly. Two weeks came before you new it and it was time for Major and I to go back to L.A. I hugged my future husband family before I left and told them what a wonderful visits I had. On the way back to the boat to take us back to Miami Sam and I smoked our last joint before I left. On the way back I was so excited to get to L.A. to tell all my friends and family how my stay on the Islands was. It wasn't a big fashion show and everything was close together people was all about life there and I had a great time. The work schedule was different and the people were so friendly. But, it was time for the trip to be over and for me to take steps back in my life on Jay Jack corner and The Roxy's. It was an experience of a life time.

Chapter 6

The sail on the boat to Miami was about sixteen hours. When, we got to Miami, Florida Major and I got on a train to go to the Miami airport. I had never been on a train before in my life and I liked it. The train made it to the airport in no time. It stopped right in front of the airport and Major and I got off. Instead of driving in a rental car to Jacksonvillie we decided to take flight. The flight from Miami to Jacksonvillie was a resting stop and the next step for Major and I was to catch the next plane to L.A. The route was longer but it was amazing riding on an airplane. I got a chance for the three time to see how pretty the sky looked in the air. By, the time we had made it to L.A. it was the next day which was a Tuesday. I was well rested and had slept on the plane the whole way back to L.A. When, I reached L.A. Major and I got in a cab to ride to our apartment in Up Living. We had left all electronics in L.A. so I couldn't wait to get to the house to use my phone. My cell phone was fully charged and I had a couple of miss calls. I decided to unpack everything and prepare to call Reese and the kids. Unpacking didn't take very long at all. And

before you knew it I was on the phone with Reese. Reese was eating some leftovers that grandma had cooked the way she was smacking in my ear made the food sound good. I told Reese about my experience and she really was into the conversation but I had to make this short and call grandma. The first thing I said to grandma was hello grandma and I love you. "Baby you back." "How was the trip and did you have fun?" I told grandma all about Major family and how we went out at a tent house and she say she knew I would have a good time. I asked her did she have some more of that food that Reese had but she was out. I talked to grandma for and hour before I got off the phone. When I finally got off the phone with grandma I went to pick the kids up from Reese place. I had gave grandma word I would come see her. On the way to Reese house I called Man and told him that I was back in town and I would drop his insents off in a few. Man and I talked for about five minutes and in that short time I told him all about Major family. The part he liked most was that the tent house clubs isn't nothing like L.A. night clubs. He was surpise about my experience and by then I had made it to Reese apartment. When, I walked into Reese house I was smelling good with some oil called Super Star that I had got from Cross the Water and Reese wanted to know what it was. In my hands I had Reese leather bag that I had got from the man who make purses on the Island. Reese was already smiling because I wasn't emptry handed. I gave Reese the purse quickly which was wrap in a gift bag. Then, I picked Major Jr. and Money up at the same time and start loving on them. While, I was loving on my kids Reese told me that they did great at their doctor visit and Major Jr. weighted eighteen pounds. Money weighted fourty five pounds and I was happy that they were healthy growing kids. Reese had pictures lined up that she had took of them while I was gone and they were so nice and neat. After, Reese gave me the pictures we sat down in her living room area and she wanted to talk about my experience cross the water again. Reese wanted to know how the people talked and act on the islands. I told her the culture was very different from America and they were much friendly. I stayed to Reese place for an hour talking about my trip. She enjoyed talking to me as always. Then, I left and went to Man apartment and quickly dropped off his insents. Major was calling my cell phone by then to tell he was out in about for the afternoon. Major had just wanted me to know he was on his way to downtown L.A. to start off where he left off selling drugs. I told Major I was on my way from Reese place and I would be downtown in a few and I would stop by the apartment to let him see the kids. As, I rode to downtown L.A. it felt good to be back in my home city. Reaching the hood I saw people that cared about me and loved me like Kreme. As, usually niggas was selling crack and hoes was tricking to make a dollar too. The kids and I got out the car and walked into the project apartment so Major could see them. When, Money got in there she gave Major a really big hug. The hug she gave him was like a daddy and daughter hug. He picked Major Jr. up and start kissing on him and telling him how happy he was to see him. Major, put his son back in my hands and kept doing what he was doing. Major was cooking dope so he could trap for the night. As, we was spending time Kreme past thought the hood playing her music loud. She notice I had parked at the trap house and came to see me. Kreme pulled up on me and said, "Hey bitch am happy you back in the city." "What's popping for the night with you." "So much have been going on." "These chicken heads have been hating on our team since you been gone." "I got in a fight and had to straighten one hoe ass but other then that the streets been the streets." "Well, baby I don't think tonights going to be a night out for me." "Iam just getting back in and I want to spend a little time with the kids." "Reese have had them for two weeks I think she going to need a break so tomorrow I'll be back at it." "Damn I thought it was going to be plans for me and you." "Yeah, today am going to get me some new gear to be fresh for the block tomorrow." "Well bitch do you want me to fire yo heah off you know you just getting back we can smoke a couple joints." "Yeah Kreme that's fine with me." "Let's just smoke outside the kids are in the house and you say hoes have been popping off let's be easy." "You know I don't want anyone calling HRS you know hoes stupid in the world and would try to do a bitch in like that." Kreme and I went on the porch and smoked a couple joints. She told me how she missed me since I was gone and that she made three hundred thousand. She said she had trick with some niggas out of Tennessee State. I was like damn bitch you made all that you must really put on a freak show for them. She told me Jay Jack was up to the same old thing and I should stop in before tomorrow and see him. The thought sounded good but I knew how I was about making money once I got on the corner I would be calling Reese to babysit so that wasn't a good idea. I knew niggas missed me and couldn't wait until I get back to spend money on me. After, about three hours of catching up with my home girl I made moves to Tricks so I could get new lingerie to work in tomorrow.

Then, I was going to get my nails and toes and hair redone for the niggas I wanted to be on point that's all. Before, I left the hood I stop in to see grandma then I went on about my way. I rode though the L.A. traffic and it was thick ass fuck in L.A. Traffic was so jam to get down the expressway it took me fouty five minutes to get to Tricks. When, I got there the owner to the store had out all kinds of lingerie. I looked on the lingerie rack to find what I wanted. I saw thirty items that I wanted out of Tricks and the cost of them was a yard a piece. Trina the store owner had a smile on her face because she knew if I got the items I had the money to pay for them. It was a rule to buying lingerie and that was you couldn't try them on you had to know your size. Trina had builded on a new heel section in the store and it reminded me of my trip to Miami where I saw all kinds of colorful heels in the flea market with Mark that time we went to traffic dope. The only thing about it Miami had the most heels. Trina had all kinds of heels you wanted I looked thought the thirty lingerie outfits I had and picked me out thirty pair of new stilettos. She had every shoe I wanted in my size which is a nice size eight. The stilettos were fifty dollars a piece and the lingerie was a yard so I paid fourty five hundred in total. I left the store with much shit to put in my Bentley. Trina the owner of Tricks helped me carry all my items to the car. I rode the expressway a couple exits in L.A. to my apartment in Up Living. I didn't want a bitch robbing me in the hood while I was getting my nails and toes done. When, I got to the Chinese people to get my service done it was only two people ahead of me so it didn't take that long. After, I got my nails and toes done I went to the hair shop and my regular hair stylist was back in. When

she saw the bob that the chick had done her eyes was amazes. She ran her hands though the tracks and examine her work. After, that she put me before all her clients because I was only there for a re-curl. It took her thirty minutes to bring the bob back to life and I was gone in no time. I called Major to let him know that my day was over and me and the kids was about to head home for the day. He asked where I was and wanted me to bring him a garlic seafood plate from the seafood place. I went and sat in that long ass line that I hated to wait in but I had to get my nigga what he wanted. After, I got the plate I called Major to let him know I would be outside in a few and to step out to the car and get his seafood. When, I pulled up Major was already standing outside waiting for me. I roll down the window and gave him the seafood quickly and road out the hood to head to the expressway. The kids were hungry and had only had a snack so I stop to feed them. It took like twenty minutes to get Money something to eat and feed Major Jr. a bottle and then I got on the expressway. When, I got home the kids took a bath and I put them to sleep. Then, it was time for myself, I put the lingerie and slitteos away that I had purchase earlier that afternoon and ran me a bubble bath. I decided to put a nice sleep wear outfit on so I could look sexy for Major when he come home for the night. I turned on you tube and listened to some Jagged Edge and then I played a little bit of Keith Sweat and R. Kelly. As, I was getting out the tub I got the tub cleaner and wash out the dirty ring around the tub. Next, I brushed my perfectly white teeth and whipped some make up off my face with some make up remover that I had got from cross the water to take off the expensive Mac make up that I wear. By, the time I did that it was ten o' clock at night and my man was still out making money. I thought weather I should call and him or should I just laid down in bed and wait for him in my sexy sleep wear so I could surpise him when he got home. After, thinking I picked up the phone and before you knew it I had Major on speaker phone. "Baby where are you?" "I am on my home." I got off the phone with Major and turned on the television so I could give the dark apartment I was in some light. Then, I watched the eleven o' clock news. So much shit had happen in L.A. today. A woman throwed her baby stories down a building, five major drug buses happen. A couple bank robberies and a police got kill on the expressway. Seeing everything that happen on the news I got my bible and thanked god for another day in this beautiful world that he made. As, I was reading the bible Major walked in the house. When he walked in the back room he had a frown on his face and blood was all over him. He walked in the room and got some clothes to put on then Major went in the bathroom to wash the blood off him. The whole time I was wondering did he kill someone until I saw the firearm with an emtry chip. "Baby are you okay." "Kelly don't worry about your nigga am straight." By the time I got out the bed Major had come in the room and sat on the bed. I got out the bed and stood in front of him and rubbed Major on his back. He sat on the bed while I stood in front of him and touch me on the booty. Then, he got up and looked me in the eyes and said, "Kelly I need to tell you something." "I never thought I would have to kill a nigga." "But as I was walking out the apartment today a fuck nigga tried to rob me and I took his life." Then he went on saying it would be nice as his lady to keep my mouth close because if I didn't he would never see the streets again. "I would never go against you baby in the game and that my motherfucking word." "I know you wouldn't just go out and kill a nigga for no reason." "Baby what I want you to do is whole me all night don't even thick the dick in just get yourself back together because I know you is having flash backs." "Damn Kelly am sorry that happen just stay true to your nigga and keep that to yourself baby please." "Never go against me and the court of law baby and that will never come back." I kissed Major and laid next to him in the bed where he was still sitting up. "Major, I love the fuck out of you be easy and I will always remember to stay true to you." Flashing lights from the flat screen was the only thing you could see in our apartment. I laid next to Major all night wondering why a nigga would want to rob him. He had only been back in L.A. a couple hours and had took a nigga life that quick. I got the remote to the flat screen Samsung television and flip though the channels to find something to watch. I pass by Lifeime and didn't want to watch a murder movie so I went to BET. It was a old movie on name Waiting to Exhale. I had caught the movie at the beginning and wish I had some popcorns in the apartment to pop and sit back and watch the movie. The movie was on the part when Angela Bassett husband leaves her for a white woman. I always like the part when she put his shit on fire and go to his job slap the white bitch and take his black ass to court and walk out with all his money. Looking at the movie thoughts came to my head that's some shit I would do. The movie didn't last that long and no time I was asleep. The next thing I knew I was awake by the morning light coming from the blinds of my apartment. Major was next to me. I got up and checked both of the kids rooms and Money was still asleep and I decided not to mess with her. As, for my little man he was wide awake when I looked in his carrier. He was starting to found a personality and smiled and rolled over as soon as he saw my face. I picked my baby up and hugged him very tight. Then, I prayed that my son be more in life than me and his father. I prayed that one day he be a football player not a dope boy. I went to the kitchen and warmed up a bottle for Major Jr. to drink for his first meal of the day. Then, I got out a bowl so I could have Money creals waiting on her. "Mommy you up" "I love you mommy you are the best is the first thing Money said to me this morning. Next, she asked me could she eat some candy after breastfast like she do at Reese house. "Yes sweetie you can have some candy when you finish beastfast." I watched Money eat and then I drove to the store to get her some candy because I didn't have any at the house. She wanted bubble gum too so I got that. I told Money to make sure she keep the bubble gum in her mouth and she told me she was a big girl and she would do so. I was so proud of her. When, we got back Major was up and was taking a shower for the day and his clothes was laid out on the bed. I went to the bathroom that only had a sank and tollet in it and bath and wiped the kids off. By the time I had done that Reese was already on the phone asking me was I bringing the kids over for the day. I start smiling and told my sister that she was a blessing from god to me. I told Reese I was almost finish clothing them and I would be on my way. It took me no time to get the kids ready but I waited for Major to get out the shower. When, I saw that he was fully dressed I asked him was he okay and did he have clean thoughts and could he make it thought the day without me. He kissed me on the lips and told me damn I don't know what I would do without you. Kelly you is a down as female. "But baby am a man and I can handle my own from what I did last night." "You just get ready for today make sure whatever you do it's a come up for our family." "We in this shit together no matter what okay baby." "Damn right." "By the way am about to drop the kids off at my sister crib and go on Jay Jack corner and make some money." "Do your damn thing and remember you my thug bitch for life." I start smiling grabbed my keys and headed to Reese crib. When, I got there Qunicy was there and I see Reese had been spending a lot of time with him because Money knew his name and face and ran right up to him when she saw him. "So what ya'll kicking it again or what." "Yeah, we have been back together for months." "I'll be moving back in once my lease is up in my apartment and hopeful Reese and I could be getting ready for a marriage and a new baby in the next couple moths." "Damn Reese why you didn't tell me you was expecting a new baby girl or boy?" "Yeah, I found out a month ago and I was trying to find a right time to tell you everything." "Which is when Reese?" "That Qunicy want to marry me and he already bought the ring and everything and that we are trying to come up with a wedding date and time." "That's wonderful Reese am very happy for you." I walked out Reese apartment thinking how the lord blessed me to have a strong relationship with my sister. I headed down L.A. Blvd. back to my apartment. There I found myself going though the lingerie I got from Tricks so I could look sexy on the block for some niggas. I got five lingerie outfits to last me thought out the day and night. I picked up the phone and called Kreme to see was the hood jumping. As, she was picking up I could hear niggas in the back ground asking junkies what they need. "Bitch what's going on over there is money coming or what?" "Yeah baby money coming both ways though this shit today." "Hurry yo ass out hear so niggas can see that pretty face of yours and you can get some money." "Word, am getting ready now and I'll be there all day long making it do what it do." I got off the phone fast as I could. An, before I left that side of town I called Man to see did he want to make a play for the day. He was to busy trying to set up his new strip club that would be opening up less than six months. I hung up on that shit Man was talking about quick. I rode downtown L.A. and when I pulled up in my Bentley niggas was like get out and show a niggas some love baby. I parked in the back of Jay Jack and I already had on my lingerie ready to work the corner. Jay Jack told me happy to have your money making ass back and the first thing come though is yours today. "Okay Jay Jack it's my world today on these motherfucking streets." In seconds a nigga from uptown L.A. pulled up in a gray MC. Jay Jack ran up to the car like he was a drug dealer and asked him what he wanted. "I want that pretty lady in the pink and black stilettos with all that booty." "Great because she up next to make money." "How much are you charging and where should I take her." "The cost is five hundred dollars and there is an ally apartment upstairs where you can take her." "Okay let me park." Dude parked the MC and past the money off to Jay Jack and walled up the stairs. As, any other man that was new to this he talked and wanted a converstion to make a bitch feel like tricking was about making friends instead of making money. "Look sweetheart I know you want to talk but it's time to get to business because I have more money to be making." "Oh so that's how things work round here?" "Yeah, so do you want to fuck or do you want some head." "I want a head job because my wife like to smell my penis when I come home." "That's fine." I pulled down his pants roughly and grabbed his dick like it was a hotdog. It was that easy. I put my mouth around his dick and start moving my head up and down. As, I was giving the man head his shoes came off and he start wiggling and curling up his toes to the good head job. "Baby am about to cum in your mouth come up." An, as soon as I was about to tell him I swallow he shout off in my face. Cum was everywhere but it was quick and easy. "Damn baby you did a great job you did something my wife never done in her life to me." "Is this where I can find you on a daily basic?" "Yes, and just ask for Kelly if am not here I got one other home girl name Kreme that can do the job like me and make sure you straight." "Nice details I will remember to only asked for Kelly or Kreme baby." "Thank you for your service I got to be going." I walked downstairs and before I could make it on the corner Jay Jack was asking me to go back upstairs with another man. Unlike, the first man this man was turned up and asking me all kinds of nasty shit before he could un-button his pants. "Baby don't take it lite on the wood suck all nine inches of that dick I want to get my money worth." I come though hear often and Terri was my regular trick but she don't work the block anymore and they said you is the next best thing to her." "I heard around here you and Kreme have the block on lock." "If the service is like Terri you would be seeing a lot of me." "An, no am not a drug dealer am a regular professional business man." "Well with all that being said you can start by kissing on the tip. I like when a woman kiss and lick on it. I did as he told me to do. An, as soon as I got it on hard he wanted me to suck it from the back. He then wanted me to put his balls in my mouth. The whole time I spent with him he cocah me on every little thing he wanted. I didn't like that but money was money so I just let him coach me though the whole time. Next, he picked me up in the air and fuck the shit out of me. By, the time we was done dope boys from downstairs was upstairs in the ally apartment about to make it do what it do. That wasn't nothing they always cook crack in the apartment in the ally. The guy I had just made two fifty told me he could get used to the way I trick and he would be back some other day. Before, he left he asked me did I know someone to do a threesome with and if I founded someone to give him a call. I told him that wouldn't be a problem me and my girl Kreme do that type of shit and to walk to my car and I would store his number in my phone log. "Okay baby." We exchange numbers and he told me to be easy. Jay Jack was on the corner and said, "I guess everything went as planned with him." "Yeah, if he come back around here just remember that's my money so don't let anyone do business with anyone else." "I got you baby girl." "Ya'll keep doing the things ya'll be doing around here and I'll be a million dollar pimp in know time." By that time of the day it was time for me to take a lunch break. I figured I could smoke a joint or two and have a sub sandwich. Shit, I was hungry and this was going to be my first meal of the day. I call Jay Jack up the sidewalk and told him I was about to slide. Then, I went to the weed man that live in the last building in the project and bought a quarter from him.

Next, stop was to the cocaine man. Then, I finally got something to eat. I sat in a local park in the hood and smoked my head off and ate my shit up fastly. I called Major on my break to see did he have his freedom still and for two to see what his day had been like. Major still had his freedom but he had already had lunch and all for the day. Then out of the blue he asked me to come though and give him a hug on the way he wanted some dime cocaine bags from the corner hood store. I ran across the street to get some dime bags instead of driving. There was no need to waste gas. Then, I walked back to the car and drove Major the bags. I got out the and gave him a hug and put the dime bags in his hands. While, I was there Major bagged up a grand came though the projects that fast. Major said he had called his supply man two times today and a couple more sells he would be on round three. "Damn baby are you making all that money to spoil me." "You know am trying to make you stay in all that high price shit you be wearing." "Baby what's our plans for tonight". "Shit, wtch a movie at the drive thru and seat in the car in talk about the future would be nice". "You could never get tired of making plans to better yourself for you can see a better day." "You right about that part, but baby I was talking about when I get home from the Roxy's are you going to beat that pussy down because last night you skipped out on me." "Damn I forgot tonight you dance but damn right baby when we make it home I can been that ass over and put this dick in you if that's what you want girl." "Yeah, baby and make sure you hit that shit nice and slow and make me go crazy afterward on that dick." "I got you boo thang." I walked out the apartment and hopped in the Bentley I felt good and I was high and I had ate a nice little sub from the corner store so I was good. I rode down to Jay Jack spot and Kreme was out there servicing. By, that time Mark, Red, and a couple more cats had made it out there and shit was lovely on the corner. Mark gave me a hug and told me to work that ass but not to hard because I was first on his payroll because he had missed this ass while I was gone. A nigga name Max came on the block. He did a little talking telling the niggas how the police was hot on Late Ave. He said this was the only place humping with dope money and hoes that was tricking so he decided to come make money our way. Niggas knew him so they were friendly about him making money on the block. Max had on a fresh pair Jordan's and a Ralph Lauren Polo fit with a Micheal Jordan jump man hat. I was already looking his way. I wanted and hoped he would talk to me. Shit any nigga I had heard about and that was in good health on the streets I wanted to make play with them. Before, he could set his eyes on me I was already walking up to him. "Yeah, Max my name is Kelly am one of the females that make money out here.""If you down I want you to make memories with a bitch like me today if it's okay with you baby." "Damn ya'll get that type of love on this block.""Baby, if that's the case who your pimp I can pay that shit for your fine ass right now." "Jay Jack the pimp that collect money around this way". "Hay Jay Jack how much it's going to cost me to take this pretty girl name Kelly upstairs and make memories with her." "Five hundred bucks." Max pulled out the money paid Jay Jack and he gave me my half which was two fifty and I went up upstairs and the ally apartment. When, we got in there he had some Trojans condoms and his dick was already on hard. The smell of his polo cologne smelled good. I asked

Max did he want to fuck or just get head. Max said both would be fine and dropped his boxers. I directly got on my knees and did what I do for a living. "Damn baby am happy I came on the block today.""You must be young because I never saw you around in L.A. I lifted my head up to tell Max yeah, but I never told him I my age. After, he got his nut from the head, he told me baby you know what to do next suck that wood and get it back on hard so I could lay between that pussy for the first time. I did what dude said and in no time he was back on hard and we was in the ally apartment fucking. Max eight inch dick wasn't the best but I could make it do. I kissed on his neck while he whole me in the air. It felt so damn good. An, it was a hell of a memory fucking with a new nigga from another block. By, the time I thought Max was nutting him and Mark was running a threesome on me double teaming my ass. Shit was so real niggas was taping a flick of me throwing my cash in the air. The way my ass was clapping was remarkable and I couldn't wait to see the flick on replay.

Chapter 7

Last, night I end up watching the flick on replay then dancing at The Roxy's I fucked around and did a threesome and it was video taped. A group of hoes from Miami Florida came to The Roxy's and Kreme got mad and hit this bitch with an Exclusive Liquor bottle. I ain't gone lie that bitch beat the hell out of Kreme ass. Kreme face fuck up and I haven't seen her today. All, I know is I grabbed a table from under some chairs and throw it at a bitch. Her home girl that was in The Roxy's with her spotted the table and blocked it and start fighting me. I was toe to toe with the hoe and came out on top. I couldn't even make it over to where Kreme was because so many people were in the way of her getting her ass beat. The bouncer to the club saw the fight and came and put all our ass out the club. When, he saw it was us he let us back in the club. That bitch had cut Kreme in the face. An, I had to take her to the emergency room last night. I didn't stay with her I had money to be made uptown L.A. I went to the niggas house and did a thirty minute dance. It was some old ass white man that had came in the club before and been had my number and finally wanted to use it while his wife was gone to Altanta for her daughter wedding. When, I got there it was a small old house and it looked like they had been living there for years. I did Tom a lap dance and I charged the fuck out of him. Tom end up paying me ten grand to work my ass. I wasn't there that long and I went home to hug up with Major. Now, it's morning am trying to find Kreme so the first thing am going to do is hit her up on her cell phone. Next, step is call her grandma house and see what's going on. Kreme grandma answered the phone and luckly she had just got there. She said the cut wasn't deep enough to get sticking so she got some ointment so her face could heal. I asked her did she want me to come rub it on there for her just to be nice because I felt bad I couldn't make it to her in the club last night in time before that hoe cut my friend. I knew she had to feel pretty badly for a mark to be left in her face. I told Kreme that I was get off the phone with her and head downtown L.A. to check on her for the day. She said okay and I told her to give me an hour. I went in my closet and got a DKNY outfit out that I had recently bought from the mall. It still had tags on it because I didn't try it on and the store so I didn't pop the tags off. When, I put the jean DKNY outfit on with the rips in it, it fixed my body perfectly fine. I went in the bathroom and put on some MAC make up with some Candy smelling lip gloss and spray on my Coach perfume. By, the time I got ready I was looking like a million dollar bitch. Then, I put on some jean and black shoes. I got in the car and went downtown L.A. When, I got there I went to Kreme grandma house. Niggas was standing on the sidewalk to see if they could find someone that had a video tape of the fight in The Roxy's so they could go kill the female from Miami. Kreme was standing out the door with a mirror in her hand keep looking at her face. She was fucked up. An, the hoe had blacked both of Kreme eyes. I got on the phone and called some niggas I knew to see could we find the bitch. Rome a nigga from around the way came just in time and gave all her information. The female name was Carmax and was a stripper who travled from city to state making money because she had played out in Miami. Carmax was standing right at The Hideaway Inn and had fucked and tricked with Rome all night. He said that he would go kill the bitch and rob her and take the money he paid her back and used a crack head car as get way car to go throw the body away. When niggas heard the plan some of them left with a promise not to tell about what was about to go down, five cats stayed while they was making plans to go to The Hideaway Inn with Kreme to end Carmax life. I told her that I was about to start my day on Jay Jack corner and I would catch back up with her later. Kreme meant the world to me but for one I had children in the world and for two she was a millionaire in the streets which I was still about to become one and had dreams and that wasn't to end up in prison. She looked at me and gave me the okay. I told her to report to the block after she made sure the hoe Carmax was dead. I gave Kreme a hug just in case it was my last time in both of our lives seeing each other. I jumped in my Bentley and rode to Jay Jack block when I got there it wasn't that many niggas on the street but it was money coming so I was about to start making it for the day. Red, Mark and some nigga that they had met was chilling in the ally apartment, I was the first person on the block making money so they

went down stairs to Jay Jack and paid the usually amount for a corner hoe. Since the day was moving slow I decided to get a cup of drink from the bar they had builded in the ally apartment. It was some gin and I got a little tipsy and took my time. It was no need for me to make all the money. I already had heads up because I was the first person out there. I walked around to entertain the niggas as I drunk on my liquor. I danced in a slow pace for Mark them I would use eye contact with Red and the other niggas. While using eye contact I would lick my tounge and pop kisses and rub my hands all over my body. Dude them thought the shit I was doing sexy and tipped me more money on the side. As, they gave me the money I put the money in a duffle bag. As, I was putting the money up Kreme had walked in. She saw I was busy and walked outside the door. I told Red and Mark it was time to make it happen. I gave them a quick fuck and went outside to see was Kreme still there. But, when I got outside she had already left. I hit her on the hip to see where she was and she was back at her grandma house in the project. I told Jay Jack that I was about to step away from the block for a little bit but my day wasn't over. He said okay and I walked those few blocks to get a work out for the day. When, I got there I asked Kreme how did everything go. She told me Rome shot Carmax five times in the head and rape both of her home girls and shot them too. I was like damn am sorry all that happen over a fight in the club. I was happy it wasn't me. An, I wished like hell Kreme just had beat the hoe ass instead of her getting beat up. Kreme was happy as fuck that those hoes was dead. That's all she wanted to talk about. Until, I told her I was bout to go back to the corner and make some money. She told me to wait until she wash up and put something on to work the corner in for the day too. Kreme say as Carmax was dying Rome took the million dollar he trick with her back and fucked her right in front of her and fire more gun shots to the head. He put her body in a garbage can on the other side of L.A. Kreme said. By, that time she was done getting ready. We walked back up the corner to Jay Jack block. When, I got there Jay Jack called me to go up the ally apartment to make some money. When, I got there it was a nigga name Jay waiting on me. He said he was in the mall and Reese and Qunicy gave him my address on the streets when he told them he was looking for a stripper. I told Jay nice to met him and that I would rather go to a small hotel. He said that was fine and we could go miles away if I wanted too. In the room 150 we got it on. In the room it had double beds and I had sex with him. Jay had a nice size dick and the movement he was doing was a great sex beat. When, I got done my hair was messed up but I combed it back down to make it look nice. He program my number in and gave a extra token because he couldn't take me back downtown because he was a drug dealer and had runs to make. That was fine with me and I took the train back downtown. On the way there I looked out the window and saw all the cars in the busy traffic in L.A. It was something I had never done before and it was great. I went back to downtown L.A. to Jay Jack was a little bit upset for me leaving the block with Jay. I explained to him that I wanted to go to a new spot and fuck off. He gave me a hug and told me if I wasn't one of the best he would make me leave the corner. I start smiling to hear the word best and walked off. When, I got upstairs Kreme was in a freak show and the television was on. News reports had

found Carmax body just that quick in the trash. They say she was shot five times and there was no witness. They also said if anyone out there knew the killer to give them a call. All I could say was god. I notice I had still had on the DKNY outfit and I worked in it all day and decided to go but on a lingerie. At, that time all niggas was announcing for all hoes who wanted to be in Kreme freak show to go but on a lingerie. When, I changed into my clothes Mark pulled out some money and told me to put it in my money bag. He called me over to him and said, "Baby fuck what you do on the streets and how you been doing count it it's a quarter million dollars in cash." I bent over and start working my ass for him slow and letting him feel up on my fat pussy. Mark was licking his tounge at me and telling me to open up my legs so he could eat my pussy. I got on the table and told him to climb between my legs and to eat my shit slow so I could cum. Then, I told that nigga to reverse that shit to the sixty nine so we could do each other at the same time. Dope was selling and niggas was videoing me get a quarter mill on the streets. I was happy ass fuck. I already had a couple hundred thousands and before you know it I will be at my goal. Mark asked me to turn over so he could slap me on the ass from the back while another bitch fuck me with their hands. I say okay and laid down and let them finger fuck me. It was Candy that worked at The Roxy's who I had dislike for a minute about Major who finger me. She saw how I looked at her and told me to minus my head with the drama shit and let's make money. With that said I got on my knees so she could see the back of my pussy so she could finger me. That shit felt so good and she put her head down there and start kissing my click. Mark was smiling as he got some liquor and filmed us at the same time. While they were filming us Red had Kreme ass front the back and a seprate film fucking the shit out of her. The excitement that was going on had me want to entertain them niggas even more. I got on the table and start dancing shaking my ass off the music they were playing. Candy came right behind me and start eating me again. I ate every bitch pussy in there and walked out with another quarter mill. I notice I had a million dollars because I was keeping track of what I made. I got the money and went outside to my car and drove to my apartment in Up Living to put the money up. When, I got there I counted the money up then let my main man Major know his bitch was a million dollar bitch on the streets. Major was like damn baby am proud of you. I call Reese to tell her about the million dollar and anyone that was close. Reese say that she was asleep for the night and call her back tomorrow. By, the time I had got off the phone with Reese Kreme was calling telling me she was at the police station and they had proof she had something to do with Carmax death. She say the police knew everything because one of the girls who Rome thought was dead made it. I was like damn call me if you get a bond. In my head I thought damn am happy I didn't get in that shit with her. She got off the phone and before we hung up she told me she didn't have a bond and that she was going to be charged with murder. I start crying and hung up the phone. That night I called everyone I could think of and told them about Kreme. While, on the phone phone I got all kinds of news from calling around. Mark and Red got charged in the process with all kinds of guns and dope and all the other niggas in the ally apartment was gone so they where left on the streets. I got a cup out the kitchen and poured me some liquor. I needed it after all that bad news. I grab my keys to go to the police department and check on Kreme. When, I got there they told me everyone had been charge and visitation at the jail was over and to come back tomorrow. They, gave me a paper with the rules to the jail and I left. All, night I was wondering why all that shit had to break out. I went back home and laid down and by the time I got in a deep slept Major came in with the late news. I got up and start hugging him for him still having his freedom. I told Major I wish Rome and Kreme them had never went to murder Carmax. I start crying again for the second time. Major put me in his arms and healed me real tight. He got a joint to smoke that was already rolled and lord knows I needed it. I hit the shit a couple times and got high. It felt better to be high but my head was still hurting. I got a early start making money so by that time it was eleven o'clock and the news was coming on. The called out all there government names and ages and what the fuck they was going to be charged with. They even told hand prints was on the guns in the ally apartment. They got fingerprints off the plastic bags and all the dope was Anthony Clip and Mark and I missed what Mark last name was because it was raining to bad that night. All the lights went off when the news was on and they came back on about eleven thirty. I watch the same story when the news came back on for the second time and Mark last name was McDay. They had so much dope in the ally apartment which it's always like that in the apartment I knew the feds was going to pick up the case. They talked about how they were going to stop the tricking and drug selling on that block. I guess everyone was watching it because Jay Jack called me and told me that the streets was going to be close down until father notice. I told him okay and got off the phone. Shit I was a million dollar bitch. Shit, and I still had a job at the Roxy's so that wasn't a problem for me. I hung up on Jay Jack and got some rest. When, I woke up the next morning Pimp the club owner name was on my cell phone call log. He asked me was all that true about Kreme them I told him yeah. Then, he asked me did I have anything to do with it. Pimp said he would hate to lose another dancer because that's how he make his money in the club. He said millions was in the club last night and I missed out on Young Swagger surpise party for Candy. I was mad but shit something happen to Kreme I couldn't make it. I had to get myself together. By, the time I got off the phone with pimp and got ready the jail was open for the day. I got in the car and the first thing I did was stop by a store to get a newspaper to see what the daily paper had to say. When, I reached the jail it was crowed but I sat down and waited for them to call my name. When, I got upstairs to the top level I picked up the phone and called the deputy in the part to tell Kreme she had a visitor. When, she got there she was crying and asking me to call around for her a lawyer. I told Kreme that I would find her one of the best lawyers in town. She was my homie that what I was suppose to so. She told me okay. We talked and she said she was going to tell the lawyer she wasn't the killer and to see could that less her time. By, the time Kreme got done crying and talking visitation at the jail was over. They only gave you thirty mintues to talk. Next, I went and saw Mark and Red and they were find like most niggas be in jail. The conversation with them was short and I left the jail house.

The next step was going to find a lawyer. The attorney I found name was Mr. Menu and he said it would cost me thirty thousand for a case like Kreme case. I asked him how could I pay for that. An, I had an choice to pay in full or by a payment plan. I told him I would be paying in full and with a credit card. Mr. Menu said it would cost more with a credit case but only by a couple of dollars. That was find with me. I took out my card and he processes the payment. The machine took a minute but I waited. After, the machine went thought he gave me all the paperwork. LiKe his contact number and when he would start on the case in the meanwhile he said he would go by the jail and see Kreme. Mr. Menu was one of the best lawyers in L.A. I went back up to the jail. After, going back up to the jail house and talking to the captain about giving Kreme her the information from the lawyer. He finally said it would be okay if I give her the paperwork. He told me I had thirty mintues to see Kreme but to make this my last time coming up there two times a day. It ready wasn't that much information but his name, number and address with the paperwork that I had paid for Kreme lawyer by credit. Kreme was smiling and happy that she had her a lawyer. She thought she was making the right choice and that she would get less time due to the fact Mr. Meun was one of the best in the city. I talked to Kreme and told her that he would be to the jail to see her and my last words to her was that I would send her some money J-pay. Then, I told her I would send a copy of the information about her case as I get it from the lawyer. I left the jail house having doubts about my friend getting out. An, to tell the truth I really did want Kreme to be release from jail. I wanted to be top of the line in everything I do. I rode down the streets and it was a Winn Dixie to the left hand of the other side of the road. I got in the turning lane and went to the Winn Dixie to pay some money J-pay for Kreme to have some money on her account. While, I was there I decided to by Travis some whites and send him some money a long with Mark, and Red. It was another local club call The Comfort Zone and it was open during the daytime. I heard it was a money spot. I drove down Broadway street going to The Comfort Zone on my way there I saw all kind of niggas in cars on rims Bently and all just stunning. I spotted the club and pulled up in the parking lot. I jumped out the Bently and walked to the front door. When, I got there the niggas that was down the raod in their show off cars was there. I got out the car in some bad ass jeans from a hotline call Flirt. Every nigga in there was looking at me from head to toe. I was feeling good about myself and walked thought the front door and asked could I worked the club for a couple hours. When, I got in there niggas was in there left and right trying too holla at me. I walk to the dressing room and put on my clothes. I walked out onto the dance floor and start dancing. Candy the bitch from Miami that work in The Roxy's was there and she told me she worked in Comfort Zone in the daytime too. Candy told me she was dancing to open up a perfume company in L.A. but the line was also going to be ran in Florida in the down south area of Miami. I was happy for Candy I had begun to be her friend. After, talking to Candy for a little bit thoughts came racing to my head that I was going to tell the police that Kreme told me that her and some niggas was going to kill Carmax at the Hideaway Inn. I was a friend to Kreme but now she was locked up for murder which is something a bad bitch won't do I was having second thoughts. She didn't know it but I was going to the police station and tell on her ass. For one with Kreme locked up that was a way for me to make more money on the streets. I wanted to be top of the line in the game so if it was to get rid of a bitch then that's what I had to do. At The Comfort Zone I made plans to be with Candy. An, we made so much money in the club that day. We did threesomes and niggas paid us big money to dance and eat each other pussy out. I like Candy pussy so long she came in my mouth three times back to back. While Candy was cumming in my mouth niggas paid us more money. After, the threesome Candy and I danced until it was time to dance at the next spot. In the Comfort Zone there was a female in there name Clay trying to find out what happen to Carmax in the club. I told her Kreme and Carmax got in a fight and they somehow tried to cut each other and Carmax end up cutting Kreme and the next day Kreme got niggas to kill Carmax. After, talking to Clay I did a lot more things that night. I got to know Candy. I didn't tell the bitch any of my personal business put we did make money and I got in a lot of niggas pockets. Kreme was sad at the county jail that night and had the deputy to call me. I was mad ass fuck with her and told her to never call me while am getting money in the streets. She was kind of shook and got off the phone but I did tell her a bitch from Miami was looking for her. Kreme asked me was the bitch asking about the murder. I told her yeah and her I also told Kreme that I mentioned to the female name Clay she was involved. I got mad at her on the phone and called her a low life. An, I told her that I was going to call police and tell them she had something to do with the murder. She start crying very quickly and wanted me to change my mind. It was time for her to know I wasn't her friend anymore. Bitch, Had been making to much money on me she needed to be in jail. That how it was on the streets if a bitch made that kind of money on the streets a hoe or nigga would get mad at them. I was that kind of bitch. I had lost my mother to the streets and had never experience that kind of love. In the hood all afternoon I chilled at my grandma house. I thought how it felt to be on top. Major and I had been in the world doing big shit. I loved Major and haven't seen him all day. But, I damn sho was about to call my baby. I picked up the phone and dial Major phone. I got a little down but it was okay. I walked outside to see if I could find Major and talk to my man and enjoy the conversation we was about to have on the phone. When, I walked outside every car was parked in the hood. When, Major got on the phone he was happy to talk to me and told me he was on his way to grandma house to see me. I told Major I would wait out the door for him. When, he got there he hugged and kissed on me. Major made me feel so good more than any nigga ever have or ever would. Major had to go make a sell so he couldn't stay that long. That was find with me. I went back to Up Living to make some arrangements to go to the club and dance. I looked though the closet to see what was in there. I wanted to make some money at The Roxy's. I know a bitch was about to get paid Kreme wasn't dancing in the club. I found me a couple laces that plans was to get my strip bag ready was new that I found in my closet that I had found out of Tricks. When, I left the house I went to Starbusts a shoe store in L.A. to get some money. A nigga I knew was over there and they wanted to make a couple moves with me. I called the nigga B-Low to see what kind of money he wanted to spend. When I got on the phone I start putting my game down to B-Low. I asked him what kind of money he was trying to spend for the second time. Then B-low said what kind of money you trying to make. I told him I was looking for a hundred grand. That was good money for me if a nigga was going to do that in the game. I told B-Low I was on my way to Northmore to get paid I made love and fucked the shit out of B-Low and he told me how I had the best pussy the world. I had wanted him every since Kreme told me he was a money man in our city. After, I fucked B-Low it felt good to ride with the cash he gave me in my Bently to the other side of town. I was about to live all the dreams I wanted to live out in L.A. Travis was still locked up and six month was moving slow to me because I had a lot going on. I had been over seas and lived my life to the fullies. That meant the world to me. I loved my life living the fast pace and doing what I needed to make money. Starbust was open and I had planned to walk into there and buy me some shoes. I walked into the shoe store to get my shoe game right. When, I got in there Step the store owner had so many shoes to choose from. I looked on the wall and looked for all the shoes I wanted. Next, I put on each pair heels and walked around I them to see did they fit right. The shoes was one of a kind and I knew I would get much money in them. I paid three thousand dollars for three pair shoes and man was I ready to rock my ass in them. I walked out the store with my mind set on going to the club to dance. When, I got to Up Living Pimp called me to see was I working the club. I told him yeah and rushed and got ready to make the other end of my million dollar plan add up.

Before, I went to the club I stopped in the hood to see what was going on. Major was still over there and junkies still was buying crack. Every nigga was hanging out doing their thing. Some more hoe was in the hood. Some fine bitches I could get own with and eat pussy. Those was the kind of females I was looking for. Before, I left to hit club I called the police to let them know Kreme had planned to kill Carmax. For some reason I was mad at Kreme and wanted her to get life even though I had got the lawyer. One of the reason I did it was because I thought Carmax was a badder bitch than Kreme that didn't have to die because of some bullshit. Kreme was just jealous ass fuck and wanted the spot light to herself. In my mind I was going to set anyone up that didn't like a bitch because they was on top. I finally made it to the club. Many niggas was at the club and trying to get at a bitch. But my main focus was those hoes that was on the corner. One of them did a freak show with me in the club. She ate my pussy on stage in front of so many niggas and we made thirty grand. Most of the niggas in the club that night was throwing up game signs and getting toast to all the strippers. Major wasn't in the club I called him but I didn't get and answer. Fruity, the female that had ate me out danced next to me for the rest of the night. At, the end of the night I gave her a hug and headed towards my car. When, I got to the car some nigga jumped in and rob me and told me he would put me under the grave if a nigga do life for me and he was talking about his brother. So, I guess Rome was his brother. He took the thirty grand and hit me in the head with the pistol. I was a little scared but I drove home that night.

Chapter 8

Late last night I got my shit fucked to sleep after I told Major I got robbed by some nigga at the club. I loved what Major was doing to me. That nigga made my pussy feel so good. He didn't show know remorse on this ass. That nigga dick was so big off in my pussy. My shit was jumping all night. I laid next to Major and he felt good and his skin was so soft and I liked the way the touch felt. Major was king in the bed to me. Major was street when it comes to fucking. Not only did I enjoy sex last night but the club was jumping. I really enjoyed myself expect when I got robbed by the dude Rome brother. He hit me in the head with a gun and everything. I was sick to my stomach he had robbed me for thirty grand. Thoughts race to my head about that shit as I got out of bed. I went in the kitchen and got the house phone and called Reese. I told her as soon as I clean up I would be over to her place to get the kids for the day. Reese said okay and got off the phone as usually. I clean up the apartment and it smell just like bleach and I mopped the floor and sprayed airfresher. As, I was cleaning up Major woke up before I could tell him I already called Reese he was on the phone with her again asking about the kids. Money and Major Jr. was eating and Qunicy had my son in his high chair feeding him. I told Reese to put me some beastfast up so I could put something on my stomach. Major and I press end on the touch screen phone and got off the phone with Reese. We hugged and kissed on each other and I told Major I was having thoughts about having another baby. He slap me on the booty and told me to go take a shower and get ready for the day. I turned on the hot shower and took a bath and got out and look thought my closet to put on a Jimmy Choo dress. Jimmy Choo was one of the new hot designs that were out. I laid the Jimmy Choo dress down and though how wonderful it would be to stand next to Shonda again in this Jimmy Choo designer dress. Before, I could get out the bathroom Major was in there trying to fuck me I left his fuck ass standing right in there and went and got ready. While I was getting ready Jay Jack called me on my cell phone and asked me did I want to work his online stripping business that he had just opened. Hell yeah I wanted this ass to be part of a booty call. I wanted some new niggas to spend some money on me. Jay Jack said I could make money on the corner and from the online cite at the same time if I wanted too. All, I had to do was go and resigter my name under the website and post a picture so client's could know who they where talking too. I went on the cite and put my name and told my sex hobbies and posted a picture. As, soon as I did that a nigga name Made tried to holla at me. I gave Made the address to The Hideaway Inn and told him I would meet him there in thirty mintues. I called around to a few people to see if anyone knew Made and Candy say he was a money man. I start telling Candy that my pimp had an online cite now and Made just popped up on my screen. I start getting ready by the time I was done Candy had told me about all the hoes Made fuck with. About all his cars that he was married once and he have ten children and he fuck with Trisha on the side. I finally made it to The Hideaway Inn and got off the phone with Candy. When, I got there I called him on his cell phone. Made answer that bitch like the man with the plan, he told me what room he was in then he answer the door with his boxers on. I pushed that nigga on the bed and gave him the best ride of his lifetime. Made turned me over and fuck me all up in the air and that shit felt like he was a king to me and I was his queen. After, the quick fuck and I made the money I went to Reese house to get the kids and back to grandma house in the hood. When, I got to Reese house Qunicy say she was gone to grandma house for the day. I went to grandma house and when I got in the hood I had on my strip fit and every nigga say I looked just like a model in a magazine. Grandma was happy to see me and told me I reminded her of my mother in her younger days. Money looked at me and said bitch I want to be just like you strip and get money when I grow up mommy. I looked at Money and couldn't say nothing. That's why if my baby wanted to be just like me I needed to step my game up. I loved what my life was about. I was a bitch with a plan. Not a hoe on the streets not doing nothing. A bitch was making memories of a life time. I liked being a street bitch and didn't care what anyone had to say about it. I looked on the cite and seen if any more niggas wanted to see what I was talking about for the day. A lot of niggas was trying to get at me but after that million I was trying to love up on my nigga for that big success. I called Major to see where he was and to see did he want steaks for dinner. By, the time I had made it home the phone had rung and grandma had lost her life that fast. Now Reese was the only person I had in my family. By that time Major had made it in the house I cried in Major hands all day long. I knew that would be something I would never forget the day I lost my grandma. An, that's on everything. I loved my grandma and wished she could have lived in the world to see me with all this money I had just got. I called Reese for the second time that day and she was at the hospital with grandma body. I told her to stay there and sign every paper she had to before she leave. I wasn't over the funeral and grandma policy and that was find with me. I knew Reese would handle everything she needed to. I got off the phone with Reese and call around for a dress to wear. I end up getting a Chanel dress with some Chanel shoes to wear to the funreal when ever Reese was going to be having it. My heart was in so much pain. My body was about to go under. That's how much I loved my grandma. I gave Major the print out of what my grandma wanted her funeral to look like. An she wanted it just like my auntie that had pasted away. I called Reese and she had all the paperwork she needed to gone and do grandma graveyard service the same day. There was no need to wait. But, when I called Reese she wanted to whole off on things. I was like damn as soon as I was about to turn on Kreme I lost my damn grandma. I knew shit liked that wasn't suppose to be. My grandma was the nicest old woman in the projects and a nigga had took her life just like that. I knew I was going to miss her. I knew it was

because of me in the game. My talking ass had hurt my grandma so much. Kreme problems was nothing like mind I had lost grandma. I knew I was about to be lost in the game. I was upset for losing my grandma that day. Earlier, I had decided to stop making money for the day, but after that I got my ass back on the online website and made L.A. light up. Pain was still inside of me but I had to do what I had to do. I suck a little dick and made love to all kind of niggas and that shit meant the world to me. I just wish my grandma could be here to enjoy the money I had made. By, the time I had made it home I had several missed calls and Reese was one of them. I phoned Reese back to see what was going on with her and she told me she was still at the hospital with grandma body. I wish I knew how to tell Reese it was my fault grandma had got killed. I didn't know how to tell her that it was Rome brother who killed grandma because I had told on Kreme and Rome just some days ago. I finally got out my hoe clothes and went and viewed my granny body. You hear one day and gone the next day is all I could say to her. When, I put my hands on her my grandma body was cold and the only thing I could do was cry. My ass had made the mistake of my lifetime. I couldn't stay to the hospital that long because I was sad about my grandma death. I went back home and by the time I had got there I had cried all my make-up off. I went in the bathroom and took a shower to go and lay next to Major for the rest of the night. I listened to Kirk Franklin all day long and cried myself to sleep. I found myself up and the next hour and got all my photos of grandma and looked at them. It made me all upset that grandma had died all over again. The news came on and grandma landlord from the

projects had put on television for her to be a special part of the community. My phone start ringing and all my friends over L.A. wanted to tell me how sorry they were that my grandma had losted her life. That shit made me feel good about myself. I looked at my phone for the tenth time and it was Reese. She wanted me to know that grandma had planned for a outdoor funreal. That was good too it was whatever she wanted. My dress would go with the sun light from outside to even though it was white. Morning came so fast and the first person called my phone was Kreme from the jail to tell me sorry grandma had died. She wanted to know was I good and when was the funreal. I told her it was today and I was at my apartment in Up Living getting ready to go to Reese place to go to the funreal. Money was at the house with me and wanted me to love on her because we had lost grandma my baby was close with my grandma and she was going to take this hard too. I went to Reese house and Major decided to go with me. He was already dress so only me and the kids needed to get dress for the day. It was cool outside and L.A. today so I didn't want the funreal to last that long like they could. Major was upset and cried more than me at grandma funreal. After, the funreal Reese had a little dinner for all the friends and family and the food was good as fuck. Reese ready showed me that she could cook good ass fuck. When, we got to the house we was home alone and Major wanted to know could he fuck me. I was ready to get that wood in me. Shit, it had been a couple days and we were long over due. I sucked my man dick and made love to him and what we was doing we was working on another baby. I damn sho hope we was working up on baby number two I was deep in love with this nigga. A third child at this time would not matter. I was a million dollar bitch and another baby just would make me get more money. After, making love to Major he stepped out to make some money in the hood so I got on the hotline to see what was up. I end up calling this nigga name Jamal and he had some lovely shit to talk about. Jamal talked about going to Florida for this one day past event to a water Park. It was a cool outside so I couldn't make the trip. Jamal end up calling me back and me, him and his brother got a room and the next city over where they ran a train on me. Hell, the dick was so good with Jamal and his brother I gave them their money back and told them they could keep it. Shit, I had much money some good dick is all I needed. Now, I was moving on to the next level in life. I planned to get myself together and do what I needed to do to be on top in the game. I wanted a shoe company and I also wanted to go to business school. That's how it was in the business world bitches was coming up and doing there thing in the world. After, coming up with a business plan for the rest of the day I played in the field and made more money with niggas of all kinds. Night came fast and my day was over working the hotline. I went home and prepared for the next day. I decided to not work The Roxy's for a couple days due to the fact I had lost grandma. I thought of away to get my day going so I could go help out at grandma house so someone else could move in the house grandma was living in. I cleaned up grandma apartment to the tee. After, cleaning up grandma apartment I went and checked on my apartment in the projects. Everything was in order and Major had everything nice and clean. I saw everything was put up nice and went back to Up Living.

When, I got in Up Living I got on the online website and every nigga in L.A. was trying to holla at me. I call Jamal back first and went and made money with him. Then I called a nigga name Key-O from Washington D.C. he was in Westgate and wanted to send time with me and another nigga. When, I got to Westgate Key-O was having a strip party and there was more stripper there making ends meet. When, I got there money was in the building and I was ready to get paid. Key-o on the other hand wanted to fuck Candy. Money was all over the party and niggas at Westgate was walking past the room like look at those hoes stripping in there. Especially, that bitch with the booty shorts on. Candy was the female with the booty short on she start smiling from ear to ear and that made me laught. I hit one niggas up all day at Westgate and he end up spending two million dollars in total for me. I half the money with Candy and told her she could have it because she didn't make that much money for being with Key-O most of the time. We had a ball at Westgate and they even had the news channel on and Kreme was on television having here case heard by the judge for the first time. My thoughts had change about Kreme and I wanted her to win her case again so she could be home. The investigation department said Kreme would only get about ten years since she wasn't the one who actually killed Carmax. I was excited to here that because that was no time for her to do if she did that. I had paid for one of the best lawyers in L.A. After, Kreme was on television for the third time since the murder all kind of niggas was calling my phone to give money for her. Then, Kreme called when she got back to the jail house. She wanted someone to call her lawyer to tell him to come to

the jail house and see her. She say she wanted the newspaper article that was going to be in the paper the next day. I told Kreme that was no reason to call him for a visit I would just tell him to bring a paper by the next day. Then, she asked me was I coming to see her. I put on my clothes quickly and racked up my money I had made at Westgate and went to the county jail. When, I got there I talked to Kreme for thiry minutes and I told her ten years was no time for a murder case. Then, I went to see Mark he had good news. Mark say the feds had dropped all his charges and was working on a bigger case. Mark told me to give Major the word that he was next on the feds pick up list. I left the jail right then and called Major I told him he needed to get in contact with the feds and turn another nigga in before they pick him up and our relationship come to an end because of him doing a lot of time. He was down with that because niggas on the streets thought he was trust wordly and it would be easy for him to set someone up. Major and I decided to meet and go to the feds and talk to them. They were nice about the case and Major end up getting out all his shit even without telling on someone. I told my man to let's go home and make love so he could celebrate with the success he had with the police. Major suck my pussy all night and all he talked about was he was happy the feds was nice to his ass but drug dealing was his life. When, I got up the next morning it felt like my ass had been renewed and my pussy was even fatter than it was the day before after Major had put the works on me. Major flesh was so warm and we were hugged up when I opened my eyes. He felt so good and made me feel like a woman on the in and outside. He kissed on me and then I got a call from Pimp. Pimp wanted to see what was going on with me because I had missed working at the club for a couple nights. I thought the police had close the club down because of Carmax murder plus I was still getting over grandma. But, I see things change. I made it my business to dance in the club on the day shift that day. It was a couple of doctors and lawyers at the club doing what it took to get a bitch paid. That what made my life easy at times, I took off my lingerie and loved how my body looked in the club mirrors and start making money. Jamal and Key-O dropped in the club that day and paid good money. I made another hundred thousand to go with the two million five hundred thousand I had saved up. It was my birthday and I had finally turned twenty years old. That made me feel like I had power. Money birthday was coming up and she was about to be three. I was thinking hard that day on whether I should go back to school and invest the money in a shoe store. I danced all night at the club and end up ordering me a party pack from one of the party companies in L.A. Candy walked in the club looking fly like always and danced with a couple of niggas and made some money to give me because it was my birthday. Key –O which I was impressed to see was in the club with Jamal and they gave me hell of money that night. I mean the club was a total success. I danced for the rest of the day and the club came to an end. Lots of niggas was trying to go home with me but I couldn't my daughter Money birthday was a day after mines. I packed my things and walked out the club. I round to my apartment in Up Living where I found my man already in bed for the day. Major woke up and went in the closet and got out a new Jimmy Choo bag for my birthday. That night we didn't have sex we laid next to each other and hugged up and woke up the next morning. When, I got up I put a Nike outfit and went to a special cake company and bought Money a Princess and the Frog cake for her party. I bought all the party items and then I called around for kids to come. I planned to have it in the projects where everyone would enjoy the day. I pulled up to the projects and went in the club house to make sure it was open and no one was using it. It was going to be lovely everyone was going to be at Money party. I called the radio station to give money a birthday shout out and to invite friend and people that wanted to come. Six months had went by and Travis was home for Money third birthday party. I was happy he was home and Travis was out to see me spend my three million dollar and be a baller. That day before Money party I went to the GED class to enroll. I wanted to start up my own shoe company name Bubble Gum shoes. I also was and online website to sell my shoes. I field out all the paper work and I took it to the clerk at the school. I felt good about getting my GED. When, I left the school I went and got a drama L.A. magazine and then I hit the mall up to get the kids something to wear for the party that was going to be in a coulple of hours. When, I got from the mall it was to late to do Money a party so I call around and told everyone that it would be the followind day in the same location. I went home and read my magazine. The magazine had a lot of things I want to know about in it. It talked about all the big time strippers and dances in their days of stripping. I was one of the strippers in there. They had a picture of me and Major at the club. It talked about how I was in a relationship with one of the biggest dope boys in L.A. The magazine noted that I had been in several articles and I wasn't a reader. I called L.A. magazine and asked to speak to Coogle a well- known editor that was over the magazine. He talk to me and stated he wanted to do a television commercial show with stripper and their lives as a stipper and I was one he wanted on the show. The show was the next day because of his busy schedule and he had to do it right away. It was a live television show program that would be viewed by L.A. cable company, night was the time scheduled for the program and he wanted me to be dressed to impress. Everyone in the world that loved stripper was going to be looking at it. I went home and sat down and refreshed my mind with a math, language, and reading book I had bought from the store that day. My mind was a little behind because it had been year since I was in school. While, I was reading over the book Travis called me. He wanted to let me know he was out on the streets. But, word travel so fast I already knew he was home. Iam not going to lie the conversation wasn't even about Money. He wanted some pussy and I rushed over there to fuck him and get that good nut from my baby daddy. His sex ability was just like a nigga who had been locked up. That was some good shit that Travis did to me. His dick was good and tasty in my mouth and he shot off heavy. I finish up with Travis and thought of how busy my day would be the following day. On the note of thinking heavy I went to sleep. The next morning I was woke up by a phone call by Kreme to tell Money happy birthday. I got up and put the kids on there clothes. I called around to see was everyone still coming to the party. Everything was going as planned. By, the time I got up and put the kids clothes I was getting another phone call from Reese. Reese wanted to know did I still want her to decorate the party. I told my sister yeah and asked her could she go to the club house with the kids and wait until I get back from the mall. I had to get ready for my interview I was having with Coolge from L.A. magazine. I went to the mall and when I got there I went in the Jimmy Choo store and got a Jimmy dress with some stilettos that matched the purse Major had got me for my birthday. I went back to the house to put my dress up and did a last minute call to the radio station again to wish Money a happy birthday. By that time Reese was calling me because so many people were at Money party. I told her I was on my way and for the first time in months I drove the Lexus. When, I got to the party Money had so much money in her hands and all kind of hoes was at my jit party with their kinds dress to impress. I play music and the party went on for hours. At the end of the party we cleaned up the tent house and left. By, that time it was time for me to get ready for the interview on television. I went to Up Living and put on the Jimmy Choo dress and heels. Next, I drove to the spot were we was going to be getting filmed live. At the interview we talked about how strippers make money and want kind of people you meet. I told Coogle you met all kinds of people. I told him I work in one of the biggest clubs in L.A. which is The Roxy's and I have danced for rappers, Lawyers, doctors, and dope boys of course. I mentioned to Coogle that the pay was good and I loved being a stripper. He talked to the other girls and they told him about the same thing I said. It was wonderful and I am happy I was able to make the show. I left the interview and went to work in the field for the night. I look online to see were any ballers trying to talk to me on their free time. Longway a nigga out of Texas was trying to spend some money. I went to see Longway at The Comfort Zone when I got there I wanted my money upfront. Longway had the money and I gave him a show out this world. I shaked my ass and made my ass bounce up and down on the floor. Longway had a truck on twenties with tv's in the back. That nigga made my pussy come so many times. An, even though I didn't make millions like I did with Jamal and Key-O I did make two hundred thousand dollars and that was for the dress I saw out of the L.A. magazine. I saw it on this girl name Alexis last night at the interview. It was a knock out dress and I wanted it as soon as I saw the dress. I went and got in the car and looked at the magazine where Alexis had got her dress and went to this store call Top and got it. The dress was so beautiful and it looked great on me they had it in all colors. After, I got the dress which I got it in pink and charged my credit card for another red one I went home to my apartment. When, I got to the crib Major was there and he wanted to play some cards and enjoy the little time we did have together. I got out ten grand to play Major in spades and for hours I sat down and won all his money. After, that part of my day I called the gold man and went and got an eight piece in my mouth. The gold man didn't take that long and for the rest of the day I smiled and looked in the mirror to see how pretty I looked with gold's. I called Pimp to see were the club open so I could go to the club and dance. Pimp said the club was going to be open all day and night. I rushed over to the club and it was full because Pimp was doing a happy hour also where they drink for free. I danced in a nice outfit and got what I needed for myself and that was cash. My ass was fat from the back and the more I bounced it niggas paid there money. That night when I left the club I had made enough money to get my ass pumped up. I called the booty shot man in Miami and scheduled an appointment to get some shots done. He wanted me to fly in right then so I called Delta Airline and got a ticket to Miami. When, I got there he had so many strippers ahead of me I sat in the lobby and wait for my turn. By, the time Black got to me it was midnight. Major called to see where I was and I told him I was in Miami getting my ass done. Major was surpise I told him that and thought I would just ask like I was getting bigger from the sex. Black finally got to me and it didn't take him long at all to do the injection to the ass. He put me to sleep and when I woke up my ass looked like one of those female off a video. It sat up just like a horse ass and it was beautiful. I stop at a motel and got a room for the rest of the night and the next morning I went to the Saw Grass Mall in Miami and Fort Lauderdal exit. When, I got there I went in Sak Fifth and bought me a dress to wear for the day. Then, I got on the bus and rode to the airport and took my flight back to L.A. When, I got back home it was late that night and my Bentley was parked at the airport. I got in the ride and the first thing I did was went to the strip club. When, I got to the club Candy was there and she notice my new booty. I told her that a nigga name Black did then in Miami and that he didn't charge that much. I went to the stripper locker room to change into my dancing clothes. My new ass was so fat when I walked it would shake from side to side. Niggas at the bar was buying drinks for me and by the time it was time for me to dance on stage I was tispy. Pimp was happy to see me in the club because for months I had only worked a couple nights out of each month. So much shit was going on. When Pimp told me I looked nice that made me get up and dance my ass off so I could make the most money. Candy and I did a team dance and made stacks on deck that night. Those niggas were loving us so much they was touching all on us and had their heads between our legs. The Hideaway Inn was crowded and most hoes was tricking that night.

Chapter 9

Oh, last night was popping bitch. It went down. The club was on blast and niggas was spending there money left and right. Shit, was real in there and hoes with the most money had the most ass. I had all kinds of sex items to make my show right. My gold's was shinning and I was excited about my new look. I lusted over my booty all night and many niggas paid to see me shake my ass. It was real out there. A couple niggas had got shot and killed out there to rest in the grave. It was some out of town niggas though. After, that I went to The Hideaway Inn, now it's the next day and I am up ready to make moves in my life. L.A. shinning and Travis out of jail to make a living and he was at me heavy. Travis had on Polo and that dick was so good had me wanting more. Major was uptown and to make sure he wasn't coming anytime soon I called him on the phone. Travis came thought the back door of the apartment and laid my ass down to sleep and if Major had came to that shit he would have beat the fuck out of me. Travis and I told each other how good it felt to be next to each other in the same bedroom. We fucked and after that I made him feel like the man he was. But between me and all the shit I was doing I was still going to fuck with my baby daddy. Kreme called and I had forgot all about her the other day I had so much going on. I was late with the newspaper and took it to the jail. I visited her for a little bit and enjoyed what she was talking about. I told her Travis was out and she said he had been by the jail to see her. After, the visit I talked to Red them and told them everyone was cooling it on the streets and it had been a minute since I was last on the block. I told them that the club was back opened and they said they couldn't wait to jump that shit again. Mark and Red said I had gain some weight in the ass but that was from the booty shots injections that I had got in Miami. I left the jail and went back to the hood and went to Travis and Kreme grandma house. "Damn Kelly yo life got shit going on straight out here on the streets everyone talking how my baby mama balling and shit." "That pussy was damn sho good and I see you twenty now you getting older and shit looking sweet for you." Then Travis told me he knew how Kreme and I were doing good on the streets. "Give a nigga some of that money to get on his feet." "I damn sho will." "You my first love a bitch will do anything for you to make you happy." I went to the bank and got some money to give Travis. Some how I had went to the bank and placed those millions in the bank. When, I got to the bank there was so many peoples in line I had to wait. I waited until I finally got my money and went back to the projects so I could help Traivs out. My baby daddy told me when he get on his two feet he was going to start helping out with both of my kids. An, to just keep that shit on the low. On the low sounded good. Shit, what Major didn't know want hurt. I went to my apartment and looked on the online website. Nothing was going on so I went back to Travis grandma house. At Travis and Kreme grandma house I talked on the phone with Kreme and told her how happy I was that Travis was back on the streets. I told Kreme that Travis and I had messed around and she thought that was sweet. She always wanted me and her brother to get back together. I told her to keep that to herself because I didn't want everything to come to light. Travis was on the corner and was calling my phone back to back. Talking about if he made enough money in the coming years on the corner he was going to buy Money a house to live in when she go to college when she get older. I thought how great that would be for her future. But, that would be years from now. It was Monday and I had to go to a GED class. I had my notebook and everything with me in the hood so I could go straight there. The GED program wanted me to take a test to see where my skills was. It was only the math and lauguage part of the test. The school was one of the nicest schools in L.A. I went in the testing center and took the hour long test. After, the test I went to the park and sat down and wrote Mark, Red, and Kreme a few lines and put it in the mail. Then, I forgot that orientation was at the school also and this was the day the teacher was suppose to meet the students. I rushed back up to the school and went in the class. In orientation the teacher Mrs. Smith say she was going to treat us like it was the first day of class. I took out some paper to write my notes on. I paid close attention to what was going on in class. She taught the basic math first. Some hoes from uptown L.A. was talking in the class and got there ass kick out of class. I know they were some bitches that went with another bitch man that was balling because that all they talked about. Mrs. Smith had everything explained and for the first day which was orientation she did a pop quiz. I took out my calacutor and start doing the quiz. I look at the clock a couple of times to make sure I had enough time and I was doing well. All my answers looked right and that made me feel good. The GED class was only six months and I should know everything that was going to be on the test. When my teacher dismiss the class which was a hour long for the first day I called Travis. The first thing he said was yeah I am at the spot and I would love to eat that pussy. I told Travis I was going to Jack's and get a bottle of liquor and I would be right his way. I went to Jack's and got a bottle of Moet for Traivs to drink. I pulled up in the projects and got fucked good for the day by my baby daddy. I moaned and rounded my pussy all over his dick. After the good fuck of the day I went online to see was some niggas on there trying to spend some money. I decided to keep on my same outfit and make it do what it do. My ass was on fleek so I know niggas would be happy. Tae was my first client if the day. He had a freah haircut with a Lacoste outfit on out of Macy's department store. His gold's shinned like a rich nigga out the hood. Allen and a couple of his road boys stopped in at the Manson and got a spot for me to lay my ass while they ran a threesome on me and made a bitch want to stay all night the way they was putting down on my ass. I sprayed some Fresh Me Up on to take away from the body odor that I had got in the last couple months for having to much sex. After, fucking ex amount of niggas that what it would do to you leave a body odor. He didn't smell the odor because the perfume spray worked a lot. As, I was laying on the bed with Allen waiting on him and his road boys to make the next move on me his dick became soft and his body became cold. That made me call the police right them to take him to the hospital. When, the police came I went to jail for having sex and tricking. At, one point I thought it was a set up. The other niggas that was in the went to jail. The jail center was pack that afternoon and it took forever to process my paper work. An soon as I got in there Shonda fought me for calling the police about Kreme case and caught another charge. She beat the fuck out of me and the police locked her in a room in the center. My head was hurting and the jail center gave me some head pills. It was my first time being arrested and some ugly bitch from Florida that was a run away told me if it was my first time they would release me on the first day after my points come back. Since, it was over night I end up leaving that morning and going straight to my school. My teacher of course was in class before the students. All the tests were on the desk and the grades was on them. I knew I was on top of my game and made and A plus on my test. She went over everything to make sure that the class understood what was going on. Everyone had done good on that first test and I still was having though of being locked up last night. I was happy to be from the place because it was so cold in there. For the rest of the class period I sat and took notes. Yes, my math class was over and my next class was language. Monday I missed orientation for my language class after my teacher in math class gave us a pop quiz. It was my first day of my language class and she did the teaching for the day on verbs. Just, as math my language teacher gave us a pop quiz on nouns. I asked her could I make it up because I had missed that part of her notes. Like any other teacher on the first week of school she said yes. I did the best I could do and all that I done so I know on the make test I should make and A plus. Shit, I was young pretty and smart. I left school that afternoon and the police was on the answering magazine of my phone. I called back because that was important. They said Tae was not dead and that was a good thing. He was cold due to the fact of a heart attack but he was going to be okay. I went thought the hood and got on the online cite and called around for the Tuesday special. That's was when Jay Jack call around and tell niggas that stripper are going to be doing special's at The Manson. The direction online was for anyone that was going to be doing privates to report with lingerie for the runway event. I rushed to the apartment got some lingerie and headed to The Manson. When I got there am not going to lie it was some bad ass female in there with a credit card and for the check to be sent to Miami Florida for them. I did wonderful but I think the females from Miami put on a show. Kalil a man with wealth called me and put me on some money to be made after the show. He say I looked new to this and that's how he liked his women. I took him in on the afford and danced with him all night. The money from the payment magazine was at the money gram by the time I left and it was somewhere around ten grand. Kalil gave me three thousand and he was professional with the way he treated you. My smile with the gold's made him love looking at me. He like my ass and told me I was very thick for my size. I had ass out on Major enough and it was time for me to go home. I left and made my way back to Up Living and made it my business to lay with my man and go to sleep. Major and I fuck on the bed and I sucked his dick and he loved what I was doing. I bounce my ass to make it move fast and slow while on his dick. He ate me out and I came so many times. Reese had Money and the baby so we had the apartment to our self. After, Major ate my pussy I got up and moved on his dick one more time. I then got up and took a hot shower and took out a duck commander outfit to wear to school. By the time I got in bed Major was sound asleep. I slept all night next to my man and woke up the next morning and got ready for school. At school in math it was our math class first day working on algebra expression. I took notes and we had another quiz. Next, was language arts and I walked in to my class and took my make up quiz. My teacher graded right then and I made and A plus on it. My test paper was all I needed to save to study for my GED test. After, school Travis called me to check on me for the day. Lately, I had been on the go and my rent in the projects was behind. Major was still asleep when I called him so I went to the bank and got the money out and told Major to pay me back when he get to the hood. Major told me he would call me when he get on the expressway and thanks because he see he had slept all though the day. I went to the corner where Jay Jack was and it was some new cats making money and selling drugs. Candy was the only trick out there and people were making money to get ready to start tricking for the day. Some niggas from uptown L.A. came to see what was going on with the streets downtown. The ally apartment was back open that quick with tricks jumping their ass up against the pool table dancing. Mark surpised me and walked in there with a pocket full of money. Skittles a well known rapper from L.A. was playing music in the ally apartment and everyone was vibing. Skittles was playing Rich Gang. I saw

Mark and asked him about Red. He said Red was home taking a shower but they both was out of jail. I started dancing taking care of my main nigga. He was my money man on the corner and I was happy Mark was out of jail. Mark tipped fourty grand that night. Red walked into the spot and all eyes where on him. He came to the spot Mark and I was and I still was dancing. Red asked could he hang out with us and I told him yeah I missed the two of them on the corner putting it in me. I jacked both of their thang at the same time and they even licked my click after I made them feel with comfort. Later on that afternoon I made the ally apartment niggas spend all their money. I went uptown L.A. afterwards because it was a big time basketball player birthday I hung out for a little bit but then I went to Reese house to get the kids. They had been there since Money birthday. When, I got to Reese house I talked to her for a few. Reese was in love. I liked to see her and Qunicy together. Qunicy and the kids were asleep. I told Reese that Mark and Red charges had been dropped. She said something smart out her mouth. "Yeah and I know you tricked with them too bitch." "What hoe?" "You heard me I know you tricked with them." That hoe was mad for some reason but I got off the subject. Reese was a beast when she got mad. Hell I did't want to go though anything with her. "Qunicy woke up and went home while I was there. "Damn Reese all you got to do is tell you baby sister you don't only work at the hospital." "Hoe tell her you a stripper too." "Bitch tell her since back in the days you have always fuck all her boyfriends." "That would be the safe thing to do." "Kelly on the real start keeping your kids.""I look out for them when Reese is in the streets I see." "Yeah Kelly Reese know how to do her shit she is a little bit better than you at what think." "Now on note." "Hear this from the horses mouth I am not prenacy from Qunicy he is just going to take up the resonibleity." I did believe shit I heard. I thought they where lying. I guess talking to her was a bad ideal. I got Money and Major Jr. and went to my apartment two blocks away from Reese place. Major Sr. had not made it from the projects yet. He was surpiset to see me and the kids home when he got there. We had much to talk about. I told him about what had happen with Reese and I. Major said Reese was lying she was pregnace from Qunicy and she wasn't a trick she just didn't want to keep the kids anymore for me. That's what I thought. I laid down for the rest of the night until it was time for me to go to The Roxy's. Time went by quickly and niggas was all over the parking lot. When, I got out the car about twenty niggas rushed up to me ready to trick. I went to The Hideaway Inn and pulled my G-strings to the side and let them hit me from the back each for a grand a piece. Frank a nigga from California came inside of my pussy. I licked the tip of his dick and rubbed his dick across the click of my pussy. I went and the club afterwards and the entertainment that was going on were wonderful. Strippers was swing off the pole and they where sharing the tips that was being made. Candy and I worked the three level with all the finest lingerie on. We had on a bra set to match each other and it was black and pink with white lace around it. Most of the club was full and it was like old times because Mark and Red were back in the building. My night went smooth and I made lots of money. Major wasn't there so that was a good thing because I was able to make more things happen with other niggas that night. By, the end of the night

I had made ten grand. Mark and Red had became extrelmy close since they were in jail together they was acting a ass and clowning in the club spending money on bitches and taking all kinds of pictures. I know it was going to be a lot turned up with those two niggas in the club as friend now. I changed clothes in the stipper locker room for he second time and when I walked in the dressing locker room a new bitch that was working the club wanted to know how much money be coming thought The Roxy's a night. She had a flat ass booty but she was pretty and her tiddles was a nice size. I told her enough if she knew what she was doing. I rushed into my second strip gear of the night. I figure if I made enough money Iwould beable to get my beast down by tommrrow. Surgery went by fast up in L.A. The cosmetric surgery place was a hot topic. Next step for tonight was for me to dance at the backstage bar that had free liquor going on for all strippers. When, I got done getting dress I went to the backstage area I made another three grand and called it a night at the club. After, I left The Roxy's I went back to Jay Jack corner. It was open late night and hoes were out there tricking and making money. "Hello baby you must be new out here." "No, but this is my first time out here I work the day shift Iam just out here trying to make extra money to get my beast done." I want a bigger size for the business I work in." "Okay just let's go to The Manson." It was a little far out but it was worth my time. For me to make money so I could make and appointment first thing in the morning. I had money but the million dollar was for an investment. "What the night without a beautiful lady like you?" "Nothing I guess". By the time I had reached The Manson I was sleepy. I still got out the car and worked my ass and performed well on the client I was working with. I put the white cat almost to sleep how good I rode him. Well, after that job my night was over and I had fifteen grand to get my beast done. When, I arrived home Major was awake. It was six a.m. in the morning and the first thing I did was give him a kiss. I laid in the bed and thought how good my night was working as a dancer and waited until it was time to call to get my beast done. Major laid next to me and put his dick against my leg and he wanted some ass. I rounded over to fall straight into Major arms. The warmth I felt was so good to the feeling of my body from him rubbing on me. It kind of reminded me of the way Travis used to hold and look at me with his thick eyelashes. Major moved up and down between my legs and his romance was so good it felt like I was eating a T-Bone steak. I was fast asleep after he put the dick down. I laid down for the rest of the night and enjoyed my sleep. The sun came though the blinds of the apartment very quickly and I woke up. I rounded over like I was on drugs because I was tier from the night before. I continue my sleep because I needed it. The phone rung and I really had to get up. It was Reese apologizing for the lie that she almost forgot she told me. I looked over the fact that Reese was a little upset. I smiled because she invited the kids into her house again for stay at anytime. Just that quick I had forgot about my class. I was running later getting up, but school still haven't started yet. I got up and put on some faded jeans to make with and Aeropostle shirt I had got on sale in the mall. It had rhinestones on it and it was a nice choice. Felicia a girl from the school called me because we where suppose to study. She wasn't that good in school and wanted me to help her out. That was find with me as long as she had her head on her shoulders. Felicia came from a family of computer techs, and technology was something she like doing and had dropped out of school and had a baby at a young age and went the other way in life. I told her I was just like her but I was a stripper. I rushed off the phone with Felicia by telling her I was on my way to the school. I went in the kids room and got them ready and rushed them to Reese house in my Bentley. When, I got to the school I called Felicia on her cell phone. It was still early when I got to the school so we had a chance to do a study section. While studying it were some older dudes at the school scoping me out. It was fine for the most part of it but they didn't look like they had money. One niggas at the school called Nate Thang was finer than a motherfucker. He had a pretty smiled with nice white teeth in his mouth. Nate Thang walked past me and Felicia while we was doing out study section and I decided to get his seven digits. That day after school was over Nate Thang was the first nigga I hit up. "Damn Kelly you touch the pad that fast." "A nigga must was on speed dail to your mind." "Yeah and fast to spend some money on you I heard about you most niggas in L.A. know you and your girl Kreme ya'll getting paper." "Of course I am a professional dancers." "How old are you?" "Twenty one, he said." "Am twenty.""Oh that's what's up." "So are you in GED." "Yeah, and yourself." Yeah am in GED to I end up dropping out of high school when I got ten children from this bitch name Dric back in the days. She had one when she was young and keep having them and her grandma put the children off on me." "But, I got to give her credit she been doing what she got to do over the last years she have became a book writer and everything." "Damn

Nate Thang seem like she was an important part of your life." "No, I just fucked her but I like her come up plan about the kids." "She bought a nigga a hundred birds and I been rich in the game every since." "Meet me at The Hideaway Inn.""Damn Kelly you don't wanted talk and get to know a nigga like me." I end up talking to Nate Thang and meeting him at The Hideaway Inn. I rode him up and down and he had a ten inch. The way I rode Nate Thang had him want to fuck with me on a regular. Nate Thang and I decided to make this an everyday thing after school. He was cheap he only gave a grand, but the sex was good. Shit an everyday fuck with a smooth down south nigga was cool with me. I left T he Hideaway Inn and went to the other side of the hood. Everything was jumping. I put on my Gstring and got out the car on Jay Jack corner. Shit, I didn't want to walk that many blocks looking like a trick so I walked right up to the nigga I wanted to trick with. Mark watched me dance for a while then he fuck with me on some serious type sex shit. Mark money made me feel like a star and my head was to the sky. I was riding solo and I had no one to answer to. I was on my shit. Kreme was gone and I didn't have no one to ride around with and half my check. I put on my sunglasses and decided to look gangsta for a nigga to fuck with me on some real G shit. I put on my sexy lady and start dancing for Mark again. He was rubbing his head of his dick in my pussy. I fucked around and got some Exclusive and that was it. Time went by fast and I called Major to check in on the kids because Reese had took them back home. I know Major was a little upset about that and wanted me home. But, first thing and the morning they were going back to daycare. That was going to be my everyday route. Next, I called Pimp and he told me to check the magazine on my phone. When I check to see what he said Pimp wanted to put the club strippers on a payroll and we still keep the tips. Last, I called Shonda about the heels and perfume. I wanted to open up and she said it would be easy. The only steps I needed to take were to have the smell I wanted and the money. Shonda said I could go the Macy's Department store and they would order different smells for me. I rushed to the mall to see if what she was telling me was true. An, yes it was right in the store you could buy the smell that you want. I went and got an apple, grape, watermelon three of my favorites. Next, I went to the perfume company that she told me about and in weeks I had a perfume design on the market. The heels was still in progress. But, before long I would have it together. I went to school that day and for the last couple weeks I had been doing fine. I worked all day to get the jobs done that needed to be done to make money. On my progress report at school I made all A's and I was on the road to success. Not to forget Nate Thang and me balled until we could ball any more. I got some perfume as a gift from him called Taken of Love. We went back to The Manson and fuck. My pussy was so wet Nate Thang licked all between my legs. The Manson had bottles of Pink Ice for the guest. After, Nate Thang Iwent to The Roxy's and danced for the day. I checked online before I went to the club to see how my perfume was doing and it was doing well. I had made a billion dollar sell. Next, I calledaround to see how I could set up some heels for sale and talked toa rapper name Brick. Brick sells was on top of the game in the heels department in every store. I dance in a lot of his heels and they where the bomb. We

discuss business and latey after that we a set up a date so he could draw the stilettos for me and put them in the store. I was at The Roxy's by the time I got off the phone. I just knew I was going to make a whole lots of money that night because I was looking fly ass fuck. I jumped out the car with my big booty and niggas was trying to get at me as usually. They were trying to trick with a bitch. I worked in the club and Pimp wanted me to work the private room for the night. That was good because it was laid back and I didn't have to slpit my tips. Traivs came to the club for the first time in awhile and he had money on him to spend. I continue to dance where I was. Steven had paid me foutry five hundred dollars and that was enough money to make me get loose. He had some cocaine and I hit it a couple of times and got high. It was some clean. My nose was in the air after that. The night went by so fast and it was time to go home so I could relax for the next day at school. Major and the kids were at home waiting on me. An, when I got there they was at home watching the Four Litlle Princess's on DVD. I walked pasted them and got in the shower. I bathed with some Jadore' so my body odor could go away. As, I was bathing Major enter into the bathroom to bath my backside. He rubbed on my pussy to make me get freaky. "Damn Baby stick that wood in so I can feel you." Money start crying but it was to later the robber had already shot her. The niggas was looking for money. Just that fast some one had enter into our apartment. Major and I got out the window in the restroom and called the police. Good thing we didn't keep drugs in the house. The police came and we told them the story. That we were in the shower making love and that's when someone enter into our apartment and shot my daughter. When the police got to Money she had already was dead and they came back outside and told me. I went crazy. The first thing I did was call Travis to let him know that Money had been killed at my apartment. Travis almost lost his mine. He couldn't stop screaming. Tears rounded down my face as I was talking to him. Money was only three years old damn my baby was gone. I called the amubalance and some more police man came out to see what was going on. Th the police that came out next was from the investigation department. Major told me to lie to the police about getting out the window because that would bring charges against us. I told the police the story that we were taking a shower and someone enter into our apartment with a dangerous force and tried to rob us and shot Money. After telling the police the story I called Reese to tell her that Money had been shot and killed. Weeks ago I had lost my grandma I went to jail for tricking now I was losing my daughter. I thought to myself if it's not one thing it's another. Up Living was back with investorgators and they had the dogs and everything trying to find a gunman. It was the most saddes day in my life. I hated what was going on. After the police left I went back upstairs but I couldn't get any sleep. I just sat and prayed that it be a better day for me. I had to stay strong.

Chapter 10

Money died surpised the fuck out of me. It was my first time losing a child. I cried all night all night long. An, for the most part of it I wanted to know who the fuck was the murder to my child. Money was three years old and had lost her life in the game. I called the school aand told them my daughter had just got killed the night before and I couldn't make it because I had to do the funreal arrangements. That was fine with my teachers and she said she would have my work when I get back. I got on the phone and made plans for the body to be picked up from the hospital. The funreal home services Right Funreal Company went to get Money from the hospital. I went to be to do all the things I needed to do for the home going of my daughter. I finished the plans for the funreal in about eight hours and then I went to the projects. Just like grandma death so many motherfuckers was telling me sorry about Money death. The bad thingabout it I didn't have a policy on her so I had to pay cash good thing I had the money from the life style I was living. When, I got to the projects I went to Travis grandma house and he was locked inside of his room crying. It was his only baby and Travis couldn't take the death of Money. I wish I could bring Money back for Travis and I both. Today was the day Reese went to get her ultra sound at the doctor. An, I was not going because I couldn't take Money death. While at Travis and Kreme grandma house she called from the jail and said they was going to be having a speedy trail. The trail was to gone ahead and see weather they would be dropping the charges or giving her ten years in prison. That was some good news. Then, I told Kreme about Money death and she got upset. She wanted to know detail from detail about what happen to Money. I told her and she was crying and wished like hell she could be here for Travis and I. Major called on the phone while I was at Travis and Kreme grandma house. "Damn baby you at school." "No am in the projects visiting Travis for the lost of our child." "I'll be that way soon do you need anything?" "Yeah a fourty pack of cocaine to make a bitch feel better about this nightmare." I stayed over Travis grandma house all day and night and the next day I had the funreal so I could go back to school. Thursday's in L.A. usually don't hump. But it was all kind of niggas on the website trying to holla at a five star bitch. Even though I had lost my child I had dreams so I went and fucked around with this nigga name Bean on the northside of town. It was my first time hanging in those projects. It was some nice little apartments set up with only about a hundred units. When, I got there he had the smokes and drinks and everything. The parking lot had one car and it was a small Totoya. I got out walked upstairs and went into Bean apartment. Inside the apartment he had funitune and a television. An, he had the air cool ass fuck. Murray was on and there was a lot of baby mama drama going on. Murray had some hoes out of L.A. on there and they were fighting about some nigga from Texas. I used to live by one of the females in Northwood projects with my auntie on my father side for a while until she dead of a crach overdaose. Anyways, Bean gave three grand. I let him hit from the backside because that's the way he wanted to fuck me. Bean was a big nigga with a nice size meat on him. I wasn't in love of anything but it was some great sex. Nate Thang was the next person for me to call for the day. "Nate Thang what's up as the phone picked up." "Nothing on my way to The Manson to see you." "Nigga Iam in route grab some liquor and shit for a nigga can ease her mind." "My daughter funreal was today.""What happen new thang." "A nigga came though the apartment and tied to rob me and killed her on the spot." I met Nate Thang at The Manson and damn did he ride my ass from the back. Bean shit wasn't nothing like the shit he did. After having sex with him I laid in the bed for a while. Next, I got out of bed and washed my pussy up. Nate Thang had a bird of cocaine for me to sell for myself. I went to the hood and sold all thirty- six ounces for one grand a piece. My shit didn't have any cut on it and it was humping. Major was still upset about Money death and felt like it was my fault she dead because I move out the hood. He felt like in the hood she had a better chance. Travis was back on the corner. I called Reese to see what see was having and it was twins boys. That's the kind of shit I was talking about someone left our family and we blessed with two more. I was about to spoil those babies. After, Talking on the phone with Reese I called Major back because I wanted him to enjoy life. Money was in a better place. I sat on the pourch

and finish selling the dope I had. Major pulled up as I was on the phone with him and talked to me and told me the investigators had found out who killed Money. He say it was some nigga that was from G.A. robbing hoes that was in the strip game. It was time for me to call back my heel connect to see how much it was going to cost to get a heel line started so I got off the phone with Major. The nigga said it was going to cost me four hundred thousands dollars. Shit, that was no money. I had that all in the bank. I set up a time to go to the bank so I could pay the money so I could get the company started. After going to the bank I went home to put on something nice. I wanted to look like a business woman. I left the house to go give dude the money for the heels and I told him that wanted them to be name Designer heels. He said no problem and the heels should be out in a month so I could fine a building to rent or buy now. Directly, after meeting dude I went back to the hood to make some money. I sold the last couple ounces that I had which was nine of them. Jay Jack called the phone to see was I coming on his block for the day and I told him yeah. He had become nice since Kreme had been locked up. When, I got on the corner Ice a new chick was the only one working and she was tricking with a nigga name Tony. Ice was this bad ass female with diamonds in her mouth and since she had been on the streets every nigga downtown had spent money on her Ice always had this rock star look about herself but she was also on crack. Ice wanted me to join her and Tony in a threesome so I went and laid in the back room with them. She was smoking crack and shotting up with a needle. I was shocked ass fuck and decided to not fuck around with Ice. For the rest of the day I was pissed off that Ice had even asked a bad bitch like me to fuck off with her and she was on crack and needles. Chip, was the next nigga on my list for the day. He was a big time nigga from around the way that had just recently got out the federal pirson system. Chip was well respected in the hood and had did a long six years in feds for selling drugs and was out on the streets spending throwback money. Not only that Chip grandma had won the fantasy five and she had like a million dollars. All his hoes had left him while he was in prison so the first place he came to get some pussy was on Jay Jack corner. So, happening I was standing by the door and when he came my way I stepped in front on him to block his walk way. Right then he wanted to know was I down for the plan. Nigga only had the regular five hundred. I told him I was top of the line of the streets and next time to have a grand. But after a talk we came to the conclusion he could spend five hundred for each day out the month. Shit, that was good for a nigga just coming home. He said after a month he should be back on his feet and he would start paying me three grand each pop. "Yeah, that would work I'am number one on the streets most hoes that come out here don't make the king of money I make." By that time Chip and I had already start fucking. Chip was like damn this good fat pussy is all I need. After the quickie Chip gave me the ups he would be though everyday. Next, my baby Mark came in with a hand full of liquor and money and you know I had to fuck off with him. I got drunk and he fucked the hell out of me until it was time for me to go to my next money making spot and that was The Roxy's. Some hoes out of Tallahassee was in the club and they danced in The Roxy's for the first time. One of them was name Moet and she surpised the fuck out of me. Moet danced for the first time amd she rounded that phat pussy all night. She made me like her how fat home girl was. Niggas gave boo money all night long. Most of the night I fault to make money with those hoes in there, Candy thought it was funny a bitch wasn't making that much money with those hoes in there. I end up going to the back private area to make what I needed to make for the night. For the first time Pimp was sercurity over the private room. He usually let his brother run the spot. When, I got in the private room it was all kinds of doctors and lawyers in there and it was one man name Malcom that made my day. Malcom paid me five grand to roll my pussy back in front for him all night. I thought I would never make that much money with those hoes out of Florida all over the club. Closing for the night came around and I end up leaving the club with only five grand that was no money for me. That's what I used to make when I first start strippig a couple years ago when I was eighteen years old I was used to some big money. After, the club I went to a all night spa in L.A. and got my nails and toes done it was mostly strippers in there. I was at the spa for almost three hours and when I left it was six in the morning I called Chip to see did he want to pop things off early so I coulde spend the rest of my day making more money. He was up and already on the block so he told me to meet him at The Hideaway Inn. I fucked Chip and got the five hundred and went on about my business for the day. He schedule and appointment for the afternoon when I was about to leave too. Then, I called Reese to tell her I was on my way to get Major Jr. Reese said the baby was already up and dress for school. When, I got to Reese apartment to get him it made me sad for my son to go to school alone without Money. I remember those days going to get my baby girl. But, she was dead and gone now. While dropping Major Jr. off Felicia called my phone to see was I coming to the school to study with her for the day. I told Felicia I was blocks away from the school and to go to the libracy and I would be there. I liked my life dancing going to school having an online perfume cite and last but bot lease about to come out with my own heels and have a store right in L.A. I thought to myself how I had come from nothing and was at the top. I was a big time stripper bitch that was making everything in my own life happen. At the school that morning I study with Felicia and she told me that they had a test while I was gone. When, I got to class I sat in the computer lab room and worked on my test all day. I did the class work first. Ms. Kim a teacher aid watched me to make sure I wasn't cheating. I finish my work and went to my language arts class. Class was cancel in the language arts area so I called Nate Thang so he could meet me at The Hideaway Inn. When, I got there he was playing Young Thug. That shit sounded so good to my hear with the beat down in Nate Thang car. When, Nate got out the car he had on some hundred thousand dollar jeans. That nigga was so clean. We went to the front desk at The Hideaway Inn and paid for a room. Nate Thang got in the room and I danced my ass off for him. I liked that shit chilling and having fun with a balling ass nigga that had a dress code out this world. After, dancing for Nate Thang for and whole hour he beat this pussy off Young Thug Bestfriend. I end up playing around with Nate Thang all that day and when I finished I looked outside the motel window and there was cars parked at The Roxy's I went home and packed my bags to go to The Roxy's. I packed my bags really quickly and drove in the night air in L.A. where I loved the night life. When, I got to the club Candy was there and it was a gain of niggas in the building watching the Dream Team Girls dance. Most girls that danced on the team was red bone chicks with lots of money from back in their stripper days. They danced to the new hot music that was out Young Thug and I really like their entertainment. Mark and Red walked inside The Roxy's and I went over to their section with the attitude of a godest and start dancing on him to make some money. The club was live and all the niggas that had money was in ther even their old ladies that night. Bubliouis a stripper name after some bubble gum danced on stage first to some slow R. Kelly. She had a strip lingerie on that made the club stop what they was doing to see her work her ass on the pole. The Roxy's was on point. It was just like a Friday it was jumping and the DJ was playing all the hottest music. Mark paid me as usually to shake and dance for him. He was my money maker and I was the collector. I paused for the camera that was going around to make sure all my pictures and films that was going to live as a league was perfect. Mark told me I had the game on lock. He was popping and throwing money my way left and right. A nigga that did underground music in L.A. came to join us by tipping me some money too. I had on some bad ass shit that came out of L.A. magazine. The club were the place to be and I was live. As, the night went by I made more money as usually on a Friday night. I worked the poll and came down real fast into a hand stand and worked my way to the floor and start making my ass clap both ways. "Damn Kelly work that ass and make a nigga come home to you every night and spend money on you too, Major said." After dancing in the club on stage Major was ready to get me out the club for a night of a freak show at home. When, we got in the car he wanted to stop by a store that sold late night sex toys and get some to play with while we was having sex. I didn't give a fuck I was down I was drunk and I was over heated and ready to get in the bed with him. We stop by the store and got all kinds of shit that end up costing us a grand that night. When, we got to the crib we put on and laid each other to sleep. We ate chocolate off another and made love to really slow music. We grinded slow to the beat until the sun came up. He pounded that ass so hard he made me make all kinds of faces. He told me how much he loved me and I hit some good ass cocaine in the process of doing it. He made the feeling feel real and that was the best thing about having a man that night. When, I got up I had tatts on my body and I didn't even remember getting them done. I was that fucked up last night. Major said before we got home from the club we had went to a One Shop Tatt place and got them done. He said the man got the ink and needel and start working on my thigh and I didn't say a word so he let him finish. The only thing I remember about our night was the sex. Imean Major had put down on me. I remember I was suppose to fuck Chip twice and forgot about him yesterday. Looking at the tatts made me feel good. They were fly as fuck and I decided to wear some shorts today. I got up Major was up and dress and he left the house I called Chip and he was hustling already and wanted to know did I want to go to Calfornia to a water park. When, we got there the water park was close for the day so we end up hitting a strip club.

I went in the spot and since I was a new face I made millions of dollars on the spot. The name of the club was Wildstyle. At the club I meet a nigga name Shawn and he had so much bad shit on his mind. Dude was one of those killer type nigga and wanted to fight some of the strippers because their serves wasn't quality. The body guard had to put his ass out. Wildstyle was some where I didn't want to leave. The money was good and the dope boys all had a mouth full of gold's which was my type. Chip went to the ATM to get some money and he showed love like Mark. Chip had just got out but he was on his feet and somehow found the money and the time to get out of L.A. Calfornia was the place to be and I met some niggas that wanted to go back to L.A. to see me dance at The Roxy's. It took a couple hours to get back to L.A. but when I got there I looked on the online cite to see what was going on in my city. Speedy a nigga I never tricked with was on my page trying to make moves with a bitch. It took me a minute to get from the airport to the crib and when I finally met up with him I met Speedy at The Hideaway Inn and he laid the stick down to me. Speedy was an original gangsta out of Orlando, Florida. After, the section with Speedy I rode around L.A. until I got my next call which was Nate Thang. I bought some dope from Nate Thang and rode around with him and sold my shit. After, I road around with Nate Thang and jumped the brick I went on Jay Jack corner and worked there for the rest of the day. When, I got on the corner Pee Wee, Tubb, and Swagger was thugging it on the corner. Those was some niggas from around grandma way. They all had on some free my nigga Rob shirts and was shinning making it do what it do. For, the last couple days I had not been paying Jay Jack so today

I decided to give him his cut. When I got in the apartment in the ally a nigga out of Alabma with dreads wanted to trick. Showtime was the nigga name and he had a mouth on him. When, he took out the small size dick I couldn't believe it because he was talking mad shit like he had a big ass dick. I got him on hard and rode the fuck out his dick. The pay was everything though. Showtime gave ten grand and that was it for the day for me. I went to the projects to my apartment and when I got there Major was on the phone with his mother and sister. Major said his cousin had been stoppedon the borders with dope. The officer say it was hard to detect him with the dope because he wasn't the only one trafficking on that day. Major cousin Micheal was lucky and got off on that. That was one of Major cousins I didn't meet when I was in the Islands. "Damn Major lets go home and get some time in with each other." Major was down and we called Reese to babysit for the night. Major and I had a candle light dinner with steaks and ribs and French fires. We laid and cuddle and talked all night long. It made me feel good to be under my man. Sunday came around so fast and it was time for me to get up. I had made up in my mind that I was going to church. I went to L.A. Baptist Church to praise the lord for all that he had done for me. Even though it wasn't the honest way. The preacher preached about evil people and their ways. An, it was a really nice message. I stop by the jail to see Kreme and her case was about to go to trail. She told me that Monday was her first day of trail and depend on how it go she might not have to prison. That was some good news for me to here and I told Kreme I would be there to support her. I went home took a shower and put on some Bath and Body Works with something sex for Major. I laid in the bed and waited on my man to get home. When, Major arrived he layed that wood to me. I rode Major dick for the longest and he ate this phat pussy. Major put me against the wall and fucked the shit out of me. I know the people next door heard us because we were loud. I fucked him in the shower and suck his dick to he came all night long. In the middle of the night Major and I was still having sex and Reese called the phone to come get Major Jr. because he was up all night and wouldn't get any sleep. I stopped having sex with my nigga and rode two blocks up to Reese house to get my son. I was upset she called me that late especially in the middle of sex but that was my child so I had to go get him. Everytime I would go get Major Jr. from Reese house and I knew Money wasn't there would make me sad to know I had lost my baby girl to gun shots. When, I finally reached Reese apartment I got Major Jr. and drove back to Up Living where I didn't get any sleep until that morning beause my son was up all night long. Just the happy as he wanted to be. The next day came and Major woke me up to get really for Kreme court case. I am happy he did that because I would have over slept. First, thing first was to get Major Jr. up and get him ready for daycare next thing was to take and have him there before eight because that what time I had to be at the court house. I rushed and dropped my son off at the Los Angeles Enrichment Center then I went to the Los Angeles courthouse. In the first hearing which was today the jury was picked. Kreme was dressed in a suit that Travis had bought for her. The friends and family of the victim was there and they was happy justice was about to be sevre for the case of Carmax. I am not going to lie Carmax was a beautiful girl that lost her life to some violences. The judge of the courtroom schedule the court date for the next day because Lisa Terry a Fashion Designer which was Carmax friend spoke at the trail and speeded things up. She was a business type lady and was an African Queen. She wasn't the flashy type. I left the courthouse and prayed that Kreme came out on top of this murder case she was in. Some how the nigga that killed Carmax got off because he was a resigter crazy man and they sent him to the crazy house for five years. Kreme was left in this shit by herself but she had a lot of shit in her favorite she wasn't the shooter. That's what the jury stated in the first statement. Even though I saw Kreme hit her first. Whatever, it came down to I hope Kreme got off too. She wasn't the killer and it was self defence in the club after the female cut her. Her lawyers was one of the best. By eleven o' clock I was in school. Felicia my new homie was already in class. I joined Felicia to make sure she was doing it right. Than, I took out a piece of paper and decided to start on my homework before school end. I was late to school and my teacher was kind enough to let me sit end on the last part of class. "Damn baby you look behind today.""Yeah I'am and we won't be going to The Manson today." "Just get up with a nigga when you get time." "You know that's the best thing I got going on these days is you." I hopped off the phone with Nate Thang and went to my language arts class. The same thing happen in my language arts class my teacher wouldn't let me take notes because I was late. So, I left school and rode to Kreme grandma house to see what was going on around her way. All she talked about was how she missed Money and wanted Travis and I to have another baby. I even consider what see was saying because I knew Travis wasn't going to get anyone else pregnant. After, talking to Kreme and Travis grandma for hours I went home. When, I got there I watched BET on television and looked at what was going on in entertainment. Young Jezzy had a new CD out called The Snow Man and it was on top ten. By that time it was time for me to get Major Jr. from daycare. When, I picked him up L.A. was having a grand opening to a new park and I went throw there to see what was going on. When, I got to the park couples was out there so I called Major to the park to hang out with me and his son for a while. He said he would be there in no time and he would bring some snacks for us to snack on. Major made it to the park and we jogged around the park. Major and I talked about getting married in the future and how our relationship was a success. I loved my man and he was the best to me. After, being at the park with Major and our son we went home. At the crib I called Pimp to see what time the club was going to be opening and he said it was already open for the day. I told Pimp as soon as I called Reese to see would she baby sit I would be in. I got off the phone with Pimp and called Reese up. Of course she was at home chilling doing nothing and said the baby could come over. I got up packed my Gucci bag and went to Reese apartment to drop Major Jr. off. When, I got there Reese was home alone and asked me could I picked him up after the club because she had to do some shopping for the baby early tomorrow. Before, I went to the club I called my friend from school Felicia to see did she want to join me stripping tonight. Felicia wasn't down for those kind of activites and told me all she wanted to do was finish school and that it. Before I left to go to the club I looked on the online cite to see if anyone wanted to spend some money. Clip was the only one on there to spend his coins and make ends meet. I called him on his cell phone and when I got in contact with him he told me he was at the ally apartment so I got on the expressway and went there to make the money. Clip had came up just that fast and for me not charging him that much at first he gave me fifty grand. I laid that dick to sleep. An to my surpise Clip was just getting out but after the trip to north California and tricking with him at the ally apartment he had went and bought me a new Acura off the car lot. It was black with some twenty-four inch rims.

Chapter 11

Chip surpised the fuck out of me with the new Acura. I called Felicia on the corner to take the Bentley home for me. The Acura had a red ribbon on it to show it was a gift. We laught and I took photo's and posted them on facebook of my new car. Clip was a nice ass niggas because we had just start fucking around and he had already bought me a new car. Mark was on facebook at the time and hit like on all my posts. Felicia followed behind me in the Bentley to drop it off in Up Living. It was nice having a new car sitting on some Thangs to Thangs. I dropped the Bentley off and checked the online cite to see what was good. A nigga name Tony was on there trying to trick again. I called Tony back by saying, "Tony what's up baby what you got going on?" "Nothing but trying to spread those pussy lips open." "Well meet me in Northwood Plaza and we can fuck in my new ride." "That would be nice to have sex in a car but I want you to meet me at The Manson." "Okay Tony I'll be to The Manson in twenty minutes." I rushed to The Manson and tested the speed of the new Acura I was riding in. When, I got to The Manson I called Tony to see what room number he was in. After, the second ring he answer the phone and Tony told me he was in room one twenty. I walked upstairs to his room and when I got there he gave he ten sacks. I laid across the bed and Tony rubbed his dick across my pussy until he got it hard. Then he turned me over from the back and fucked me. By, the time Ifinish withTony it was time for me to hit the club. When, I got to the club Clip was there and he bought the bar for me. I drunk all night and shook my ass all over different niggas. Felicia wasn't into dancing but she did come and support me. In fact she had a couple of drinks and was tipsy when she left the club. I went to the back locker room and put on a Bebe outfit to go to The Hideaway Inn and get fucked up on some cocaine. When, I got there Clip called the phone to see what was up with me. I told him I was at The Hideaway Inn getting on some cocaine and if he liked he could join me. I told Clip to bring a bottle of Henessy so I could drink and get fucked up. I matched up a joint and smoked the hell out it. The cocaine joint mixed with weed was loud and I liked the taste it left in my mouth. I had laid off drugs for a minute but now I was back on them lacing was my thing. After, a couple of joints it felt good to be back on drugs getting fucked up. I smoked my head off until I couldn't smoke anymore. I open my pussy up and start playing with my insides. Clip had a video camera videoing me. I pulled down my bra from top to bottom and put on a sexy walk. I rap my legs around him. "Damn Kelly your pussy is one of a kind you got that phat phat." Laughting out loud I kissed him and said, "I know daddy." The night ended on a good note. After, that the club came to an end and I went to Up Living. When, I got home I found my man rolling up a joint

and I decided to roll me one up to before I go to Reese place to get my son because she was going shopping for the baby. I smoked in a rush and went to Reese apartment then I came back home and got some rest because I had to meet the dude tommrrow morning about my designer heels. I said a couple of bible verse and went to sleep. Major and I laid arms and arms all night. That made me feel with comfort knowing I had a man next to me. That night we didn't have sex and morning came rolling around fast. I got up and cooked some beastfast and got ready for my appointment with the shoe man. Brick was a rapper that designed shoes and was a major part of the game. When, I met with him for the day he had the lay out for the whole set up for the store and I had found a building. I decided I was going to buy the rest of the shoes for a hundred thousand and sell each one of them for a yard a piece. The spot I was going to be using wanted me to pay them in cash so I did that. I called the bank to get what I needed. Next, I had to go to class for the day. I called back to the apartment and told Major to take our son to daycare because I had to go get the money out the bank for the building and head to class. Last, I called Felicia to tell her I was on the way to the school so we could study. I got to the school took out my algebra expression notes and logged all my answer in on the homework keypad to check them. Felicia and I study for about an hour and then it was time to go to class. When, I got in the class my teacher gave us a pop quiz for the day. Felicia smiled at me knowing we had just studied and would do great. After, math I went to language arts and we wrote a grammar eassy and that was easy. Class ended early and I went to the libracy to type my homework up. Next, Nate Thang and I decided to go to The

Manson and make something happen with each other. Nate Thang didn't want any pussy but he did want some of my head game. I licked his dick to make Nate Thang feel good. As, I gave Nate Thang head his toes balled upand his face made a funny face. I liked what was going on. I still didn't get any dick. He contact the dope man and we got a couple of birds. That was some big shit for me. My plans were to give the birds to Major so he could sell and make some extra money. It didn't take Nate Thang connect that long to bring the birds to The Manson. When, we got the work he gave me my cut and the first thing I did was call Major. When, I told Major I had some keys for him he told me to meet him in the projects. It didn't take me know time at all to get to the projects. When, I got there I got out the Acura that Clip had bought me and walked up to my apartment door. Major wasn't there yet so I just waited. When he arrived I gave him the dope and he was smiling and all and gave me a big hug and kiss. Major said with the money from the free birds he was going to try and get me a manison and do it big with me. I open my desktop and looked online to see what nigga was trying to trick. An, for the last couple times it was Clip. I called Clip back and told him to head to Jay Jack corner and make arrangements with Jay Jack for a section. Shit, it have been a while since I paid Jay Jack to work the corner I needed to clean my face. Each section I did that afternoon was an hour and when I got there Mark and Red wanted some action so that made three shows for me. Clip just wanted a lap dance and for me to shake my ass all over him for some sacks. He knew every nigga in there had to get a chance so he was easy on me. Mark wanted a head job. They all paid three grand a piece and I gave Jay

Jack some of the money. After, the small fuck in the ally apartment Brick the nigga with the heels wanted me to go check out the building. When, I got to the building Brick had every set up for me and the store could open whenever I wanted it to. I had a couple females out the projects that was jazzie and was going to work the store for me for a small fee. I posted some photos on facebook of my new shoe store and I got so many likes of the whole set up. It wasn't a big shoe company but it was a start. I had a little online cite to order shoes from too. I started off with a million pair heels to sale. That impresses me to know my dreams were coming true. I got a phone call and it was from Kreme. She was calling to tell me some good news that the jury had found it self defense in Carmax murder. She said she would be release sometime today and she would give me a call when she get out. When, I got off the phone with Kreme I call everyone I thought cared she would be coming home and told them. Everyone was happy about the good news. Her grandmother was like thank god my granddaughter is coming home too with be her son. "He have been so upset his mother have been always I know this child is going to be happy." "He hasn't been doing good in school or anything since Kreme was alway." Next, I went back to the projects. When, I got there a bitch name Tammy and Angel was fighting over Mark. Since, Mark had been home he had left Tasha and was messing with two hoes that lived in the projects. Mark knew that shit wasn't going to work. They were two crazy ass bitches and they both lived in the of back of the hood. Creeping around in both of there apartments they found out about it and start going thought it with each other about what they called Mark to be and that was their money man. Angel beat the hell out of Tammy ass. "Bitch what you doing with those bitches fighting over you, I called Mark and said." "You know you owe me more money for messing around with some other female." "Iam a badder bitch than both of those females I mean you need to pay me a hundred grand to keep you spot Mark." "Damn baby okay I got you." I looked at those bitches kick and hit at each other for almost an hour. The police rushed in and that shit made me mad. A nigga ran in the house and watched those stupid ass bitches be arrested and the same day the rent lady put their shit on the side of the road. Dumb bitches fighting over a nigga and got kicked out the projects. Kids going to be homeless and they broke hoes with no money saved up. I got up off my ass and went to the mall. It was enough of watching those broke down ass female get put out the projects. I decided to go get me a new handbag that was out of the Micheal Kors Store that we had in the mall. When, I got to the mall it was jam pack with niggas and females. I went and got a purple Micheal Kors handbag that went with this purple and gray Aeropostle short set that I had found last time I was in the mall. I left the mall very quickly because I was only going there for one thing then I went to get my hair done in some waves for the first time. They were the deep oceans waves. I throwed on the throwback look to make myself look like the seventies you know something different. It was getting late so I stopped by the house to put the Micheal Kors bag up and grab a couple things to work at The Roxy's. It was payday at The Roxy's so I wanted to get there early to make sure I get my check before late night. When, I arrived at the club Pimp gave me my check and I started my day off early that night dancing. I had made another million dollars in one month and I had four million dollars to my name and I was still in the stripping business. I worked my ass off hoping to make another million. An, for the first time I hooked up with the club owner Pimp. I was surpised Pimp and I even did what we did. I sucked Pimp dick and made him feel like a man should feel when a woman go down on him. He told me straight up I had the best head game and cut me a check for another million dollars and told me to keep that to myself. As, I was walking back in the club from The Hideaway Inn Kreme ass was out of jail. "Damn Kreme you look good ass fuck and we on payroll around here now." "It's not only tips so make your money you got to do." "Since you been gone a bitch have came the fuck up I have made four million dollars and just got and do what another million from Pimp for some head game but keep that to yourself." I love what the fuck I saw my home girl back on the streets and she was really to shake that money maker and get some money. It wasn't know new shit to her she knew just what to do and knew how to do it. All night the club was on point that Kreme was out of jail and back in ther. We were in VIP shaking our ass and making up for the time we had lost with each other. Kreme looked over the fact I tried to tell on her and still showed me love. We worked VIP until it was time for the new stippers to come and take our place. Iam not going to lie they put on a show to make some money that night. Niggas was at Kreme and me all that night and I not going to lie we made money out the ass. Rappers werein the club that night and before the night ended those hoes out of Tallahassee was back in there to make some money. Iam not going to lie it was so much money in the club one of the bitches made a million dollars and gave her goodbyes to stipping all in one night. I loved the fuck out of that. The club was about to end I wanted Kreme to see me pull up in my new Acura so I left minutes early. When, she walked out I pulled up on her and told her Clip bought it for me and not to fuck with him he was my new money man. That night Kreme and I had a long talk and I explained to her that since I hade turned twenty I was in GED school. I told her about my perfume company online my heels that I was selling out my store and the online cite that I had selling heels. She was like damn Kelly Iam so damn happy for you. I see you have been doing a lot in the last couple months. I talked to her about her future plans and it was to get her grandma out the projects and support her family like she always do. She said the paperwork got messed up some kind of way with the house she was building her grandma and she was happy to be out to deal with that. The next day home girl was up early trying to get her grandma out the projects. The house was finish and the man that she got the house with had all the paperwork it was just some small misunderstanding. But, the house was worth a quarter million. All kreme had to do was sign the paper saying that she paid for the shit for real. We went and check the place out after I came from school. That same day Kreme came to the school to enroll in school. That was just like my girl she won't let the next bitch out do her. An, she said now that her record was going to be clear of the charges she was going to get in school to be a LPN after she get her GED and maybe do private sitting. It was all good I even told Kreme that I had been arrested for tricking at the motel a couple weeks ago or more like a month. She thought that was bad and told me to stay they fuck away from that kind of shit. Even though it was on my record. I fucked around with Nate Thang because that deal I still had with him I wanted to keep him on my team. Shit, the more niggas I had the more money I can get. Shit, Kreme was bad so I know L.A. was going to on fire. She was a million dollar bitch that moved her grandma out the hood who wouldn't want her. I put her on game about booty shots in Florida. I told her about the man who did my gold's and all. I told Kreme that was going to be a coming home gift from me. She wanted to leave out for Florida that night when I told her about the booty shot man. Kreme got the number and call to the dude in Florida and he told her since she was my friend he would charge her ten grand. I went to the crib and got some money out my safe and Kreme made flight by herself that night to Miami Florida. In Florida she end up meeting some nigga name CeeCee and tricking with him for a couple of days. Off top he gave her a million dollars and was suppose to be one of the biggest ballers in Miami. That's just what kind of bitch Kreme was. She would make a nigga spend his money. An, that's the game she taught me. That's how I keep my foot in the game. After, talking to Kreme and finding out she was going to be gone a couple more days I went online to check on my perfume company and of course I was doing well. Then, I made payroll to all the woman that worked for me at my shop where I was selling heels because two weeks had went by and it was time for the first pay period. By, that time Kreme called me and told me she was at some party with CeeCee and she was dancing in Miami and she wished I had made flight with her because the party was one of a kind. She said so many niggas with money was there and she was having a

ball. I asked her did she fuck him and of course they had already had sex. She said her booty shots were done and they were perfect with her shape and frame. She sent me a picture to my phone and damn did she look good. I arranged a meeting with her so we could do a freak show Kreme was looking that damn good I wanted to eat that pussy and fuck the shit out her. In a couple days Kreme called me and she was back in L.A. I schedule an appointment with her and my new little baby Clip so we could do a threesome and make some money. Plus, I wanted her with that phat new booty. I fucked around and picked Kreme up from her flight and I was on. On her way to the car that bitch was so fat I liked what I saw. As, soon as Kreme got in the car I told her I had some money for us to make with Clip. Even though I didn't want her to fuck with him without me. She jumped in the Acura and headed to Northwood Center to hit the lick with Clip. I pulled up on Clip with a mean ass swag game and hopped out with my fat pussy showing in my boy shorts. I turned so he could see my ass and he laughted and wanted me and Kreme right then. We went in the room and I stood against the wall and he hit my pussy and told me I reminded him of a bitch off television. When Kreme came in the room I ate her pussy from front to back and he posted us all over the internet. When, Kreme and I got finish we went to the hood and fucked around with Mark. He was fleshly dress with some Addias on with my favorite cologne on which was some Polo. He got in the back sit of the Acura and his swag reminded me of a nigga out of Florida. I couldn't believe that Mark, Kreme and I was hooking up for a threesome. I didn't give a fuck because Kreme was on point with her new booty. Mark and Kreme talked on how they used to go to Westgate and play on the playground when they were little. I wasn't that old so I didn't know what they were talking about. Next, Mark asked us to stop by the store to get some sex toys. At The Manson that night Kreme, Mark and I had a great time fucking and getting high. Kreme was doing all her stripper moves and she was turning me on. I got on top of Kreme and start riding her face so she could eat my pussy. That's how it was going down in our section. Kreme was fresh got but she still got on cocaine with me. "Damn Kelly ya'll on that dust too." "Yeah we get pretty fuck up." While riding Kreme face she ate the hell out my pussy and I came three times back to back. After, Kreme got done eating me out I got on top Mark and start riding him to sleep. He put his self in a relax mode and I put his body in reverse and start hopping up and down. Kreme start licking Mark from the back and he was making all kinds of nasty faces. This time I was riding him slow so I wouldn't touch her tongue when it was on his dick. When, we was finish he gave us three grand a piece. Kreme looked at him and start fussing. "You know next time I do a threesome with you boy you better have more money." "Mark you heard what the fuck I said coming from a bitch that's about money." "Yeah Kreme just meet me tommrrow in the ally you and your girl and I got you." "What a nigga owe you." "Fourty grand nothing more nothing less." "Damn that's eighty grand." I got you baby girl. I kept my mouth close and Mark told Kreme he will make sure he continue to make something happen on the tricking level with me and her. It was late as hell and as I was entering the hood Major and the baby was leaving in his Bentley. Major must had took his Bentley to a one day paint shop because it was baby blue with some floaters on it. I start smiling knowing I was the bitch with that balling ass nigga with all that money. I pasted on by Major and pulled up to Kreme grandma house. When, I got there Travis was outside with his mind thinking a hundred miles and hour. He must was thinking about the death of Money. From time to time he got like that. I know he was thinking about Money. That's all he been thinking about lately. I blowed the horn of the Acura and sat in my new Acura that Clip had just bought me. Next, I drove to the ally and it had been my first time in a long time being in the ally at three o'clock in the morning. I rode though to see who was out there. Jay Jack was asleep in his car and I woke him up. He got up and I told him to go home. He rode two blocks away to a two story building that just had been builded in the hood. For the most part they were some nice apartments I never knew where the hell Jay Jack lived until then. Now my next steps was to be on my way to Up Living so I could get me a couple hours of sleep so I could go to school in the morning. I was back on my regular schedule and that was trick with Nate Thang and Clip after school and study with Felicia before school. I had some shit to do with Kreme the next day. An that was take her to the tattoo man so she could get tatted up and look like a million dollars stripper like all the bitches that strip looked like in our days. She end up making my day when she came back in L.A. tonight. I had just told Clip about her and Kreme was making flight. I made it to Up Living and thoughts about how Kreme had told Mark that we needed some more Money made me feel like he had been getting over on me. Shit, he always gave me three grand but it didn't matter I liked Mark swag game anyway. When, I got in the house Major was bathing our son in his baby tub. I went in the restroom and ran me some bath water so I could get ready for a busy daythe next day. Next, I called around to the cheek bone doctor so I could get my cheeks done. They wasn't open but around six in the morning they called back so I could get a appointment to come in later on that day. I made an appointment to get my cheeks done for five o' clock that afternoon. Morning came and I got Major Jr. up so he could put on his Enyce outfit. Then, I got ready to go to Mrs. Parks class. He was smiling and winter, spring and all the seasoning of the year had past and it was almost my son birthday. An, I was going to make sure his party was going to be a blast. I was going to get Major a clown and everything. I even was going to get my son a pony ride for his first birthday was going to have it in the projects for a bitch and the hood could call over L.A. and tell everyone that Kelly doing it big for her son birthday. After, I got ready Major wanted me to go to the corner store to get some cigars so I did that for my boo thang. At the corner store I got Major cigars and then I went back to Up Living. I called Kreme for her third day in the streets and beating her court case. She was at her grandma house about to smoke a joint for the morning. I rushed upstairs and gave Major his cigars and got my son so I could take him to daycare. My plans for the day was to go to school and fuck with Nate Thang and Clip and go get the fourty grand from Mark. Before I left the house Ilooked online to see how my perfume and heel company was doing and everything was still in order. When, I got in the car the radio was jamming 2Pac and I blast Hell Mary all the way to my son daycare. Next, I stopped by the FoodMart and got me one of those hood beastfast meals for the morning. I sat in the school parking lot and ate my beastfast and waited on Felicia to get there so we could study for the morning like we always do. The school had short section today and class let out early. Nate Thang was posted in the student parking lot to make moves with me. We didn't hit The Manson up for the day we went to The Hideaway Inn. At The Hideaway Inn Nate Thang wanted to visit Mexico Islands. I never heard of that in my life but he said that's where he got a lot of his cocaine from. Next, I went to the store so I could get some cigars so I could smoke my head off for the day. I went directy back to The Hideaway Inn and got fucked by Nate Thang. I had my laptop to see was any niggas on there to make money with with me. It was one nigga out of North L.A. name Jon looking for a female to spend some money on. You could go to his page and see the selection that he had picked from and Kreme was one of the bitches that Jon wanted to spend some money on. I guess that meant I would have to get up with Kreme later on that day when she finished her date with Jon. Other than that I still was at The Hideaway Inn with Nate Thang. While at The Hideaway Inn we made plans to go to Mexico Islands next week. That would be good timeing because all my school work will be done and I could experience something new in my life. I called my next trick of the day which was Bean. He was in uptown L.A. and that was a minute to drive but I damn sho was about to make that move to make the extra money. My life in L.A. was everything at twenty I was a millionaire with a perfume and shoe company working on my GED in a amazing relationship with some one that understood the grind and what it meant to make money. I had some up's and down's in the last couple months like the lost of grandma and my daughter Money but other than that I was eating on the streets. Pull wasn't nothing for me in L.A. I knew all the big time niggas and they loved me too. I pulled into the road from the side parking lot of The Hideaway Inn and went to Murphy USA store to get some coffee to wake me up. I was kind of sleepy and needed a wake up before I see Bean. I called Bean to let him know I was on the way to see him in uptown L.A. He said he had a million dollars and a bird of cocaine for me. I mean at once I was just getting grands but now I was getting millions at a time. When, I got uptown L.A. I went to Up Living first to put on a pink leather pants set with the vest out of Wilson Coat Fatory. It took me about and hour to get ready and Bean was calling my phone out the ass. My waves were still looking good and I had on some pink makeup. "Bean I am on the way I had to stop by the crib to refreshing up." "Where the hell you live?" "I live in Up Living.""Okay cool because I was about to clear the spot if you live downtown in the hood." "I am at the motel called Uptown Skyline." "I got everything you need." I ran out my apartment and got in my Bentley and rode to Uptown Skyline where Bean was. The motel front desk clerk told me Ed Wilson was in room three thirty. I knock on the door and he was surpise to see me wearing a ten thousand dollars pant set. "You looking gooder than a motherfucker Kelly." "The leather got my eye." "Come on in so a nigga can get some of that fat ass." I walked in and Bean sat on the bed. I start dancing right away and he started to tip me money. I danced the whole time with the leather pant set on and still made a million dollars in cash. I gave him some head instead of fucking him. Bean told me the job was worth it and I asked him did he know someone I could get a clothing line from. I was making progress with all my plans now that I had millions of dollars in my bank account. My plans was to open up a store in the L.A. Square Mall where old Finish Line used to be and make it out of a urban store. Most female would by from an urban store in the mall. Bean said he didn't have the connection with the clothes but he would look around and if he found someone he would give me a call on my cell phone. By that time Mark was up and wanted to meet him at the ally for the fourty grand. He said he couldn't get in touch with Kreme and I told him she was gone with this dude name Jon. I hit Kreme up on the phone and asked her could I grab the fourty grand from Mark for her and give her part to her later. "Sure why not." "I am busy for the rest of the day anyways." "Tommorrow Saturday right." "I'll get it tomorrow when I go get the tatts and the gold's put in my mouth." "Love you and see you later." "Love you to Kreme." After, I got word from Kreme I called the L.A. Surgery Client Center back and asked could I come in early so I could get my cheeks done. Ms. Brown the front desk clerk said yeah that would be okay and three o' clock was my new time to come in. I drove to the center looking nice with my leather pink suit on. I had one million and eighty grand on me all of it was mines but fourty grand. When, I got there to the center where I was getting my cheeks done I talked to the doctor and made plans to get my cheeks done the next day. I hope my face surgery come out on top and everything looked nice. I smiled at him and he gave me a compliment on how pretty my gold's was. As, I was leaving Reese called me and talked on the phone with me and told me how much she cared for me and loved me as a sister. Since Reese was in a good mood I told her to never lie to me and tell me she was apart of the tricking business again. Reese thought that was funny. Reese asked me how were I doing after the lost of my three year old daughter. I explained to Reese that life went on and I was in the game of making a new day always better for myself, butI would never get over Money. She gave me some thoughtful notes on going to school. She told me that was a real plus in the game. I don't know if Reese was in it on the deal but I told her about my new shoe store and my perfume company. I explain to Reese that I was a millionaire. An, she couldn't believe it. She was proud of me. I got off the phone with Reese after an hour and found myself just driving in L.A. "Damn I was on the phone with Reese for a long time." I couldn't even remember what I was about to get myself into next. Now, I was thinking about my next step and I thought to call Major to see what he was doing in the projects. On the phone with Major he talked about hustling and making money to get us a manison. I told him to save up each month for a whole year and the dream of having a big house should be true.

Chapter 12

Kreme was with Jon all last night and called me early this morning and woke me up. She had a date with a dude name Heavy. Heavy wanted to do a threesome he was a nigga from the down south area a little before you get to Miami. It was straight for the most part of it but I had to get up and get the house cleaned and all before I leave. My face surgery was still schedule for today in the afternoon. I had a lot of shit to do for today. Kreme still had to get her gold's in her mouth and her tatts. I already had gave her the money on that part. But, since I made a million dollars with Bean I would just pay that over and charge what she already had in her pockets to the game. I grabbed a red, yellow and troquise Enyce outfit to put on with my red, yellow and troqusie high tops shoes. I told Kreme it would take me a minute because I had to get ready plus clean up. She was a little upset and I decided for her to hit Candy up on the hip to see did she want to make the money. Shit, I really didn't want to miss out on a million dollars but I had other shit to do. I picked up the phone to call Reese and she was excited to hear from me early this morning. "Kreme and I got some things to do so could you keep the baby for me." "Sure Iam off today just bring him over I got everything he need at my house." I slipped on something to run two blocks over to my sister house to take my baby where I know he would get the same love I can give him. After, I dropped my son off I got back in the Acura on floater and rode back to the apartment in Up Living. When, I got there Major was up cooking me beastfast. I got my laptop to follow up on my facebook page. Then, I came across pictures of Major with some bitch name Shontae. She was a dope girl who sold bricks in the city. Major and her was out on a date and whoever posted it online posted detail from detail. I didn't even care about that shit. I said fuck it and went ahead and took a shower for the day. I put my clothes on the toilet and sat in the tub for a hot bath, I washed up with some Jadore' that I had bought from the mall. I bath and my body smell refreshing and I felt good. I got out the shower and put some gel on my waves thinking of how Major was on facebook with some other bitch. I had the most going in my life so that was funny ass fuck. I was fucking around with so many people. I did my make-up and put on my lipstick to bring my lips out. I packed my makeup for the day because I was having surgery done on my cheeks and afterward I would have to put some more makeup on. Next, I picked up around the house to make sure everything was in order. The weather was bad outside and my computer was down. But, dudes still called me on the phone. I got a call from Law a nigga out of Tampa Florida that was in town for a business meeting on some drug shit. He was a fashion designer to so I know he had thehook up with a clothing line. I finished getting ready so I could met Law at The

Manson. It was my first time sleeping around with him but I damn sho was about to enjoy myself and have a laughter of a lifetime. I put on the Enyce outfit after I got done with the cleaning at my house. When, I got to the parking lot my Acura was gone. A nigga had come to Up Living and stole my shit. I called the police to find my car. I gave the police the vin number and the registration to the car. In minutes they had a state out over the whole L.A. the dude jumped out and ran. "Damn niggas was silly and didn't know how to act without taking people shit." I went three blocks over going the opposite way from Reese house and got my car. The stering wheel was messed up and I had to drive the Bentley for the day. I called Law and told him I was running behind time because someone had stole my vehicle. Next, I got the stering wheel fix and made the moves I needed to make for the day. It took Shawn my engineer about one hour to fix my car. After that I called Law and he had found another female on the website to fuck around with. Shit, I missed out on that money. It was raining hard in L.A. and it was a good time to go and get fucked up to buy some cocaine. I went to the hood and founded Clip and got an ounce of cocaine so I could get high. I went to the ally apartment and start taking hits to my nose. Clip sat with me. The ally was cold from the rain and I wish I had bought a jacket so I could keep warm. By, the time I took the whole ounce to the head the ally apartment was full of niggas and I was the only female in there. Mark had more cocaine and wanted me to buy some so I went to the ATM and got money. A grand to be correct. I pulled back up and bought another ounce of cocaine and sat all day until it was time for me to go and get my surgery done. When, I got to my appointment I filled out all the information I needed to so I could get the surgery done. The doctor I saw the day before wasn't in so I saw another doctor. He put me on a table and got some needles to put me to sleep. I laid down and the last thing I remember before I woke up to a new face job was going to the hood to get high that day. I looked in the mirror and everthing looked great. I thought that was one of the nicest face jobs I ever saw in my life. I looked just like a movie star. I called Kreme on the phone to see was she done making her money doing business with Heavy. I got off the phone with her and went to get my third ounce of cocaine for the day. When niggas saw my face they could tell I had surgery but all of them said I looked finer than a motherfucker. Before, I got there I had to stop by the ATM to get another grand so I could put up my nose. Clip was there and niggas had made money for the day and hoes was tricking. Jay Jack was on the corner and my lick of the day Law the nigga out of Tampa had called back. I went to The Manson and for the whole day I had been getting on cocaine. On the way there I got wasted and smoked a couple joints. I had let Candy whole the Acura and I had the Nissan Altima that I still had from years ago which was my first car. When, I got to The Manson Law was on the twenty first floor. The Manson was one of the biggest hotal in L.A. He felt directly on my pussy and kept fucking around with my G spot until I got wet. I pulled off the Enyce short set and laid on the bed. I was smiling and licking my tongue at him. "Kelly your pussy gooder than a motherfucker.""It's one of a lifetime gir." I sat on top of Law wood and start riding him, Law money funds was low but he did have ten grand. I went to the mall after I was done because I needed to get some new clothes to go to Mexico Islands to get some cocaine from the borders. I went and got all kinds of nikes, Addias, and Jordans. I needed on teenis shoes just in case I needed to run. It took me a while in the L.A. Square Mall. By the time I got back to the hood Kreme was at the ally apartment. She had been with Heavy all day. She told about the whole deal and had got a mill out of him. I gave her the fourty grand from Mark and went to the tattoo man to get her tatts done. She got the gold's the same day too. I had been on Jay Jack corner all day and didn't make any money off it. I asked Dave a new kid on the block did he want to spend some money on me and he had already paid Jay Jack his half and that was fifteen hundred dollars. I went up in the ally and opened up my pussy then I put my legs in the air and let Dave fuck me. Dave moaned and fucked me to a beat in his head like we was listening to some gangsta music. Next, on the list were Mark and Red. I even ran though Travis that day. Travis of course felt the best. Thoughts of how we made our child Money came to my head. Thoughts of her death even rushed though my mind. My day was over and Major was no where to be found. I guess he was somewhere with his new bitch trying to fall in love with her. I had to get control of that by falling back into Major arms. Nann bitch was going to take my place. I drove to Reese house to grab Major Jr. and rushed back to the crib so I could play around with him for a minute and give him sone kiddy love. He was in such a great mood and I wanted to love on him for the rest of the day. I called Major because me and his son was home alone for the rest of the day. "So what you with you?" "Nothing just finding me something to get into.""So what you out cheating now?" "No that's not

it I was on a blind date that my home boy sat up for me." "Oh well it's about time for you to end that and come home". For the rest of the afternoon while waiting on Major I played with my son. He laughted and he liked to called me daddy daddy. I turned on the television and looked at Lifetime. That was one of my favorite channels when I was home. Major Jr. had went to sleep and I was up by myself. I was scared ass fuck because I watching a love movie based on a husband killing his wife. The Saturday sun was coming down and I stayed up waiting on Major. By, the time he had got there I was asleep. His so call blind date lasted for a minute. All I know this was Major second blind date. All I know I was going to make a suggestion that he stop going on blind dates. I laid there for a minute and then Major started to touch on me. I found myself getting hot very fast and wanted him to have sex with me. I didn't want him leaving me for another female. I wanted Major to myself. I told him about the trip to Mexico Islands with Clip. Major was a little impress. I mentioned to him about the success I had made and the last couple of weeks. Lately, Major and I had lacked up our conversation. He was selling drugs. Major was working every other day. I guess that blind date shit had him going. He pulled out a condom and told me to lay on my back. In seconds he was putting the beat down on my pussy. I knew right then the way Major was having sex with me he had not had sex with another woman. After, having sex I got up and took a shower. I looked inside Major Jr. room and he was sitting up in his baby bed. "Dad Dad", he called out and Major Sr. came to get him so fast. He was so happy that our son called him Dad. "What lil man you want to see whats going on in the house." For the rest of the night

I laid next to Major Sr. while he talked to Major Jr. They were in such a deep conversation. Major Jr. was laughing and talking baby talk heavy. I dosed off and went to sleep and the phone went off and it was Kreme. She was calling to tell me her grandma had a heart attack but it didn't kill her. She was just in the hospital. I got up in the middle of the night and drove to the elderly care client and visited Kreme grandma right away. At the hospital they ran a couple test on her grandma and they said with all the reports she would be in the hospital for two weeks at the most. After, hearing from the doctors I wanted to go home but I couldn't. I think it was because of the death of Money I had to support her grandma. I would feel bad if I went home and something happen to her. Morning came and Kreme and I were still at the hospital. We decided to go to the Light of the World and have church in L.A. that Sunday morning at pastor Thomas church. They had serve at eight o' clock and that's the one we was going to catch. Both Kreme and I packed up by grabbing our pocketbooks and leaving the hospital. We did a little prayer and we were out. I had to be there for her. I know if she wasn't in the jail the day my grandma died she would have been there for me. I got in the car and it was about to be six thirty in the morning. I told Kreme to rush home and get ready so we could go praise for the day. At the church called the Light of the World the pastor preached on the twenty third song. He basically said how god would guide you down the right path if you are going down the wrong path. He would always have your back. After church I called Major to see what him and Major Jr. was up too. They were at home watching some wrestling on television. I finishd up the conversation by telling Major

I was on the way. I made it to Up Living and walked up the stairs. I changed into some more clothes so I could go back to the hospital and see Travis and Kreme grandma. It was sad because today Travis and Kreme were moving out the projects. At the hospital her grandma was in good condition and we left to unpack the apartment. Kreme grandma house was full with things inside of it. It took us all day long. Then, I helped her move in Orange View. I was a nice neighborhood and there was no dope over there. Travis and Kreme would be the first to move into this type of community. I wish Money was here to see her family take in a beautiful home. I walked inside the four hundred thousand dollars home and helped Kreme and Travis put away there things. With the three of us it didn't take that long to unpack it was the moving it from the projects. Then, I got a phone call from Clip saying we were going to leave out for Mexico Islands tonight. Good thing Travis and Kreme had a moving vanand her car. I left to go home to pack my things up. This was Reese first week going to be off while she was preganant for the rest of her months so she could keep the baby. So, I phoned her to see would she watch Major Jr. while I was out of town for two days. Reese said no for the first time so I had to drop Major Sr. off some cash and bring that nigga some dope back for him to watch our son. I packed the Nike, Addias, and Jordans outfits that I had got from the mall. I went in the bathroom to get my personal items. Clip was calling my phone all day to see where the fuck I was. We end up missing the first flight and had to fly next round. By, the next flight I was ready to go. Clip couldn't come by the house to pick me up so I had to meet him at the airport. Major didn't mind me going out of

town with a nigga but that would have been disrespectful for a nigga to come where we laid our head. When, I made it to the air port the flight attended took the bags and I got on the plane. A famous model and leading actor in films was on the flight with us. She looked fabs and she had on one of the baddest pants suit. She gave Clip and I a compliment on how nice we presented ourselves and looked together. The trip to Mexico Islands was sixteen hours away from L.A. On the plane Clip and I ate fruits and talked about how excite to be home from prison. He say it was a lot of gay men in there and that shit got on his nervous to see a black man go down. I laughted at the thing he was saying. When, we arrived to Mexico Islands we got off the plane. It was so beautifl over there and the water was so nice and clear. Clip and I rented a cabinet for two days and we fucked almost the whole time we were there. The fuck up part about it was the dope man wasn't answering his phone. He was busy making deals with a bigger connection. When, he finally answer Clip call he put in his order for a hundered squares. He was doing big shit and I got Major five blocks of cocaine. That's the only thing I could pay for. After, we got the dope we decided to fuck around on the beach. The night air was great and tommrrow we would be getting back on the plane going back to L.A. On the beach the fmous actor and her party that she was in Mexico Islands with was hanging out. We played a little tennis at the cabinet and I really enjoyed it. She was a very talented person and she was so beautiful. We had bottles of liquor and we got fucked up. It start getting late and Clip and I went into the cabinet. I wish we were going to be staying more than one night and a full day which made two days in Mexico Islands. At the cabinet Clip ate the fruits that were on the table off my pussy. He did a damn good job at it too. Morning came fast and the front area that was also a cabinet room had beastfast for the guest. I went and got Clip and I some pancakes and eggs. It damn sho was good. The morning went by fast and before you knew it flight time was near. On the plane we rode back without the famous actor and her party they still was on the Islands. I wish I could stay because the weather was so nice. When we got to the airport in L.A. my car was parked in the front of the airport and it was safe to drive off with dope in the car. I called Major to see where he was and he was in the projects. I drove Clip to the ally apartment and dropped him off with a hundred birds. Then, I took the five blocks of birds to Major that I had for him. He was happy all over again like when I got that work from Miami for him that time. Major broke the dope down and start selling it that same day. I sat in the projects and watched him sell three or them. Ninety ounces went fast as fuck. Red bought the last bird for fourty thousand. Major was in such a good mood he bent me over and start fucking me right from the back. The baby was looking at us like what the hell we were doing. I told Major to hurry up because I didn't like that. It was to much for the baby to see. When, he was done he prayed I was pregnant from his ass too. That's just how much he loved me. I got up and left Major in the projects counting up money. That dope I got him went fast. Before, I went home I took the back way to Reese house to see what she was doing Reese was getting fat ass fuck and she ate a lot. Qunicy was over there for the first time in days. I couldn't wait to see the day come when she have the baby and she become a mother. I didn't stay to Reese house that long. My laptop was at home but I wanted to see what niggas was calling in on the hotline for me. I phoned Kreme to see how she was living large in her new home. I talked to Travis but we had to get off the phone because they were at the hospital with their grandma and you wasn't suppose to be on the phone in the hospital. Next, I call Man the dude who I had the apartment in his name. It had been months since I talked to Man and he was doing good we talked and I stopped by his apartment and gave him some ass to keep the apartment thing going. Last I phoned Nate Thang to see what he had going on and he was riding around L.A. selling his dope as usually. Iasked him was my home girl Felicia at school and he say he saw her in the libracy studying for the day. Then, I phoned the shoe store to see how many sells I had got on the Designer Heels. The shoe store was doing good and some cusmoters wanted to see the owner so I stopped in there. It was late ass fuck in L.A. It was almost the next day which was a Tuesday and I had missed Monday at school. I went home to refreshing up and got a shower for the night. When, I talked to Major he had made a million dollars off the dope. He say he was going to call some home builders to build us a home too. I wanted him to wait so he could sell a little more dope so I could get one that cost more money. By, the time I got off the phone with Major I was fast asleep and had went to sleep for the night. When, he made it in I was in a deep sleep and all I heard was the key turn. I went back to sleep and I heard the shower turn on with Major getting in the shower to wash his ass off. Major our son must be was sleep because I didn't hear him talk baby language. I got up to check on him to see what was going on and see was he asleep. He was sound asleep and next I went in the bathroom to wash Major back. Major felt on my pussy and wanted to stick it in. I pulled off my night wear and hopped in the shower and gave Major a fuck out his world. He beat the pussy down and told me that I was a million dollar bitch and he would always pay for my pussy. Major told me to stop fucking around with so many niggas and he would just take care of me. Hell for the first time in my life that sounded like something I wanted to do. Next, I fucked around and gave Major some of the A1 head and got in the shower with him. When, he got out in the shower he kissed on me. He showed me all kind of attention that I needed for the day. I laid back in the bed and by time I got in a deep sleep the night air had turned into morning air. I jumped up out of bed and decided to put on my addias. I got in the shower to wash my ass back up because Major had fucked the shit out of me in the bed while I was asleep. I thought carefullu about what he was saying and wanted him to know that the next chapter of my life was about being a business woman. I still had in mind that I wanted to get my clothing line and make the best out of it. I called Felicia to let her know I was about to met her at the school so I could study with her for the day. Clip called and checked in on me and were still selling dope in the ally apartment that morning. Shit, sounded good but I was still thinking about what Major told me last night. I pulled up in my Acura with the music playing loud. I was looking my best in the addais oufit. Of course the first person I saw was Nate Thang. He was dressed in an all Polo shirt with the Polo jeans. I saw Felicia and she went directly in the computer lab in sat down. I walked in behind her and she took out her notes for math so she could start the study section. I sat next to her and wrote down all the notes I needed for the class since Monday I didn't come to school. After about studying for and hour the bell at the school rung and it was time for all the students to report to class for the day. Each section was an hour and thirty minutes long. School went by fast like it did each day when you take notes and do work. At school was always the shortest three hours of my life. I packed my school bags up and went to start by day in the streets. And that was first to fuck Nate Thang. At The Manson we got it on and smoked all day long. I was so damn high and I didn't want to leave him for the day. Then, I laid up with Nate Thang some more. The romance that he gave me looked and felt like one of those hoes off a movie. I asked him did he know anyone I could start a clothing line up with and yes he did. Tim a nigga out of L.A. was a new cat to me that I had never heard of. I asked Nate Thang could he get the digits so I could call him and hook up. He told me that would be know problem. Then, I opened up my laptop and seen who all wanted to fuck with me today. Shit was looking dead at first until I scrolled down the page. It was a list of niggas from Bean to Law and many more on down trying to get at me. The school didn't give us homework for the day so that was a plus for me to fuck around and make money. I called Bean back first and he was at Hill End motel in L.A. some place a lot of rappers go to and make underground music. I jumped in the Acura and rode to Hill End and he was shooked to see me in a Addias outfit instead of having on my stripper gear. Bean took his shorts off and start trying to get on hard. He had fifty thousand dollars in the room. Some more niggas out of Texas was there and I let all of them knock the pussy down for the fifty grand. I danced on the table and drunk Exclusive. Cocaine was in the building and I got fucked up. I was so high a bitch couldn't tell what was going on in the room. All I know we were turned up. Bean let me keep the room and I called Law so he could come up to the room. When, Law got there my high had went down a little and we made love. I had a high sex drive that day and wanted some more of his sex before I left. I laid on the bed and had him put his dick back inside of me. Then he moved up and down in the inside of my walls and shit was so real with him. I didn't know wheather I was coming or going. Next, stop for the day was home. It was still kind of early and lately I have been making other moods and was far from my usually person. I open my closet to see did I have any clothes to dance in for the night. It was at least nine o'clock and the strip store Tricks was still open. I left the house and got some clothes to dance in. When, I left the store I stop by Wal-mart instead of the L.A. Square Mall and got some make up. Then, I rode to the club. I parked into the VIP parking so know one could steal my car. I walked into the club and saw some of then Florida hoes. This time a bitch name Pink, Faygo and Dynasty was in there. All of them look to be like eighteen and they looked nice. The DJ introduced them on stage and they did a strip show. They climbed up and down the poll and after Pink, and Faygo alone with Dynasty had their time to dance it was time for me to dance. I climbed to the top of the poll and came down on my head shaking my ass at the same time and made way more money than they did because I was an older dancer in The Roxy's. That night I maintain in a stable mind. Just in case Kreme got out of line. She already had beat one murder case I didn't

want it to end up being two murder cases. After, I worked the bottom level then I danced on the second and third level of the club. Mark my money man was in the club. He was watching television in the t.v. room. No one was paying attention so I went in the t.v. room and started to dance for him. I had the floor to myself. I rolled and popped my ass all over the floor and danced all night, He grinded the back of my ass, An, before you knew it Mark and I was in The Hideaway Inn laying in the room fucking and having sex. I sucked the head of Mark dick and rode his penis all night long for the rest of the night. The club was deal because I had made ten grand in ther plus Pimp had to give us our pay check for the month so I know my shit would add up. Time went by so fast and I had to go home. Wedensday was the next day and I had to get up for school. When, I got there Major was asleep and the back room. He had some information of building a new home on the bed. It was going to take a while to build the house so I decied that I would re-funitune the apartment. I wasn't sleepy yet so I looked online and found a nice Lacoste set that would look nice in the apartment. It was a hundred grand but it damn sho was nice. I paid by credit card and saw it would take three days for the shipment to come though. By, that time I was sleepy by the eyes but was still awake. I got in the shower before I laid down. When, I got out the shower I went to sleep and felt so good laying in the air condition cuddling with my man. I thought in my mind about what he had put down and said the other night. I laid down for the rest of the night and found myself restless. I got up and start reading a book called "Fly Girl" it was a book I read back when I was like eighteen years old and I decided to read it again. Major rounded over in the bed and as I was laying on my back he wholed me and put his arms around the top of my body. I was on the part of the book where she had broke her vaginal with a boy a couple years older than her. I always liked that part of the book. That reminded me of when Travis and I had first had sex. I felt grown and I felt in love with him he made love to me so much. I put the book down and laid on my back so Major arms could stay wrap around the front of my body. We slept there all night then we woke up around six o'clock. It was hard for me to get up the next morning because I was sleepy from reading late the night before. "Get up lil man so you can get ready for school." Major was still sleepy and I never saw a baby look like that but he gave me a crazy look. I put him in the tub in washed him off. Then I put him on some Lacoste for babies that I had founded in Macy's. I put on some coffee to wake me up. Then, I sat at the table in the kitchen and ate an egg sandwich. I called Felicia early to see was she awake. More than likely we were going to have a quiz in class today. She was still in the bed and I told her to meet me at the libracy so we could study. My perfume company was doing great and for the first time the professional tech that was over the line had changed the name to Major Spray Connection. She thought it would make more money and I did too. My company was a number three seller after the Trina Line and the Pink Line.

Chapter 13

By the time I got ready it was time for me to go to school. I had on an amazing DKNY outfit and it fixed my perfectly shape frame well. When, I got to the school Felicia was running behind. So, I sat at the table in the libracy and went over my math notes. The school was crowded and I could hear the noise from the outside hallway in the libracy building. I did my geometry homework for the day. I kind of figured my teacher would be giving us page three sixty for homework so I went ahead and did it. By, the time I finished my assignment Felicia was walking into the libracy. She was dressed to impress for the day. Felicia had on an addias outfit that she had went to Champs in the mall and got like me. I gave her my homework paper and let her copy it on a sheet of paper. We went over all the rules we needed to know about the work. The bell rung for class and I went into my math class ready to learn what my teacher was about to teach for the day. In math class that day some bitch made the teacher mad, Our math teacher put her out of class but before you knew it Toni the student that was dismiss from class hit our teacher in the face. To bad for Toni she got kicked out the GED program and the police came to arrest her ass for a battery charge. For the last thirty minutes of class the students just sat and talked about her. Then, it was time for me to head to my language arts class. Felicia had a different language teacher from me so we went opposite directions. I sat in language arts class and waited on my teacher to arrive to the course. I took out some college rule paper and start doing all my notes for the hour and thirty minutes. The class time went by and I called Nate Thang and he was already at The Manson and wanted Candy and I to put on a freak show. Candy neither I had and idea that Nate Thand knew both of us. My first stop was to the hood to get some molly. Cocaine was still popular but I wated some molly. I got a fifty bag of molly and went to The Manson. When, I got to The Manson I got out the car and went upstairs. Candy had on a lingerie set and I didn't. So, I took off my DKNY outfit to lay with my bra and panties on. We ate each other pussy and fucked all over the motel walls. We made videos on how freaky we was getting. Time flew by and I hit Clip up to see did he want any dealings with me. Of course Clip did. I went to the ally apartment and for some reason he was the only nigga out. We went in the back room where I got high and rounded and I hit a couple joints to keep shit going. Clip and I laid down on the mattress and he had sex with me in the from the back for the first time. That was some painful shit. I laid down and took the pain like a G. When he was done he broke me off ten thousand dollars. An, told me next time to relax while he fuck me in that spot. It was still early so I hit Major up to see what he was doing. His connection that he got dope from was out of work so he needed to know where he could get some dope from. I put him back on his feet by going in the back room in the ally apartment and getting Clip. "Yo Clip my nigga need some dope." "Do you have a couple of those birds left." "Yeah they going for twenty grand." That was high for Major and he didn't get the shit. I finish freaking at the ally apartment for the rest of the day after Major gave me word he was't going to get the shit. Rameo came though for the first time and paid for some pussy. All the females wanted to trick with him because he was giving out ten million dollars. We did line up for who was going to get the money. A bitch name Rhonda won that. He had bread on him and he took her ass to a little cheap motel call Runaway Inn and knocked her down. L.A was full of little dope spots that had cheap motels and that's where most niggas went to all day long. Rhonda was gone for the rest of the day on the corner. Jay Jack had enough money out the deal to stop his pimping business but shit still continued. Next, some old cats from the projects came in and I was hoping that was my come up. They came around to sell some guns, cocaine, dope, pills, ex and ten nines. Red bought all that shit and sat in the ally apartment and played with the clips to the gun to see were they working good. After, Rameo sold the shit he spent his money on some pussy. Lisa a stripper right out of the projects tricked around with him because he was some like a crack head and I wouldn't trick with him. Any nigga that sold guns and side the road shit was on a different level from me. Guns were used for protection not a nigga to sell them after they were used in the streets. I sat for a moment then I ran down the stairs to get some cocaine for Eddie. He was back on the streets looing gooder than a motherfucker. Eddie walked up the stairs to the ally apartment and by the time I reached the door hoes was dancing all over the wall. I took Eddie to the back room and made him feel good. I open up my pussy with my hands and let him stuck his dick inside of me. “Eddie baby make this pussy feel like one of a kind.” “Rub that dick across my pussy walls baby.” “After that make me never stop tricking and stripping for a lame ass nigga.” “Damn baby you want Eddie to do all that.” After the quick fuck I was back doing cocaine and Eddie paid three grand up front. It was about time to get Major my son from daycare so I had to leave. I called Reese to see did she want to watch him for the rest of the afternoon. She always didn’t mind watching my son or daughter when she was alive. That always left me with time on my hands. I left the trap so I could go and take Major my son to Reese house after I left Reese house I went to the mall. I got in my Acura and played the music loud ass hell though the city so a bitch could see me ride by. So many hoes was looking at me as I pasted by I only had a couple grands on me and that was the money I made at the ally apartment. I looked at the money and counted it and damn to bad I didn’t have ten grand on me. I rode to Bank of America and got the other money out so it could equal up to ten grand. I was about to go on a ten thousand dollar shopping spree. At the mall I got seventy Polo shirts and seventy Aeropostle short sets, with seventy Pink outfits and seventy pair shoes that I found all on sale. I wanted to redo my closet with all new shit so I could stay fly for the rest of the year. When, I walked outside of the mall with all those mall bags hoes and niggas was like damn she did a lot of shopping. I didn’t even now the mall was having a sale I just was going shopping for the day. I bought some dresses on my credit card and opened up a Wet Seal account for the first time in my life. By, the time I was leaving out of L.A square mall it was closing time. I pulled out the parking lot and drove to Up Living apartment. When, I got there Major was still questions me on wheather I was going to stop dancing. "Hell no motherfucker and the dick was good at the time that's why I told your ass that." "You nasty bitch I just got off the phone with the home owner people so I can build you a manison and get you a name as one of the baddest bitches in L.A with a manison on the hill. Major hit me and the eye and gave me the second black eye of my lifetime. I was to pissed off I got my bags and went and stayed in the projects. I knew not to call Kreme. She would tell Reese and it wasn't that serious this time with me. I knew I neede to stop dancing if I had a man. I just wanted my owe money and that was any bitch dream in the game. In the projects that how shit was. I pulled back in the hood and pulled up on Red and got some cocaine for the night. I went back to my apartment in the projects and got high for the night, at the peak of the night Major came baming on the door. That shit made me mad and I cut his ass up for giving me a black eye. The cuts wasn't that deep so he didn't have to go to the hospital. Major and I end up sleeping in the projects that night together because he wouldn't leave without staying the night, junkies saw the car outside and was knocking on the door all night long trying to get something to smoke. I got mad about that too. He always fucked up my next day of sleep when we stayed in the projects. The next morning came and my eye was fucked up but I still went to school. I wanted to make the best out of getting my education. Thoughts of Money crossed my mind and I just start crying because I missed her so much. I missed her beautiful face and she was so smart and young damn I hated my baby was gone. When I got to the school it was a school holiday at the school and I forgot that it wasn't no school so when I got there I had to go back home for the day. I had on a pair of glasses for no one could see my black eye. Major called the phone to see where I was and told me it was Labor Day. He said that most of everyone in the projects was cooking out. I headed back to the hood to see what was going on for the day. When, I got there so many people was on their grills cooking out. Good thing Major Jr. was at Reese house I went and got me some cocaine to hit for the day. When, I got up there Jay Jack was on the corner. I eased by him so he wouldn't see my black eye. I didn't want him telling me not to come on the corner until it go away. Red and Clip was up in the ally apartment and I got my shit from Clip because he had that cocaine from Mexico Islands. I took a hit to the nose and got high. My nose felt so bad without cocaine I was addicted to getting high. It was fine though because I had the money to support my habit. Next, I went back to the projects were Major and a couple other people was cooking out. I wasn't that clean like I usually be in the hood so I went to Up Living and put on a Aeropostle outfit for the day. I washed my waves out my hair and curled my hair under in a wrap. My wrap was perfectly long and I looked like a college girl. Next, I went to the nail salon and got my nails done for the day. I looked damn good for the cook out. I pulled up to L.A. DJ station and ordered Major a DJ for his part of the party in the hood. When, I got back to the projects Major had his Bentley up on the sidewalk listening to music. I had on some matching

tennis shoes to my outfit and all the hood chicken heads was looking me from head to toe. I took out my phone and start taking a lot of pictures and posting them on facebook to give a bitch something to not only talk about but to look at and remember for the rest of their life. So many hoes and niggas hit like on my page and made all kinds of special comments. Then after hours of hanging out in the projects at Major cook out I went back on Jay Jack corner to start tricking for the day. I rounded this pussy on so many niggas and fucked the shit out of them. In a hour I had made a hundred grand. Clip and Red and I had a threesome. I was shaking my ass all over the floor. Some nigga out of Miami name Paul was in the ally apartment and had twenty grand and wanted to trick with Candy. We posted so many photos of us stripping that day on facebook. Next, I went back to the cook out where Major was. I ate some corn on the cob, steak, ribs, snowcrabs, and drunk some Voka and got fucked up. After the party the DJ from the radio station never made it so I call to get a refund on my money I had paid. Major Bentley was the only thing we had music to listen out of and chicken heads didn't even give a fuck they were all around my nigga car dancing and poping their ass. At the apartment that night we fucked and made up. Major hit my pussy and rubbed his dick across it and ate the hell out of me. I danced for him off R. Kelly and the sound of making love to him had my heart fulled with love. I laughted and smile though-out the whole time we was having sex. After, having sex with Major I was in the mood again that it was time for me to settle down and be a one man woman. He was proud of me for making a discussion that I was going to change my life for him. Major told me he was going to go to Diamonds a jewelry store in L.A. Square Mall and get me a ring so we could get married. He told me it would cost him all he had expect for the house money. I got my night clothes out after Major told me that and got ready for bed feeling special ass fuck. School was going to be the next day and I know the teacher was going to give us a lot of notes since we missed Labor Day. I got in the shower and took along bath to wash the sex smell off me. I thought about what I had told Major for the second time and I know I needed to get my shit together to stop stripping and just spend the millions I had in the bank on me my son and my man. I also needed to start working on having another baby to grow with Major Jr. just like him and Money was doing before she got killed. I thought how it would feel to be married to Major and how my life would be. In L.A. a twenty year old could get married. Reese would love for me and Major to get out the game and raise our son. That's why I was investing in my business and that was a big plus for me. Time pasted by and I was sound asleep in bed. Major phone rang and it was a woman. My heart dropped to get out of bed and know a woman had called his phone. That's why I needed to change my life and stop sleeping around in the city with different niggas and marry my man before he found love somewhere else. That night Major told the female he was engaged and to never call his phone again. I relaxed after hearing that and it made me feel good about the phone call and made me know I needed to get my shit together fast. I felt back to sleep knowing that during the course of the next couple weeks I was going to stop stripping. Morning came and the sun was in my eyes when I woke up because the blinds was open in the apartment. It was nine o'clock in the morning and I was behind. I rushed up out of bed and the first thing I did was cook me some pancakes and eggs. That was one of me favorite meals in the morning time. I washed my face and brush my teeth to freshen up. Next, I went to the closet and got out something to wear for the day. I moved very fast and rushed to Reese house to pick Major Jr. up so he could go to daycare for the day and I could hurry up and get to school. When, I got to Reese house she already had my son ready with his daycare clothes on. Reese had a doctor appointment to check on her and the babies. I always like hearing about the update on her and the babies and couldn't wait to she have them. Major Jr. and I took the back way to his daycare and I called Felicia on the phone to see was she ready for a good day at school and her car was broke down. I guess everyone was behind this morning. Felicia car needed a battery and it wasn't starting up. I went on her side of town and picked her up and that really put me behind. I told Felicia I would be know longing stripping because I was going to get my life right get married and be with my man and be a business woman. I mentioned to her that Major and I had commitment to be together and that he was going to buy me a ring and marry me. I also told her a woman called Major phone last night. An she asked me how did I feel about that. I said my heart had dropped but he told her to never call back again he was engaged to me. At school Felicia and I made it to the school to late to go to math so we sat in the libarcy and went over some notes and waited on language arts class to start. In the course of studying Felicia went to the bathroom to make sure her make up was on right and by that time it was time for the next class. Nate Thang was at the school and he drove an old school chevy that had some sixty inch rims on it that he had got painted and fixed up. Nate impresses me and by the time he made it up the hall the next school bell rung. I went to my language class and took out my notes. In class the teaher gave us a quiz and graded it in class while we worked on a paper and I made an A plus. After, our teacher gave us the quiz back she thought everyone had did good and ask the class did we want to take our test. The whole class said yes and my teacher pasted out the bubble sheets and I got a pencil to bubble in my answers. I took the test and I know I did great on it. When, the class time was over Nate Thang was standing in the hall way waiting on me so we could go to The Manson and fuck. He told me he had the cocaine and everything and lets go. Nate Thang watch me dance and paid me money to shake my ass. I spent most of the day there. While at The Manson I called Reese so she could get my son from daycare. I kissed and loved all up on Nate thinking on how it was going to come to an end when I stop stripping. The lingerie I had on was pretty ass fuck and he took photos of me. Then, I rode his dick for the rest of the evening. By six o' clock in the afternoon Nate Thang and I was almost done having sex. I jumped in the shower at The Manson andfreshing up to get the sex smell off me. I took my time and when I was done taking a shower it was seven o' clock. I headed to the hood to see what was going on at the ally apartment. When, I got there shit was jumping like the club. My cell phone start ringing right when I got to the ally apartment, it was Pimp he was worried I wasn't working at the club anymore. I told him I was still working but I was engaged. Pimp wasn't happy for that. He sounded as he was worried the club wouldn't make that much money. Kreme

was at the trap that day when I got off the phone with Pimp. I hugged on her neck because I missed the fuck out of her. She was the one that had the ally apartment jumping that day with tricks coming in and out. So many niggas was in the apartment watching Kreme dance. All her damn clothes were off and niggas was paying her big time money to see her body. I decided to join Kreme and start dancing I took off my clothes and when I did she ate my pussy right away. Dead on the spot Kreme and I made an hundred grand. The video was playing in the apartment and we was getting our freak on. The ally apartment was like old times when I first start tricking. By, the time the freak show was over it was ten o' clock. The time had went by so fast and now it was time for me to go to Up Living to get some dancing clothes for the night. Tuesday had went by just that fast and it was night time in the city of L.A. When, night failed I usually call it a new day for me because the little time I strip at the club go by so fast and it's morning time. When, I got to Up Living I parked the Acura and walked into my apartment. When, I got in the apartment I had new strip clothing everywhere and decided to get something to wear for each hour at the club since in a few weeks I would be ending my strip career. I called Pimp and told him I would be to the club in a little while. When, I got on the phone with him he told me that Babe a big time rapper was going to be in the building with the Young Money rap group and the Hot Boyz. When, I heard the news about who was in the club I grabbed my strip bag and headed for the door. I drove to The Roxy's and no time and when I got to the club I parked in a parking spot in VIP and looked in the mirror before I got out the car at my perfectly laid wrap and gold teeth.

There were so many people in the parking lot and the club was crowded with niggas and hoes. I knew everyone would come out to show love to Babe at the club that night. When, I got in the club Pimp wanted me to work VIP. I knew I would make major ends in the VIP room with some balling ass rapper in there. In the stripper locker room you had so many bitches getting ready to go on the dance floor and shake their ass for some money. I put on my lingerie and took my time getting ready. There was no need for me to rush to the money like old times I was a millionaire in the strip game with much ends and about to end my career as a stripper and start a new life as a business woman. Candy called me back to the fitting room she was in once I got ready so I could help her put on this amazing strip gear, Candy look like she had it for a while or just was putting on a few pounds in the game from getting money riding around eating all day. I finish doing what I had to do for her and by that time it was eleven thirty. I reported to Pimp to see did he still want me to work VIP and of course he did. I walked by the bar and grabbed me a blue motherfucker to start my night out. When, I got in VIP the stippers that was already in there was doing their thing and Babe and the other rapper didn't pay me no attention. Until about one o' clock that morning he paid me and three other girls twenty five grand to do a freak show. I danced for Babe and at the end of the night I got my money and went home the rest of the girls went to Babe motel room for and after party. Shit, it was late it was no need for me to try and hit up The Manson or The Hideaway Inn to make money I had all the ends I needed. I walked in the house and Major wasn't there and Major my son was at Reese house. I took a shower to get the sweat off me from dancing and laid down next to Major once I notice he was home and I had made a mistake. Once I got in bed heput his arms around me and loved up on me as usually. That was fine but I still was wondering when we was going to get the ring from the mall for the engagement he was suppose to be getting me. A ring that I pick out the price and looks too and to top it off he was spending all his money on the motherfucker too. In the bed that night Major and I just laid in each other arms and didn't have sex. We just cuddled up like lovers do. I felt so good laying next to a nigga that cared about me and I cared about him. I end up having a handover the next morning from drinking so many blue motherfuckers in the club last night during the freak show. Wednesday had come quickly just as I thought. I made twenty five grand last night and I hope tonight was a good one too. I sat down in the kitchen and ate some cereal but when I look in the fidge it wasn't no milk and had to run down to the corner store to get some milk. I went ahead and stopped by Reese house to pick up Major Jr. He was all nice and neat and smelling good with his Baby Johnson lotion on for the day. I went back to the house and got ready for school after I ate the cereal. It was eight o' clock in the morning. Timing was perfect and I had lot of time to study for my math test before school start. On the class calendar a math test was scheduled for today. I called Felicia to see was she up. An of course Felicia was up and ready for school I went to the closet to put on some clothes. For some reason I wanted to wear a dress and some stiltteos for the day. I got some lingerie so I could go up to the apartment in the hood and make some money after school. I made sure I got more than one of them to dance in. This was my last week dancing so I could change my life for Major for good. I grabbed enough lingerie so I could do my freak show with Clip and Nate Thang. I also looked online to check my account of how much perfume I had been selling. I was still a number three on the charts. I put enough lingerie in the bag so I could dance and work online for the day too I planned to make money. By the time the Gucci bag had all the items I needed it was time to go. I walked outside and for a minute now I had been driving the Acura so I decided to drive the Bentley for the day to look like a bitch with money and class. I pulled out the parking lot listening to the morning radio. They were doing a joke about a married man cheaping on his wife. I thought it was so funny and laughted my whole way to the school. I called Felicia back for the second time to see did she needed a ride. Felicia was still without transportation so I took the back way to her house to pick her up for school. When, we got to the school Felicia and I went to the libracy so we could study for our math test. We went over the whole section and for the most part I think I will do good on my math test. Felicia and I studied well for our test in the libracy. When, it was time to go to class I went into my class took out some paper and a pencil and sat and waited for the teacher to come in and past out the test. It didn't take her long to come into the class. It took me an hour and ten minutes to complete my test. I know I did my best on it. Next, I went to language arts and our teacher gave us back our test. I made an Aplus on my language test and felt good about that. She went over the test and most of the class did great. After, that she dismissed class early for the day. I went to the restroom at the school to see how I was looking and my next steps was to call Nate Thang on his cell phone. "Yeah baby I'am in the parking lot at the school waiting on you." "I see you all back in come jump in your whip so we can do what we do for the day. I ran up the school halls until I reached the parking lot. I followed Nate Thang to The Manson. At The Manson I walked inside the front desk to get a room. The front dest repsonist was taking a longtime to do the paper work because it was so many people trying to get a room that day. Finally, she got the paper work done and gave me a room key and I was out. I went outside and got Nate Thang so we could go to the room. Nate and I went into room four twenty and made out. I had on my lingerie set for the day and start dancing shaking my ass and doing what it took to get the money I wanted from him. Nate Thang had all twenties in his hand and tipped me all evening. I made ten thousand dollars in total and my next stop was to the bank. Before, I went to the bank I had to go to Up Living and get some more money I had save up over the weeks. I took all the money to the bank and made a big desposit. Right after that I went to the hood to see what was going on with Clip for the day. He usually was my next client of the day since he got out of prison. But instead I fucked around with some old meat that I start dealing with when I first start tricking. Mark was the nigga I got money with that afternoon in the ally apartment. I danced on the table and rolled my ass around on Mark. Mark paid to see me shake my ass. After dancing with Mark for one hour we went to the back room of the ally apartment and had sex. I pulled out Mark dick and sucked the head of his balls. Then, I put his dick up in my pussy and bounced up and down on it. As, I rode Mark dick he yelled my name out. "Kelly, Kelly, Kelly your pussy is so damn good baby."

"Damn I want another round with you." Round two wasn't like round one but it was good too. When, I was done with Mark I called Clip up to the ally apartment to fuck with him. He came in the room inside the ally apartment and the first thing Clip did was break me off some money. We fucked around and I got fucked up on some raw ass cocaine. I danced on top of the pool table for Clip and made my ass shake up and down. Clip made a flick of me and I look so sexy for one of my last time dancing before I get married. I looked on the online site after the show with Clip to see what was going on. I scroll down the page to see was there anything for me do. My page looked like one of those movie star dancers and I quickly called some of the dudes back so I could meet them at a motel and make some money. Cee-Low wanted to make a move with me and that's the first thing thug ass nigga I tricked with for the day after I did my usually people Nate Thang, Clip, and my nigga Mark. When, I got with Cee- Low he had the green and cocaine and everything. I smoked so much weed I was high ass hell for the rest of the day. The section with Cee-Low didn't last that long. I only gave him a head job and sucked his balls from the back. Cee-Low gave me fifty grand for the head job. Next, on the online site was Tye a nigga out of Orlando, Florida. I don't know but for some reason niggas out of Florida loved to come to L.A. I don't know if it was the dope game or what but they loved L.A. swag game. Tye was staying at the hotel with his wife in kids and wanted to find another spot to chill and do business at. The Manson was the only spot I could think of that Tye and I could go chill at. I picked him up in my Bentley and rode to The Manson and got a room. At The Manson Tye and I end up spending hours because I was dancing and giving him a freak show out this world. My date with Cee-Low went well and it was only nine o'clock when I finish up with him. I went to the apartment to get something to dance in at the club because I had work in all the lingerie I bought that morning in my bag. I rode in the car thinking of how I was about to end my stripping career and The Roxy's and the ally apartment was damn sho something I was going to miss. At the crib that night I talked on the phone with Reese. She was just telling me how she was ready to have her baby and how happy she was do be a mother soon. I got out an Gucci lingerie set with some Gucci green and brown stittleos to make it look perfectly cute on my frame. Then, I curled my hair bursh my teeth and put on a Nike jumper to ride to The Roxy's. I grabbed the keys to the Acura and pulled out on my floater clean ass fuck for the night. At the club that night Mark and the fellas was in there playing cards and making money. I went where I always go to the back room and got ready for the night at the club as one of my last night at the club. I planned on dancing my ass off to leave my name as one of the best that ever did it in the strip game. I walked to the dance floor and danced on this nigga name Black. Black was one of the biggest ballers in L.A. He had a manison and he owned a hotel called Community Inn. It was a spot that hoes on the southside of town made money at. I was new school in the strip game to the hoes that worked that spot even though I had been in the game for a few years. From time to time I had thoughts of going to the Commuity Inn and make some money but I never made it to the neck of the woods. Now in two days I would be done stripping and just being a business woman in the game thinking of a way to get my clothing line and working in my own shoe store full time. Anyways he was smelling gooder than a motherfucker and he was making my night. Black gave me all kinds of ends that night. I made three hundred thousand dollars off that nigga that night. He was a pay master and he knew what to do to make a bitch want to shake their ass for him. Next, Bean was in the club that night. While Mark and Red along with some other niggas from the hood was playing cards I danced with Bean until Kreme came in the club. When, she came in the club Kreme made a grand entry with a Jimmy Choo lingerie on. I stop dancing with Bean to go back in the dressing room with her. When, I got back there I told her I was engaged to Major and we was about to get married. Now that Kreme had moved her grandma out the hood I rarely saw her unless it was at the ally apartment or the club. I loved and kissed on Kreme to let her know she was one of my ride or die chick. I went back to the dance floor and Bean wanted to dance a little longer with me. By, the time I got done dancing with Bean the night at the club was over. It was just my luck Nate Thang called me late that night and wanted me to stay out with him and fuck around on my nigga. I told Nate Thang that was something I was going to do because it was my last week in the game. I wanted to make memories before I was a married woman with a man that I liked before I put that ring on my finger. Nate Thang told me to meet him at the Gateway End. This was a motel like the Community Inn but strippers didn't dance and walk up and down the ally. The only thing strippers did there was meet tricks and trick with them. At The Gateway End Nate Thang decided he was going to get on cocaine with me for the night.

Morningcame rushing in and Major Sr. were hitting my phone so I could come home. I wish like hell he would stop calling me. Here it was morning and Nate Thang and I still was getting high. I got on the phone and called Major to let him know I was on the way home. When, I got there Major already had the baby at home with him and I went in the house and got ready for school. I called Felicia to let her know there was no need to study for the day because we had just took the test. She said okay and we got off the phone. I finish getting ready and rode to Major Jr. daycare and dropped him off next I went to the school. When, I got to the school I sat in the school parking lot with Felicia and talked to her. My black eye had went away fast and I was back looking nice. Nate Thang pulled up in the parking lot and got out his bubble Chevy and gave me a hug and kiss. I got out the car and made out with Nate Thang for a minute and talked to him. I told him how wonderful our night was and I was happy I was able to pulled that off having a man and all. After, talking to Nate Thang I went to my math class and waited on my teacher to enter the class to teach for the day. Felicia had stop by the restroom so I called her mobile phone and had her come in the class and sit next to me. Felicia was already coming up the hall as she was on the phone with me. Next, our teacher walked into the class. She had the test grades in her hands and I was the first student to get my back. After, the teacher pasted back all the test she went over the test with everyone that was in class for the day. I put my test in my notebook because it didn't take the whole class period to go over the test and went to the school lunch room and got something to eat until my language arts class started. By the time I was done eating it was time for my next class to start. I went into my class with a new attitude about language ready to take notes for the time. This time we were able to take notes on our computer. I opened up the windows to my computer and went to word to type my notes. Before, I start typing I went to check the sells on my perfume. I called the bank on the phone and stepped outside to talk to them. I called the bank to make payroll to my shoe company. It was a great money maker and I liked to be on time paying the woman that worked in my shoe store. It had made over a billion dollars in sells and I didn't know what I was going to do with all that money. After, I made the payroll I stepped back into the class and typed my notes up for the day. Class went by very quickly as usually and I step to the teacher desk and ask could she arrange for me to take my GED test because I was more than ready. My language arts teacher was head over the GED department at the school. I explain to her that I was ready to take the test and I wanted to make arrangements to do so. It was find with her and didn't waste no time and took the my name and told me I would take the test soon. I walked out the school and went to the parking lot and got in the car. I called my shop directly on the phone and told the manager that I had made payroll and their checks should be at the their banks in their accounts. As, I was on the phone with the store manager to my store Nate Thang came up to my car to see did I want to hit The Manson. I told Nate Thang that was fine with me to ride a couple places so I could order a cake for my last night working at The Roxy's Party City so I could get some party items to decorate the building. Then, I had Nate Thang follow me to the mall so I could go to Sak Fifth to get a Juicy dress to wear my last

night dancing. I hope the school make something come though fast so I could take the GED test by Moday. By the time Nate and I got my Juicy Couture dress and ate at the mall it was three o'clock in the afternoon. Thursday, hump day for me and I was almost done doing the last couple things I had to do before I give Nate Thang some pussy for the day. I was going to really miss my job working the club and going to the ally apartment. I can say the time I was in the game niggas showed love to me. I was going to try and make the best of the last couple times with Nate Thang. He usually showed love to me and that was always a big plus. At The Manson that night I was making plans to stay night two with Nate Thang. Shit my party was coming to an ending and I wanted to show much love to myself by inviting some good dick to my plate. Nate Thang and I pulled inside of the gates of The Manson and he got out the car and went inside the lobby and paid for a room this time we was on the last floor and he fucked the shit out of me. His dick was so good in my pussy I rode Nate Thang for a long ass time. I had so much cum back inside of me to it didn't make no sense. Now, that I was done fucking him for the day I went and got my shit ready for my party. I got all the things I neededfor the party and took everything to the club so my set up could already be done when people got there. Next, I went my ass back to the hood to see what was popping with my niggas in the hood for the day. Jay Jack was on the corner with Travis, L.A., and Roy all some older niggas from the hood. L.A. and Roy was some nickel and dimes hustlers that was just out there to sell fifty packs to junkies and fuck their money up getting high and do the same shit the next day. Travis of course was my baby daddy a nigga with a mean

come up game. He was looking good as always and making ends come up like always in the hood. I went in the ally apartment after speaking to them and talked to Kreme. I was surpise again to see her in the hood. Mark ass was in there chilling in the kitchen bagging up some dope to make sure junkies had what they needed. I took out my lap top looked on the page where I trick on to see what kind of niggas wanted to fuck around with me for the day because the ally apartment was still jumpimg with dope for the day and afterwards they was going to start paying tricks money to fuck with them when all the work was gone. Clip name was the only nigga I saw on the online site. I was wondering why the fuck he put in a order and he was at the ally apartment all the time. But, that's because he was on the move in wanted some pussy. I schedule a meeting with him so I could give Clip some pussy for the day. I spent almost all day at the motel with Clip fucking around doing nothing. We didn't even fuck I thought we was but it was a change of plans and I had to do what I had to do and that was just to chill around and keep him company. Night came around and I called Major Sr. for the first time that day and checked on him. He had Major Jr. with him and they were just chilling aound doing nothing at the crib. I told Major I would be to the crib and left the ally apartment and went home. When, I got home I hugged up on him and told him that I had went and got all my party items for my last night stripping and my party was going to be the following day. I told Major I wanted him to be there to support me and make my night a night to remember. Next, I went to the closet and got some clothes to dance in for the night and called Pimp to let him know I was ending my strip career

and I would be having a party at the club. Pimp was kind of sad I was leaving the club. I told him that I was in a serious relationship and my man didn't want me dancing anymore. I told Pimp that I was getting married I loved dancing but it had to come to an end if I wanted my relationship. I got off the phone with Pimp got in the shower and got ready for my last Thursday ever dancing in The Roxy's. Thursday was a ball in the club when I got there. All the strippers were asking me was I leaving the club for good. My answer to them was yes. I explain to everyone that Major and I was getting married and he wanted me to stop dancing. It was a hard discussion but I had to do the right thing. I was a millionaire I had much money. Not only that I had a shoe company a perfume company and I would soon be finishing school and starting up a clothing line. There was no reason for me to dance. I told the girls I would come to the club to tip and show love but it was the end of my career and I wanted them to know if I can make the money and make it out then they could do the same, Thursday in the club the DJ played all my favorite songs all night. I danced the whole club and made money like always. I really had a wonderful time that night. It was one of my best night dancing at the club. At the end of the night I did another all nighter with Nate Thang at The Manson. I had planned to make everything worth wild my last couple nights dancing. Nate Thang was the last to know about the ending of my career. At The Manson I told him I was about to take my GED test and that I had to end our relationship as far as fucking each other because I would no longer be tricking. He was pleased to ear what I had to say and was happy for me. I told Nate I was engaged and that I would soon be getting married to Major the father of my son. After, the talk Nate and I made love for the last time and I end up staying the whole night with him. I felt like a million dollar bitch in the room with Nate. I called Kreme to let her know if Major called her phone to let him know that I was with her and to call me on threeway so he could hear my voice. Kreme said okay and I was back to Nate all night long. To be accurate I called Major on three way myself to talk to him. I told him I was hanging out for my last times and the game in as soon as the sun comes up I would be walking in the door. My baby said okay and we got off the phone. I told Kreme if he called back to call me again. I got back to Nate and gave him the business for the last time. Nate smiled from ear to ear watching me dance and shake my ass. Friday came rolling in and it was sunny outside. I stopped at a store to get a coffee to wake me up for the morning and headed back home. When, I got to the house Major was cooking a morning meal and our son was still asleep. I walked in the kitchen and gave my man a hug and kiss and told him I love him. I told Major today was my last day in the game and after this I was all his's. After, making Major feel like a man I walked in the bathroom to make sure I didn't look tried. When, I looked in the mirror I was like you go girl you look damn good. I started to laid down for a while but today was my big day. I went to the closet and grabbed another dress to put on to give myself a sexy look for the day. It was my last day in the game but I was proud of myself. I made it out safe without aids or any type of disease. That made me feel damn good. I called Felicia on the phone to see did she need a ride to school and her car was running. So, that gave me more time to myself for the morning time. I got ready feeling good about making a new start in life and that was being a woman and mother to my man Major and our son. I went to school and class went well in language my teacher scheduled a date and time for me to take the GED test. It was for next Wedenesday at eight o' clock in the morning. I was off to a great start and only thing I had left to do was party and make an end to my strip career tonight. I had been waiting on Friday to come all week to make my last night as a stripper a success. I talked to Major so many times thought out Friday and he said Saturday morning we would be going to get my ring. My party end up being great and all my friends and love ones was there. I made my last ends in the game and I just want to thank god for me making it out safe and rich.

The End